Blanche Willis Howard

Aulnay Tower

Blanche Willis Howard

Aulnay Tower

ISBN/EAN: 9783743305854

Manufactured in Europe, USA, Canada, Australia, Japa

Cover: Foto ©Andreas Hilbeck / pixelio.de

Manufactured and distributed by brebook publishing software (www.brebook.com)

Blanche Willis Howard

Aulnay Tower

AULNAY TOWER

AULNAY TOWER

BY

BLANCHE WILLIS HOWARD

AUTHOR OF "GUENN," "AUNT SERENA," "ONE SUMMER,"
ETC.

AULNAY TOWER.

CHAPTER I.

THE Tower stood squarely on the old stone church and commanded the plain. In its base was a rough room with loop-hole windows, through which cool breezes played even when the midsummer sun shone hot upon giant wheat-stacks and blue-bloused reapers in the fields below, and upon parched white high-roads stretching away between lines of poplars from village to village. Skirting the meadow, the deep shades of the forest of Bondy massed themselves strongly. Gone were its storied days of demon, witch, and goblin; gone the surpassing glory of its bandit chiefs, their wild carousals and mad, late rides, when no honest peasant for leagues around dared venture out after nightfall. All, indeed, that remained of its brave tradition were a few attenuated terrors, conjured up by village mothers — according to the pleasing method of all nations — to frighten recreant children into the path of virtue.

In the wide range of the Tower, from the forest over the plain, lay many a rich farm, many a stately country seat and thrifty village. The Ourcq Canal cut sharply through the green expanse as far as the eye could reach, bearing on its slow waters traffic and merchandise to the great city. Paris itself was perceptible by the glow of light against the night skies, and when the wind was west, by the distant chiming of its bells.

Directly beneath the Tower rose the turrets of the château, connected with the church by an arched gallery through which the marquis — especially now that he was more or less an invalid — went to mass in stormy weather. The cottages of the village folk clustered close about his gates; the village interests crowded volubly and affectionately into his home, as if all distances and barriers between them were spanned by innumerable unseen arches, making church, château, and village one.

Countess Nathalie, wandering listlessly under the great drooping trees of the park, absorbed in thoughts too sombre for her youth, found the cheery bustle of the village insupportable, and silently protested against the enforced intimacy. Why could she never be alone? Why must her reveries be disturbed by the gossiping women on the common, by the sun-browned men coming noisily to and from the fields and pouring gayly into the dram-shop? Why should she be their involuntary boon companion as they sipped the solace of the little glass? Why, when the women related interesting family events, was she their unwilling confidante, gaining incontrovertible wisdom as to babies' teeth, and sheep and calves? Why must the odious pedler, with his strident voice, beady black eyes, and high, springless cart, rattle regularly into her meditations every Sunday morning, as regularly as he came to make bargains and bold jokes over his pots and pans, and disseminate his shallow, free-thinking philosophy among the workmen in the cabaret? She was not unkind, but she had her griefs, and being young, wished the world to be quiet that she might brood over them. She was not unsympathetic, but she sympathized most with herself. When the village had a sorrow, she observed that it proclaimed it from the house-tops or called in the neighbors and eased itself with demonstration. She did not realize that the poor have no time to nurse heartaches gracefully, that the necessity

of labor drives them resistlessly on, and the tyranny
of daily routine excludes fine ceremony in the presence of either love or sorrow. Quite unconscious
of its various delinquencies, the village unanimously
adored the beautiful young countess, peered eagerly
into the park to catch a glimpse of her black-robed
figure haunting the acacia-walk, rejoiced greatly
when she came into their cottages or talked with
them on the common, chattered much of her in their
own way, hoped she would marry again soon, for it
was a sin and a shame to think of the pretty dear
being a widow at her age, and the wonder was,—if
Jacques, the deceased count's stud-groom and an
Aulnay man, spoke true,—that she could mourn at
all for the old reprobate; but mourn she did, or what
meant her still ways, and her pacing, pacing, hour
after hour, her hands clasped before her, her head
bent down? So the village lavished upon her its
unrequited affection, finding a charm and a grace in
all that she did; and Countess Nathalie, although
benevolent and gracious as it was the duty of a
Montauban to be, loved the village not a whit, con-
demned its noisy lamentations as heartless because
devoid of reserve, regarded its coarse joys from
the heights of her fastidious mental distance, and

wearied unutterably of its obtrusive cackling and crowing and bleating, and the whole interminable rustic chorus.

Neither to her uncle the marquis, nor to his friend the abbé, did she express these unreasonable sentiments. Indeed there was much, reasonable and unreasonable, which it never occurred to her to communicate to them. The marquis was proud of her, and found her conduct appropriate and graceful in the extreme. What, under the circumstances, could be in better taste than a prolonged retirement from the world? Scarcely twenty-three years old, beautiful, rich, and a Montauban, a woman could well disdain any vulgar eagerness to reappear in the matrimonial market. Moreover, it was agreeable to him to retain her charming presence in his household as long as possible. In his estimation she was one of the most satisfactory women he had known: clear-eyed, clear-voiced, calm and restful in her movements, never sulked, indulged in ejaculations, or made scenes, never demanded flattery or petting,— not only a charming woman, but a woman of surprising distinction and repose for her years. He deemed himself fortunate in his surroundings; for he could emphatically affirm that the marquise, of sainted memory, had also been

a most congenial person. Of her character it was
only necessary to state that in forty years of married
life he had never known her to irritate his nerves by
an abrupt gesture or a harsh intonation. As loud-
voiced, ugly women with mental or physical angu-
larities were his horror, so a sentimental woman,
an unconventional woman, a woman with aspirations,
opinions of her own, or a history, was all very well
as a youthful pastime, but intolerable to a man of
taste as a life-long companion. Congratulating himself, therefore, upon the translucent perfection of
the femineity in the château, he would have been in
despair had he once had occasion to suspect the deplorable qualities latent in his niece, and of which
she herself was but vaguely conscious. Her sentiment, aspiration, emotion, were by no means in a
soporific state. She had a dangerous tendency to
independent thought, heretical views as to certain
sacred social fictions, and was even capable of having
what many people would call nothing less than a
history. Countess Nathalie was regarded then with
unqualified approval and pride, yet lived as far from
the château as from the village, until days came
which drew her thoughts from herself and nearer
to her uncle, — days when she longed for the village

with all its sights and sounds close before her eyes, loud in her ears, intrusive, persistent, dominant. Its dirtiest baby she would have clasped to her heart with a thousand kisses and blessings. She wished the dram-shop were crowded with the most unconscionable men. No gossip could be too vulgar for her indulgence. She would have welcomed even the pedler.

For the cannon of Sedan were silent, the Emperor Napoleon was a prisoner, the Germans were approaching Paris, where a provisional government under General Trochu had been established. The Aulnay village folk fled with their household gods. But the Marquis de Montauban, contrary to the example of his peers on all the estates in that region, and in spite of instructions from the capital, had chosen to await in his ancestral home the approach of the enemy.

By command of the French committee of defence, as well as from fear of the besieging army, the country for miles around Paris was deserted. Scarcely a living thing belonging to the soil remained, except everywhere the poor forlorn cats that lingered tenaciously in the familiar places, wailing incessantly at night about the desolate homesteads. Fruit trees and vineyards told their tale of departed thrift and peace, and afforded a welcome refreshment to the soldiers, cut off by their rapid marches from the supplies which, owing to the destruction of the railways, were often considerably in the rear. But the cattle and all means of subsistence had been removed, the grain-fields were one sad expanse of ashes, the very air, once alive with the stir of farms, the sounds of toil, calls from the meadows, voices and movement on the highways, now hung like a pall over manor and hamlet. A vast dreariness pervaded the whole land-scape. Into this silent land came the great invading army with its ominous discords of war.

When the investment of Paris was accomplished, Aulnay lay hopelessly in the German lines. The Maas army, under the Crown Prince of Saxony, occupied the right bank of the Seine and lower Marne, on the line Argenteuil, Blanc Mesnil, through the forest of Bondy to Gournay on the Marne; one division reached from Aulnay, where it touched upon the Garde Corps, to Clichy; another from Clichy to Chelles. The headquarters of the Saxon corps were at Vert Galant, a charming and well-preserved estate on the Metz road, with gardens extending to the lovely Bois de St. Denis.

In the entire district occupied by the twenty-third
Saxon division only Château d'Aulnay was inhab-
ited, and at Sévran, on the Ourcq Canal, where in
days of peace low willows drooped over slow barges
passing heavily all day long, two fishermen were
left unmolested in their hut, the fish they caught
being a welcome addition to the meagre rations.
The Germans had speedily dammed the Ourcq Canal
and Mentone brook, which, overflowing their low
banks before the line Livry, Sévran, Aulnay, Blanc
Mesnil, formed against the French an impassable
barrier, and for the fishermen a broad lake upon
which their little boats were constantly seen.

The conspicuous fact that the Marquis de Montauban and his little family remained at Aulnay
could not fail to give rise to speculations on the
part of the Germans. The château was a charming country-seat, a large, massive, comfortable, and
friendly house, but by no means so richly appointed
as many places in that region, — Clichy and Montfermeil, for instance, whose owners had, nevertheless,
not deemed it incumbent to stay and guard their
treasures. In the temporarily uncertain condition of
France no available political reasons could be sufficient explanation of his conduct. It was decided to

subject the family to close surveillance, and they were forbidden under severe penalty to cross the boundaries of court-yard and park.

It would be perhaps unjust, or at least inaccurate, to bluntly state that the Countess Nathalie de Vallauris actually enjoyed this painful situation. Still, if one has been more or less wretched in a blind way for some years, rebellious yet hardly knowing against what, conscious of wrongs which one's principles and traditions forbid one to openly resent, eager in every heart-throb yet restricted perpetually by the most adamantine if highly polished conventionalities, it is surely a vast relief to one's overcharged emotions to find something positive which it is a duty to roundly hate. Upon the Germans, then, from the moment they appeared upon her mental horizon until upon the familiar landscape of Aulnay the hostile army intruded its sullen tramp, its clang of arms, its roll of artillery, its piercing bugle-call, its swift hoofs carrying messengers of destruction, its hoarse murmur, its fatal omnipotence, she lavished the pent-up resentment of years.

And the other prisoners beneath the shadow of the Tower? The mails having ceased, the marquis read old newspapers instead of new; he contented himself, there being a scarcity of meat, with a super-abundance of potatoes and salad; and since he was restricted to his park, he tacitly reasserted his dignity by confining himself exclusively to his own rooms. But he could not and would not assume other manners for the novel situation. His antique urbanity disdained to be ruffled by the curious liberties foreign soldiers were taking with his domain, still less by the wild eccentricities of Paris proclamations. When he told his good story at dinner, — the marquis's story was always good, only a good one could last so long, — or sat down to his game of piquet or bézique with the Abbé de Navailles, his smile, though somewhat vague, was calm and courteous, his air loftily unconscious that two great nations were cannonading each other at his portals, and that the world was breathlessly awaiting the result. His table-talk airily ignored the Germans, his own aches and pains, and every other topic which a high-bred man would naturally exclude as ungraceful and unappetizing. He moistened his handkerchief frequently with eau-d'Houbigant, and mentioned one day, gratefully, that he had always found its refreshing odor a delicate consolation in sorrow.

It was a recognized comfort to every one that the

abbé remained. A man of spiritual, even ascetic
life, friend and guide of the marquis for years, his
influence on the household was boundless. He occupied himself now, as before, chiefly with his books.
His thoughtful face was unmoved by wars and
rumors of wars, and he always found time to comfort
them all with a wisely chosen word. Old Jean, a
kind of heirloom among the family servants, — indeed, the Tower itself could have been prevailed
upon to leave Aulnay before Jean, in spite of a
chronic objection to the sound of a gun, would have
deserted the marquis, — felt like a hero when the
abbé quietly praised his faithfulness and calmed his
shaking nerves. The cook ceased her lamentations
for her husband the coachman, who had been swept
away with the horses by the first detachments of
light cavalry, and grew sanguine in her views, after
a word from the abbé. Manette, Countess Nathalie's
gay little Paris maid, pronounced it a blessing and
mercy that the holy man, with his head like a real
saint, was there to say mass, — not to mention that it
was a pleasure to see his handsome face on the stairs
or anywhere; and when Pierre and Antoine, the
fishermen on the Ourcq Canal, came with their fish,
ostensibly for fast-days, — as if all days were not fasts

now, — no one could have been kinder than M. l'Abbé, who talked with them of their wives and children, dispelled their homesickness, and sat with them long in the sacristy discussing many things for their edification. But since even in the best-regulated families perfect unanimity of sentiment is rare, Countess Nathalie's voice was never heard swelling this pæan of praise. She went her way as quietly as the Abbé de Navailles went his, never opposed or criticised him. But sometimes in the library, evenings, as his interesting dark head was bent over his piquet cards, and the marquis smilingly expounded the extreme finesse of his last game, she would raise her eyes from her book with a long, searching glance; and if the marquis had suddenly turned his aristocratic profile, he might have been startled by a shade of impatience, it may be even suspicion, hovering over the brow of his young niece as she meditated upon the pleasing family group.

It would almost seem that the marquis's persistent ignoring of evils which he was powerless to remove ought to have merited something better than the aggressive precipitation of those very evils upon himself. But sometimes fate administers curious rewards to the philosopher — and the ostrich. Into

Aulnay village marched, one morning, several companies of Saxon grenadiers. The marquis betook himself to bed. Some forms of disgust are as acute as gout. His indisposition at least saved him from the pain of seeing a fresh-colored German orderly gallop up to his seignorial gates and demand entrance. Finding them barred and bolted, the rider shook them vigorously, and peremptorily repeated his request.

Old Jean, crouching behind them, trembling like a leaf in the autumn blast, — his loyalty bidding him stay, his cowardice prompting flight to the most remote coal-bin in the cellar, — unfortunately betrayed himself by a nervous cough.

Young Johann Wackermann heard him, grinned, straightened himself, saluted mechanically, stared stiffly at the wall, and roared in the direction of the cough: "You Frenchman, hiding behind that gate, I announce, most obediently at your service, that the colonel and staff-officers of the twenty-third Saxon grenadiers will quarter at this château from this day on, and that the regiment will occupy the village."

Receiving no response, he pounded on the gate with his sword-hilt: "Open, man; open, I tell you!"

"You German fiend on horseback, how dare you

pound the Marquis of Montauban's property?" screamed old Jean. "If I were as young as I used to be, I 'd come out there and teach you manners!"

Honest Johann Wackermann understood the spirit if not the letter of this greeting, grinned no longer, but glared as fiercely at the gate as the limitations of his broad, good-natured countenance would permit. "Don't rave at me in your cursed Kauterwelsch," he roared with his great voice, " for I don't know a word of it except *eau-de-vie* and *pang;* you 're an impudent French jackanapes, — that 's what you are! But you can't carry a stone wall round with you all the time, and I 'll meet you face to face before long, or my name 's not Johann Wackermann!"

Jean's aged treble responded like a fife after a deep bassoon. Both men raised their voices more and more, not only from anger, but because one instinctively assumes that foreigners are deaf. The animated scene might have continued long, — for Jean was frantic with indignation, and the Teuton's fresh-colored face was assuming a deeply irate hue, — when Countess Nathalie, followed by Manette, came into the court-yard.

"Hush, Jean," she said gravely. "What is this disturbance? You will annoy the marquis. Is it

not enough that the village is full of men and guns
and strange noises, but you must forget yourself in
this way?"

"Madame knows well," responded the old man
deferentially, "that it is not I, but this German boor,
who will not make war quietly; and where the honor
of the Montaubans is concerned, I am like a lion:
I know no bounds."

She repressed a smile; Manette giggled aggressively.
"We know your devotion, my good Jean," said the
countess soothingly, "but what does the man want?
Why, the gates are locked! Open them instantly,
Jean. He will not eat us," she added, smiling en-
couragingly at him as he still hesitated.

In rode the German orderly, angry and zealous; but
when he saw the highly respectable old enemy with
a face as white as his cravat, a broad, slow smile
broke over his own ruddy countenance, and he relieved himself by a strong ejaculation in his native
tongue. Then he turned his gaze upon the countess
and the little maid, and his smile deepened and
broadened marvellously, and his blue eye shone with
satisfaction; for Johann Wackermann had a soft
heart in his big body, and he began to rejoice mightily that he was coming at last to a Christian kind of

a place, where there was a beautiful lady and a pretty little maid, it was so long since he had seen so pleasant a sight.

"What do you want?" demanded the countess in German.

He gave his message with his stentorian voice and square, soldierly bearing, then made softest sheep's-eyes of honest admiration at Manette, who ardently reciprocated from behind her mistress's shoulder.

Great was Countess Nathalie's consternation. Ten strange men! No, this was too much! How would her poor uncle bear it?

"Very good," she said coldly. "You can go."

"May I beg to inspect the rooms," persisted the orderly, "and the stables?"

"As you please," said the countess. After which ceremony Wackermann's resounding "Gracious lady!" seemed to fill the court-yard; his salute was a credit to the Saxon grenadiers; his eyes were as tender as German love-songs as he spurred his horse, rode handsomely out of the gates into the village street, and galloped under the arch between château and church.

"That's what I call a man!" sighed Manette in ecstasy, casting a malicious glance at Jean.

The countess reflected. Looking gravely at the servants, she announced: "Ten German officers are coming here to-day."

Jean gasped, "Not to the château, madame?"

"To the château."

Manette raised her eyes devoutly to heaven. "Then war has its uses!" she exclaimed with joy and gratitude.

"Manette!" reproved her mistress.

"Madame will pardon me, but if the gentlemen are all as big and blue-eyed as that brave soldier, would that not be a distraction in this dead-and-alive château?"

"Heartless and vain coquette!" muttered Jean.

"It is not our war," persisted the girl gayly. "We are Legitimists. Can we help it if the Paris mob gets into rows with big blue-eyed nations? And can one die for one's country all day long, week in and week out?"

The countess smiled, and said gently: "It is dull here for a young thing like you. That is why I permit your lively tongue some extra liberty."

"Madame is very good," returned Manette demurely.

"Cheer up, Jean. It is not a pleasant prospect, but it probably will not last forever." That is the one consolation that never fails us, she thought drearily. "Go at once and look after the rooms. We must make what preparations we can. Give the strangers the best of everything. The hospitality of the château must not lose its reputation, eh, Jean?"

"No, madame," responded the old man gloomily.

After a pause she continued: "You may put me in my little old turret-room, where I slept when I was a child. I shall be well out of the way there."

"Yes, madame," he groaned.

"How interesting it all is! Who would have thought we should ever have had such good fortune!" exclaimed Manette excitedly. "Ten gentlemen! But, good heavens! what will they eat? Ten appetites! Dear, Dear!"

"Are there no fish, Manette?" asked the countess anxiously.

"Yes, madame; happily Antoine has just brought a quantity of fine ones."

"It is well. Otherwise they would have only salad for dinner," added the countess grimly. "One cannot give more than one has."

"Fish and salad never gave that beautiful rider his rosy cheeks!"

"Manette, if your spirits were somewhat more moderate, and yours, my poor Jean, a little less lugubrious, it might be desirable for the general good. But we must all do the best we can. Courage, Jean," smiling indulgently at the disconsolate old servant. "It's bad, I admit; but it might be worse. They are only Germans; they might be savages — cannibals. Manette, beg the abbé to have the kindness to come to me in the library."

"Yes, madame, M. l'Abbé is in the sacristy with Antoine. I will tell him at once," replied the maid, tripping brightly away as if life were one grand holiday, with music and dancing.

Countess Nathalie, in spite of her amiable efforts to comfort old Jean, felt, if not his painful tremors, equally depressed and full of forebodings. "O my poor little village, how ungrateful I was when I had you!" she murmured repentantly. "How impatient and selfish and hard-hearted I was!"

"Good morning, madame," said the abbé's gentle voice. She turned quickly.

"Ah, M. l'Abbé, you have heard what a terrible incubus has fallen upon the château?"

"The château will shake it off with time, madame."

"But meanwhile?"

"Meanwhile we must have patience," he answered with great quiet.

"And my uncle?"

"It will of course be most painful to the marquis. We must endeavor to reconcile him with it."

"It is for that reason I sent for you, M. l'Abbé. You have more influence with him than any one else. I hesitated to inform him of this last calamity. You can prepare him for it, perhaps."

"He is already prepared, madame."

The sudden question in her mind she did not express in words. He continued: "You are wondering how I knew? Antoine told me. He heard it last night. The command was brought at sundown from Vert Galant. You see it was no secret. Moreover, it was to be expected. The Germans, of course, with every opportunity tighten the coil round Paris."

"Poor Paris!" sighed the countess.

"We shall see," he returned with his curiously quiet manner.

"M. l'Abbé, I longed to go and take care of our wounded heroes; you and my uncle persuaded me to remain here. You declared it to be my duty. Good. Let that be as it may. I yielded. But sometimes I ask myself why, — and why, indeed, we are all here."

"We are here because the marquis preferred to stay, are we not, madame? Because, with his political principles and his failing health, it was his conviction, whatever should come, his chances of comfort and happiness were better here, in his own home?"

"Yes, I believe those were the alleged reasons for our course," she remarked slowly and thoughtfully, with no significant emphasis, but with evident dissatisfaction.

"But my dear madame," he began with gentle deprecation.

She looked up quickly, and smiled for the first time, a faint, doubtful smile. "Pardon me, M. l'Abbé," she said frankly; "I have grown to be a prober of motives, a dangerous underminer of phrases. I presume it is because I am restless, and because there is much that I do not understand."

"You are extremely young, madame."

"I shall never be young again," she replied in a matter-of-fact tone.

"And do you mean to imply it is my motive, my phrases, which you probe and undermine?" asked the abbé with mild incredulity.

"Yes — sometimes — often," she answered slowly.

"Ah!" he returned, with gentle regret and some surprise in his manner, as if this was news indeed, at the same time looking at her calmly and making no attempt to vindicate himself in her estimation. It was the wisest thing he could have done. His simplicity touched her.

"There are some things in the past between us," she began with an effort; "it is possible they cause me to misjudge you. I should be sorry to be unjust. I may have become too self-absorbed, too morbid, living this strangely dreary life all these weeks. But I thought it would be loyal to speak with you openly before these Germans descend upon us."

"It is loyal, countess. I thank you."

He turned away, walked to the window, and looked out. Antoine was waiting outside. She saw the abbé smile kindly at the fisherman and make him a friendly sign.

"He is a good man," she thought. "How careful he is of every one! It is I who am unkind, bad, suspicious; and what is so mean as suspicion!" The abbé came slowly back and stood before her, his gaze as clear and direct as her own.

"Madame, it would not be remarkable if you

should now and then misinterpret me. It would indeed be more extraordinary if you should not." He paused an instant. "As to the past, it is possible you may hold other views when you are older. As to the present, you surely cannot have imagined I induced the marquis to remain!"

"M. l'Abbé, your frankness shames me. Sometimes I have been capable of even that wild flight of fancy."

"But pray, what could have been my motive?" he asked with a gentle and perplexed air.

"That is what I have continually asked myself," she confessed with a little laugh. "I tell you I dream dreams and see visions; I have presentiments, revelations, second sight, like an old witch of Bondy wood."

"You are too much alone," he suggested sympathetically.

"It may be."

"Madame, there is one thing which I trust you have never called in question,— my affection for the marquis."

"Never," she returned warmly.

"Good!" A fine smile lighted his dark, pale face. "It is well that we have spoken. Let us leave old wrongs to slumber. In these strange times that are coming, pray trust me, for you may need me — I may need you."

"We do not always agree, M. l'Abbé, that is the truth. But against the Germans we are of one heart and soul. Ah, how I dread this experience!"

"Think how others have suffered. Should we alone escape?"

"Never doubt I would hesitate at any act of sacrifice, any helpful deed," she explained earnestly. "But this long inaction, this sheltering a German garrison under our very roof, — that does not help France. That is an indignity to France, to us, — odious, insupportable."

"Who can tell, countess, what your service and mine may be, and when France may require it of us?"

His voice was so solemn, that her own remark seemed petty and flippant, like the chatter of Manette.

"Who, indeed?" she repeated thoughtfully. "May France find us ready!"

"Amen!" responded the abbé softly, under his breath.

She looked at him, not without admiration for his intellect and strength, but with conflicting sentiments.

She felt that she was not malleable even under his deft touch. Her memories, convictions, and distrust of him had grown old and stern, like grim warriors whose serried ranks withstood passing attacks from momentary impressions. But he was true to the château, true to France; and there was wisdom and security in this alliance against the common enemy.

"Hark! what is that?" exclaimed the abbé, throwing open a window. Faint in the distance, gradually louder and clearer, they heard the sound of fife and drum. Far down the road, between the burnt grain-fields, came the measured tramp of the enemy, the heavy roll and drag of approaching artillery.

The two listened, speechless, motionless. Suddenly Countess Nathalie started. "Insufferable!" she cried. "Do you not hear? It is the Marseillaise!"

The abbé's eyes flashed angrily; his lips set hard.

"When I hear that," said the countess, drawing a deep, quivering breath, "I would hesitate at nothing."

The abbé turned and looked at her long. "At nothing?" asked his searching eyes.

Nearer and nearer to Aulnay Tower marched the German battalion.

CHAPTER II.

"If I have one fixed principle," mused Manette, preserving method in the madness of scarlet bows with which she was adorning herself before her mistress's mirror, and setting her lips in as firm a line as was practicable with a quantity of pins reposing between them,—"it is never to have a mistress whose style interferes with my own. When I left my first lady, Madame de St. Mars, she thought I objected to the impudence of monsieur's valet. I did not. The impudence of monsieur's valet was all very well in its way. What I objected to was madame herself. She was of excellent family, had a very decent disposition, her clothes fitted me to a charm, she was free with money, not energetic, and by no means too clever,—in short, all that could be desired in a mistress. Nevertheless, I left her. There were tears in my eyes, but I knew my duty. I was inflexible. And why? Because the conviction was borne in upon me that the want of contrast between me and

3

my mistress would be fatal to my career. I was losing my freshness. I was drooping. My originality suffered. I had no incitement to new combinations. What suited one of us, suited the other. I suspected this long; I resolved to put it to the proof. One night when she was at the opera I dressed my hair like hers, slipped into her freshest ball-dress and a pair of her long gloves, took a large fan, her best point d'aiguille handkerchief, and stood before her mirror. What a moment of anguish! *I was madame.* I do not say in every feature. As to features, there might be a difference of opinion. But the type was identical. The size, the color, the killing flash of the eye, the arch turn of the head, even the practised smile was madame. And she — did I not know that my short skirt and cap and apron would look as if they grew on her, and that she would have my own peculiar charm? We were as alike as two peas. It was heart-rending. I gave warning. And since that time, though I have had my little temptations, — and I don't say as I have always resisted all of them, — on this point I am as firm as the rock of Gibraltar: never will I go into service with a small, black-eyed, piquant, coquettish, pretty little woman like me, for it's death to my best sentiments.

" But Madame de Vallauris sets me off, and I set her off. It's ideal! It's heavenly! She is fair, but not too fair, tall, but not too tall, wears the simplest thing with an air of her own, and has such repose of manner that my little flutter makes a pleasing variety in contrast. Best of all, she is a constant stimulant to my fancy, for I can't look at her without inventing a love of a costume on the spot. Not that her mourning and the severity of her taste do not restrict my actual practice. But what of that, so long as the fantasy, the poesy, the soul of a fresh toilet is always there? Madame de Vallauris is almost too clever for a perfectly satisfactory mistress. She puts two and two together and knows they make four, which few ladies even suspect. If you don't happen to tell the same story you told yesterday, she trips you up as calm as you please. And she never scolds, which gives her an unfair advantage.

" Then, has n't this château been empty enough to ache, and me like an angel of patience with never a man about? *But* I still say, all that and worse I 'd bear, for it 's educating to live with such shoulders and such a waist; and after Countess Nathalie, no maid who respects herself could stoop to either the

scraggy or the stout, and till I die I'll declare that
for folds and colors and draping she is a divine in-
spiration. What I am myself for aprons, caps, fur-
belows, and flyaway ribbons, she is for cashmere,
velvet, crêpe. I'm the vivacious and sparkling; she
the exquisitely dignified. We are distinct, each
unique in her way. Neither interferes with the other.
I shall never get monotonous,— the worst thing in
my art, — and that's why I adore Countess Nathalie,
and am thankful for my blessings. And yet I have
my disappointments, my chagrins. Madame is as
unaccountable as she is beautiful. To-day, for example, what a field for genius! What a chance for
never-to-be-forgotten impressions! A dozen officers!
That means — oh, joy !— scores of under-officers and
hundreds of soldiers. Not a woman in Aulnay but
madame and me. O just Heaven, what possibilities! My rich imagination dressed us both in the
twinkling of an eye. That handsome rosy giant of
a German (something tells me we shall meet again!)
had hardly left the court before I saw madame
attired in subtle appropriateness for the occasion.
Some maids would have thought only of themselves;
but I am true as steel to my vocation, and to the
Countess Nathalie. Gentle severity was the key-

note of my composition : heavy black silk, of course. There it lies. Elegance and dignity in the train. Happy surprises in the drapery. Fascination in the sleeves. Defiance, pride, and patriotism in the high collar, tempered by regret in the soft ruche, with a careless bunch of violets at the throat, — as emblems of the springtime and youth which belong to Countess Nathalie if to any woman in the world, — and a cloud of black tulle for witchery. She would have been a problem and a poem; while I in my cheerful reds, my dazzling white, my decisive short skirts, my piquant shoes, my audacious apron, am a conundrum, a pleasantry, an epigram; moreover, slightly military, which is delicately flattering to the invaders. Here I stand, a success, perfect of my kind. And madame ? Alas! she disappoints my hopes, crushes my enthusiasm, — positively refuses to make any change in her toilet. I do not say that she is not distinguished and beautiful in her simple cashmere; but only once in a lifetime do ten foreign officers ride up to a lonely château where there are but two women. Great is the moment, and my design was vast."

"Manette, Manette, why are you waiting here ? I have been looking for you. You should be with me." Countess Nathalie entered the room rapidly.

"Ah, I was hoping madame would reconsider."

"Reconsider what?" said Countess Nathalie absently.

"Pardon, madame, — the toilet. It is here, quite ready. I have combined and adjusted. But five minutes, and madame would be a dream," pleaded the girl.

The countess smiled faintly.

"Manette, I ought to be thankful that you can even to-day make me laugh. Yet if I did not know what a good heart you have, I should be impatient now and then with your nonsense."

"This at least," responded Manette desperately. With one quick movement she sprang to the toilet-table, where a pale tea-rose stood in a little glass. Another bound, and she was fastening it at the countess's throat. "Madame permits —"

"Child, child, does one adorn one's self for the enemies of one's country?"

"But when the enemies of one's country are ten staff-officers! And, after all, enemies are — men!"

"I will wear the rose if it makes you happier," Countess Nathalie said wearily. "At least, it can do no harm. But, Manette, let me beg you to be discreet, with all these men about. You cannot be too reserved and careful. You are a good girl. Let me depend upon you. No chatter. No glances."

"I shall be discretion itself," and Manette drew down the corners of her mouth. "I shall be as solemn as the Tower. They shall fear me."

"If you will only be sensible and helpful, that is all that I require. And, Manette, don't put on all that red again, please. You look like a maid on the stage, or is it a *vivandière?* Come with me now. I shall wait in the library. The marquis is in despair, — refuses to leave his bed. The abbé remains to console him. Another man on horseback, this time an officer, a gentleman, just rode into the court and inquired if the marquis would allow the General von Aarenhorst to present himself. He marked names in chalk on all our doors."

"Oh! Was he tall? Had he blue eyes?"

"He was tall. I did not observe whether he had eyes."

"The dear!"

"Manette!"

"Madame was about to say — " began the girl with an innocent air.

"Nothing, Manette. There is nothing, indeed, that I can say to you, since you will not understand that my heart is heavy. I have been watching the Germans enter the village."

"I was so grieved to lose the fine sight!" murmured Manette sympathetically. "But," with an eloquent gesture towards the rejected toilet, "madame knows that where my higher duties are concerned I am adamant. Not even the military can distract my attention."

"And they are crowding in and out of our little houses, where the familiar smiling faces used to glance out and wish me good-morning," Countess Nathalie went on thoughtfully. "They are drinking beer before old Berthe's door, and grooming their horses where the children played on the green, and cleaning their guns at the baker's. They are not bad-looking —"

"Ah!" Manette clasped her hands ecstatically.

Countess Nathalie's quiet, abstracted voice continued, talking, as was her wont, to the little maid because she was the only woman near, yet unmindful of her light retort, — "Not cruel, bloodthirsty men. No, I will be just. They have honest, simple, kindly faces, these German soldiers. They are manly and brave, but gentle. They are laughing and making jokes out there innocently. They look as if they loved their wives and children at home," she said slowly.

"Wives and children! For pity's sake, madame, are they all dull old family men? Are there no young gay ones?" interpolated Manette with consternation. "Then it's no great loss if I did n't look out of the window!"

"And I will not blame them too harshly, for they are mere tools," concluded the young countess, communing still with her own thoughts. "They are forced into this cruel work. They are to be pitied. But their leaders,—their leaders I will never forgive! They know what they do. They coldly plan this work of destruction. It is a curse. It is a sin. I will never forgive them—never!"

She stood an instant pale with excitement, then, raising her head, looked out on the park where she had played as a happy child, where as a saddened woman she had spent long hours of retrospection. Her glance fell upon the little turret-room. It was a cool shrine of childhood, unchanged since she had stored her treasures there,—the ivory angel on the wall hovering over a bunch of mammoth forget-me-nots painted by her own unskilful, zealous hand; our Lady in a bright blue robe; St. Barbara too (Uncle Raoul bought that for her in Paris; she begged for it on account of the Tower); some dried grasses from

the meadow brook; a few childish books; a glass case
of toys and dolls. When she had come home from
the convent, she had been so glad to find everything
in its place. Then she was seventeen, and her uncle
said it was all too babyish for a girl about to be married, and she moved down to the stately rooms below.
She had loved to be up there, above the tree-tops and
within sight of the church-tower; but she had had
hardly time to grieve, those days had gone so fast, and
she felt so strange and dazed when she knew she was
to be the Countess de Vallauris. The count — she
put her hand to her eyes, she gave one deep sigh for
her lost illusions : " Is this the way to prepare myself
for all that must be borne ? Ah, how weak a thing a
woman is !" This was no time for memories of childhood, no time for bitter thoughts. Voices and unwonted
commotion filled Aulnay. Horses' hoofs sounded below in the court-yard. The hated strangers were at
the château gates. She looked piteously at the bright-
faced maid : " These are sad days, Manette."

" Very, madame," returned Manette dutifully.
" But," she added, her eyes dancing, " exhilarating !"

" Come with me," said the countess, turning and
going down the narrow stairway, erect, firm, her face
cold and haughty, to meet the foe.

Manette obeyed, but adroitly seized a black lace fichu, and from her convenient position, as she followed her mistress down the stairs, flung it over the countess's shoulders, reasoning: "In that straight gown, and with her repellent air, madame is too unambiguous. A touch of mystery is indispensable."

Countess Nathalie mechanically pulled the ends of the diaphanous "mystery" about her as she went bravely on, her head high, her eyes cold, her mouth determined and forbidding.

"She could n't make herself stonier if she were going to meet ten fiery dragons !" sighed Manette, regarding her mistress critically as she turned on the winding stairs. "Well, I have done my duty by her ! Angels can do no more."

Meanwhile General von Aarenhorst was in an exceptionally bad temper. Although one of the most amiable of men, as Frau von Aarenhorst would unhesitatingly affirm, this bold warrior and distinguished strategist had been for days the victim of many annoyances, to which his inner tranquillity had finally succumbed. He was of too large a nature, too successful a soldier, too much trusted by his sovereign and loved by the army, — in short, too marked a man, to escape the fate of every

mortal visible enough against the great background
of mediocrity to serve as target.   Jealousy, back-
biting, and malicious misinterpretation, not being exclusive vices of women and coffee-parties, but also
common to the grander sex and their grand situations,
had made themselves manifest in Aarenhorst's immediate circle, and ruffled his equanimity in no light
degree.   He felt aggrieved and sore from a slight mis-
understanding on the part of his prince.   He had
quarrelled with a friend, which he deeply regretted,
and failed to quarrel with a rival, which galled him
still more.   Altogether it was in no enviable mood
that the good general rode into Aulnay ; and he looked
like a very grim warrior indeed, — capable, poor Jean
thought, as he tremblingly held open the great gate
and Aarenhorst glared at him from under shaggy
eyebrows, of drinking blood from the skulls of his
victims.

The general and his suite dismounted in the
court-yard.   That quiet place became suddenly instinct with life and movement, — on the moss-grown
pavement the firm tread of booted and spurred
feet, the irregular beat of horse-hoofs, men's deep
voices in brief command, soldiers hurrying to and
fro, sabres clanking lightly, jests in a foreign tongue,

and the laughter of gallant youth ready for any fate.

General von Aarenhorst, stern and warlike as an ancient Gaul, strode gloomily toward the door of the château. His commanding presence towered above the finely built men accompanying him. His strong and handsome features, though rugged and weather-beaten, scarcely betrayed his fifty years. The square chin looked resolute as fate, the mouth indomitable, and the usual twinkle in his deep-set keen gray eyes, which made his masterful face kindly, humorous, and lovable, was to-day as invisible as the evening star on a cloudy night.

"Why is no one here to receive me?" he demanded gruffly, stopping short before the threshold of the château.

Jean quaked mightily, but forced himself to totter up the stone steps and fling open the large house door.

"Why is no one here to receive me?" thundered the general. "Where is the Marquis de Montauban?"

"Not at home," stammered old Jean.

"Not at home?" repeated the ancient Gaul, glaring fiercely at the unfortunate servant.

"Not at home to strangers," Jean gasped desperately, believing that his hour was come, but heroic in his cowardice, resolving to make the Germans unwelcome to the last.

Von Aarenhorst turned impatiently away. "This poor man is an imbecile," he said. "There can have been no irregularity in the announcement?"

"None whatever, Excellenz," replied an adjutant, stepping forward. "Orderly Wackermann announced the coming of the staff and of the battalion. I myself announced your personal visit to the Marquis de Montauban."

"I've had enough of this insolence," began the general. "I refuse to enter a gentleman's house like a thief in the night. I insist upon seeing the master of this château."

At this moment a door opposite the vestibule opened, and the irate general saw a beautiful woman, young, pale, fair-haired, stately, and forbidding. In fact, her expression as she came forward was indicative of a high and courageous spirit prepared for the worst extremity of fate.

The general saluted like the elegant cavalier that he was. The pale lady in her black dress, with a fresh Sofrano rose at her throat, drew some lace she wore closer about her, and returned his greeting haughtily. All the lieutenants in the court-yard who had been giving orders about their horses and the stables suddenly drifted towards the door, moved by the occult magnetism of a fair woman's presence. Spurred heels went together with an automatic click, hands flew up in courteous if spasmodic salute. The flower of the German army laid its homage at the feet of the pale lady, who once more returned her half-perceptible, icy salutation. Behind her a bright little butterfly of a woman peeped out and made laughing eyes assiduously, as if to atone for the indifference of her mistress.

"Jean, show these gentlemen to their rooms," said Countess Nathalie, turning to go, with a slight gesture, as if she were a crowned head concluding an audience.

"My dear young lady," began the general.

"I am Madame de Vallauris," was the frigid correction.

"You may be Madame what you please, you pretty creature," thought the general, "but you are not a day older than my Gertrud; and how would she feel, the dear girl, if a dozen Frenchmen should march in and take possession of our house at home?"

"Most happy," he returned, with his firm salute, and the humorous twinkle reappearing in his shrewd eyes like the evening star after passing clouds. "I have the honor to present myself, von Aarenhorst, General of the —— Division. I beg to be allowed to pay my respects to the Marquis de Montauban."

"My uncle for the present must deprive himself of the pleasure of making your acquaintance," responded Madame de Vallauris coolly.

The pleasant twinkle in the general's eye expanded perceptibly. This proud young foe amused him, and he admired her spirit.

"Madame, when I enter a gentleman's house as a guest —"

Countess Nathalie's eyebrows questioned his choice of words. He understood her protest, but continued blandly, "I am in the habit of being received by my host."

"My uncle can see no one. He has not left his bed for some hours."

"Is the Marquis de Montauban seriously ill?" asked the general, watching his fair adversary, with polite scrutiny.

"No," she answered, raising her honest eyes to his, — "no, he is not ill. That is, he is never strong now, but he is perhaps not much more indisposed than usual. He is disgusted, outraged, unreconciled, that is all. In his state of health he finds the situation insupportable."

"Now I wonder if my Gertrud under similar circumstances would declare war in as straightforward a fashion as that," reflected the general, studying Countess Nathalie with kindliest interest.

"Madame," he answered, "no one can regret more deeply than I that the exigencies of war compel us to seek the hospitality of the Marquis de Montauban. The facts being what they are, we shall endeavor to make our stay as little repugnant to him as possible. Believe me, in spite of circumstances, madame, we shall even hope to win the esteem, under this roof, which one may well accord an honorable enemy."

"The château is obviously at your disposal," she said coldly.

"Which is the same as saying, ' My thoughts are my own, though the skies fall!'" groaned Manette. "Oh if it were not inappropriate from me to her, how I should like to shake her well for being so freezing to that beautiful dear, and all those beautiful dears behind, like cherubim and seraphim, pulling their mustaches and stretching their handsome high boots and staring with all their eyes!"

"You will permit me to inquire, madame," said the

general kindly, but still intent upon being received according to his rank and dignity and the etiquette which he himself deemed fitting, " is there no one else in this château ?　No gentleman who can represent the marquis ? "

" Besides my uncle, myself, and the servants, there is no one in the house but the Abbé de Navailles, the marquis's spiritual adviser and friend.　Under these circumstances, I fear you will be obliged to content yourself with me," she added dryly.

"Now my Gertrud would never have thought of saying that!" decided the general, his eyes twinkling merrily as he surveyed his fair adversary and exchanged an appreciative look with Colonel von Linden.

" Madame," he returned gallantly, "to you we surrender at discretion.　We beg for mercy, not justice."

" Jean, show these gentlemen to their rooms," was Countess Nathalie's reply.　" We keep but four for ourselves," she added in a business-like tone.　" All the rest is reserved for you, with the gardener's house and the porter's lodge."

"Thanks, madame.　I regret to have disturbed you so long."

"Pray do not mention it."

With a straight look at the general and a grave inclination towards him, and another still slighter, which seemed in a vague way to embrace the walking-sticks and umbrellas in the vestibule, together with the equally insignificant staff-officers and the September sunshine on the old wall without, Countess Nathalie was gone, Manette doing as much execution as ever a single pair of black eyes accomplished during the brief act of closing a door.

The ten officers, a stately body of men with uniforms no longer in parade condition and faces which showed deep lines of fatigue and exertion, followed Jean up the broad front stairway to a series of spacious rooms overlooking the park. Several of the younger men arranged to occupy one room, and began at once to make themselves comfortable. There was a pulling about of beds and other furniture, and a tramping to and fro of attentive Bursche, and a severe inspection of defective uniforms.

Colonel von Linden smiled. "I have observed no such aspirations towards respectability among us for some weeks. Even the doctor is looking askance at his sleeves, and a panic of mending and brushing seems to have broken out among the lieutenants. H'm! and this is but the beginning."

Von Linden was a man of middle height and unusual physical strength, with iron-gray hair clustering thickly round an animated face. He was extremely well informed, and a great but good talker.

"One woman," he continued,—"but what a woman! Eh, Nordenfels?"

His adjutant turned from the window where he stood looking out on the park,—a tall, slender, blond Gardereiter, elegant on foot as in the saddle, an earnest and rather silent man. "I beg your pardon, colonel?"

"I was merely saying our chatelaine is a beautiful woman."

"Yes," replied von Nordenfels gravely.

"And a dangerous woman. That kind of a woman is always dangerous. Still and cold? Don't you believe it. The little flirtatious maid there, with the bright eyes and the warm, dark skin, — that's a cold woman. She'd estimate the price of a man's sleeve-buttons while he was kneeling before her extending imploring hands, and she'd mentally invest her savings on her way to the altar. But the mistress, there, with her clear eyes and proud air, and her mouth set as if she would n't flinch before a volley of grape,—that's a warm-hearted woman, or I'm no judge. She's a Hecla. There's fire beneath that snow, mark my words, Nordenfels."

"I mark them, colonel," returned the young man with a slight smile.

"I tell you if I were a young man, an unmarried man, I'd fall in love with that woman on the spot," said the enthusiastic colonel, waxing more and more impassioned. "I don't see what you young fellows are made of. At your age, Nordenfels, I could n't have stood there and stared at trees. I should have prepared to storm the citadel. I should have said to myself, 'In this enchanted castle is a sleeping beauty; none but the brave deserve the fair. Advance through thorns and difficulties, wake her and win her.' Thorns? Yes, there would be thorns enough on that path," he said laughing. "She's the veriest 'Dornrösschen,' and in no end of an international labyrinth."

"If I understand you correctly, colonel," von Nordenfels began with the utmost gravity, "you are advising me to entertain matrimonial designs in regard to a French lady to whom I have never had the honor of speaking. In such a trivial matter I am as wax in the hands of a friend. Pray write to my father and dispose of me."

Von Linden looked at him quizzically. "You can be as satirical as you like; but I might do worse for you, after all."

"Undoubtedly."

"Let me tell you, a little rashness never harms a man like you,—a high-ideal coxcomb, always seeking and dreaming and never finding."

Von Nordenfels smiled.

"Oh, I don't mean you're to fall on your knees to-night before the stately little lady, or send Wackermann round with a billet-doux ; but it's your want of enthusiasm that I condemn."

"Pardon me, but I don't think Madame de Vallauris would be particularly edified by our conversation," von Nordenfels ventured to say.

"H'm ! I don't believe she'd object very seriously," returned the colonel good-humoredly, seating himself and opening a portfolio, and taking out some papers. "At all events, I'm old enough to be her father. She would forgive me. And while a woman may resent too much admiration, she never forgives too little."

"Madame de Vallauris is not that kind of a woman," von Nordenfels returned abruptly.

"Ah, then you did happen to remark what kind of a woman she is! Well, I'm glad of that," said the colonel dryly. "There's some hope for you still," busying himself with his papers.

Von Nordenfels rejoined the lieutenants.

"You're just in time, Nordenfels; Forstenau is about to tell a story," drawled a dandy lieutenant familiarly known as Lily, who had parted his hair painfully in the middle, and was now brandishing two brushes and laughing hilariously.

"No, not a story," protested von Forstenau.

"He once knew a painter," explained von Gerhardt. "You think you grasp the situation, do you, Nordenfels? Forstenau says he once knew a painter. It's incredible, you know! Colossal!"

"What about your painter, Hubert?" demanded Nordenfels curtly, but with a friendly look at the youngest scion of the noble house of Forstenau, — a lank, sandy youth, whose conversation was rarely known to stray from equine subjects, and who now sat struggling with a treacherous memory.

"I say I once knew a painter — "

"Fabulous!" muttered the Lily.

"Let him alone. Let him tell his story," insisted Nordenfels.

"A painter who said — "

"Well, out with it," Nordenfels said encouragingly.

"Who said that there are but four types — "

"Of what ? Racers ?" demanded the Lily.

"No — women."

"Women!" repeated the young man, laughing. "Forstenau's actually holding forth about women. O Forstenau, Forstenau! that it should come to this !"

"Four types," persisted the wretched young man, wishing that he had remained firmly seated upon his horse and never attempted to mount anybody else's hobby. "The Marie Antoinette type — the Marie Antoinette type," he went on, feeling most miserable. "The Marie Antoinette type — "

They stared at him, smiling, expectant. The Lily turned towards him, holding his brushes motionless.

"I've forgotten the other three," stammered von Forstenau, overcome with embarrassment and hanging his head dejectedly.

A great shout followed.

"Don't do that again, Forstenau," the Lily said reprovingly. "Don't excite us in this way for nothing. I shall be cudgelling my brains unmercifully now to find those three missing types. Every time I see a woman I shall say, 'O woman, are you a type? Are you one of Forstenau's lost types?'"

"It was your fault," retorted Forstenau, rallying. "Madame de Vallauris put it in my mind. I knew the whole thing perfectly when I looked at her. If you had n't interrupted and chaffed, I should n't have forgotten. It was a very good story." He looked sullenly at his comrades and relapsed into a long silence, neither knowing nor caring why they laughed.

Von Nordenfels was examining the room attentively. It was delicately appointed, evidently a woman's room. Rising, he deliberately collected the vases, books, and ornaments, and put them in a chest of drawers in the corner, locking it and removing the key. Everything fragile he deposited in that safe receptacle. A smaller room he treated with the same consideration; but being screened from his companions' sight, he studied the few books he found, and the pictures, long and earnestly, as if he would fain penetrate into the nature of the owner. Some tea-roses stood on a little table. The vase was simple, and he let it stay. There was a low chair by the window towards the park, and, overlooked in the rapid preparations for the strangers, a small

black glove near it.   He secured it hastily, hesitated
a moment, then gravely laid it with the other objects
he had collected.   Some subtle association lingered
with a faint fragrance in the little room, or his
warm fancy invested it with a nameless charm.

"Does any one want this place?" he inquired
indifferently, reappearing among his friends. "No?
Then I'll move in."

"Are n't you giving yourself a great deal of trouble?" drawled the Lily. "One of the men could do
that just as well."

"I don't seem to be working so hard as you are
with your hair," returned von Nordenfels, smiling.
"It seems only decent to get such things out of the
way as soon as possible. Moreover, we don't know
who or what will follow us."

"Gerhardt, you need n't make yourself irresisti-
ble. It's no use. I've got ahead of you. I've
enlisted the maid on my side," said a handsome,
dark man, entering with a long, swinging stride.

"If you think that sort of thing is fair among
comrades," began the Lily. "But what have you
been doing?"

"Why I ran down to look after Claudia. She went
lame."

"Strategy, to begin with. Claudia's no lamer than you are!"

"Well, I remembered she was lame once," continued von Wedell, lighting a cigarette, "or I feared she might be lame sometime. At all events, I had to go to the stables to look after her. The reason I had to go so suddenly was because I saw a young person in red and white flitting about the court-yard conveniently for my purposes. She's a nice little thing. Her name is Manette." He whiffed, and smiled provokingly.

"I don't care about her! What did you wheedle out of her about her mistress? Tell us all you know. That's the least you can do."

"Manette is very discreet. She told me so herself," said von Wedell soberly. "She was discreetly making eyes at that huge Wackermann when I found her, and then she discreetly made eyes at me. She sighed, and said these were sad times, with the château full of handsome young officers like me and my friends, and she and the Countess Nathalie could n't be too reserved and careful."

"Countess Nathalie! Aha! that's her name?"

"Countess Nathalie de Vallauris, a widow twenty-three years old. Count de Vallauris died a year ago. Apparently the discreet Manette could tell me something highly seasoned about him, only she passed on to more vital subjects. He was an old fellow, so much I know. Since his death Madame de Vallauris has lived with her uncle the marquis. There was an aunt, or companion, or something, who fled to Paris at the first warning. Countess Nathalie is very kind, and very peculiar. 'Her hair is all her own.'"

"Wedell, don't you think we could choose a more interesting subject for general conversation?" interrupted von Nordenfels with a frown.

"Well, I don't know," replied Wedell, staring superciliously; "it's interesting to me."

"Don't be a dog in the manger, Nordenfels. If you don't happen to be capable of falling in love yourself, you need n't try to deprive other men of that bliss. I'm gone, done for, extinguished, I tell you!" drawled the Lily.

"One might think I had permitted myself unsuitable language," remarked von Wedell coldly.

"It's a mere matter of taste, perhaps," von Nordenfels replied. "My views of life I prefer to form with no aid from below-stairs."

"Go on, go on, Wedell!" cried the others impatiently.

Von Nordenfels frowned, but listened.

"Manette, that pearl of discretion, fears that none of us, in spite of our superhuman fascinations, which she gave me to understand she fully appreciated, can make the slightest impression upon the countess. Manette pronounces it a romantic situation, a thrilling opportunity. But alas! she says, what can one expect when madame remains insensible to the influence of her most devoted maid? She will do what she can to soften the sentiments of madame, but madame has the deplorable habit of thinking for herself; and, beautiful as she is, would be more seductive if—"

"Did she say nothing whatever about the Marquis de Montauban?" interrupted Nordenfels.

"Oh, you're deigning to listen, after all, are you? She said the marquis is a Legitimist and a very grand gentleman, and she, Manette, is a Legitimist too, and M. l'Abbé is a holy man who does n't care about parties or wars; but madame has invincible prejudices against us Germans."

"She's a handsome woman enough," said von Bergen, "but she leaves a man cold—cold, you know. There is nothing appealing about her, nothing sympathetic and winning, nothing piquante."

"What would you have?" began the Lily with praiseworthy energy. "Should she smirk and smile on us, and say how glad she was to make our acquaintance? No, she was quite right under the circumstances — quite! She could n't have done it better, could she now, Nordenfels?" appealingly to the older lieutenant, whom he admired vastly for an easy way of doing difficult things, and upon whose face he now perceived a shade of attention, if not of approval.

"No," muttered von Nordenfels.

"The question is now, To whom is she going to soften? It's a matter of course that we all fall in love with her — Nordenfels always excepted. All I say is, fair play among comrades. You, Wedell, — you got the start with Manette. You've got to pay for that."

"Upon my honor, I have told everything the girl said. I've shared joy and sorrow with you."

"Then I'm obliged to you. It's always important at the start to know if a woman is maid, wife, or widow. You have to make a different line of march, you know."

"The idea of that beautiful woman being a widow is preposterous. Deuced bad taste of old Vallauris. Go on, Kurt. Confide your strategy to us."

"Not a word more," returned von Gerhardt. "Mind you all start fair. That's all I have to say. For my part, I never was so hard hit. The impression was powerful and immediate," he went on calmly, unmoved by the jeers of his comrades. "I love for the first time with a reckless ardor."

"How about Countess Sophie?"

"She? Her cheeks are too round and red," he said with conviction.

"And the bright Stella?"

"Well, I was in pretty seriously in that direction for a time," laughed the boy; "but she's not to be mentioned in the same breath with Madame de Vallauris. That reminds me. Did I ever tell you of the joke about the last laurel-wreath I sent Stella? It was a crusher, with a rose-colored bow on it as big as a girl's sash at her first ball. She sang divinely, and looked mighty handsome too, but is no more fit than Manette to be compared to Madame de Vallauris, and—"

At this moment Max von Nordenfels stalked abruptly out of the room.

"What in the deuce is the matter with Nordenfels to-day?" inquired von Wedell. "The noble knight is often taciturn, but seldom so uncommonly disagreeable."

"Reason enough. He does n't like to hear Kurt Gerhardt try to tell a story," growled von Forstenau.

"Bravo, Hubertchen!" returned von Gerhardt with patronizing good-humor.

CHAPTER III.

"And, my dear Nathalie," added the Marquis de Montauban, very elegant in dinner dress, "it is obviously our duty to master these circumstances,—not to permit these circumstances to master us."

Nathalie regarded him with a surprised air. She had expected anything but this tone; and for a man whom circumstances had laid flat some hours previous, he certainly displayed wonderful recuperative power. Loftiness reigned on his brow, elasticity in his gait, and in his manner pleasurable anticipation.

Instinctively she glanced at the abbé. When anything inexplicable occurred at the château, she always asked herself, "What does the abbé mean by it?" The covert attack of her inquiry fell back as usual upon itself. His fine face was turned respectfully, affectionately, towards the marquis, and he listened as one whose quiet sympathy compensates for lack of active participation.

The Abbé de Navailles entertained the conviction that most people explain too much. He believed that a wise man never explains his own conduct. One's conduct is either understood, not understood, half understood, or misunderstood. If understood, an explanation is evidently superfluous. In each of the three other cases, by means of an explanation one may gain something, but is sure to lose more.

"There is no situation," resumed the marquis, "in which true dignity cannot prevail." Tall, slight, extremely frail, with withered hands, a striking old man with his thin aquiline features and gray hair, he walked elegantly up and down the charming room. Nathalie was weary, sad, and rebellious; but the perversity of memory is no respecter of moods, and in contrast to the repose of his sentiments and his true dignity at this moment, a vivid picture of bygone years revisited her memory, — the slight form of her uncle fleeing madly before a bull on Grosley Farm. A fresh smile softened her face.

"You smile, Nathalie. You approve. That is well. And I approve of you, my dear," he said gallantly. "Your rose, your bit of lace, show that you are undismayed. They will not fail to observe it."

“ My bit of lace, my rose, are vagaries of Manette, and no one will have any chance to study their deep significance, as I shall not appear.”

“ Bless my soul, Nathalie!” he exclaimed. Then, sententiously: “ A mistake, my child — a false move. Permit me to convince you. It should be a matter of pride with you not to let them flatter themselves so far as to imagine that their presence disturbs you.”

“ What they think or do not think, or whether they think at all, is the one supremely indifferent thing to me at this juncture,” she returned coldly. “ But I can’t climb to your heights of philosophy, dear uncle, and, as a woman, their presence is inexpressibly repugnant to me. Allow me, then, to avoid them. Manette can easily bring me something.”

“ Marcus Aurelius,” began the marquis impressively, “ once expressed himself as follows: —

— “ Ah, it ’s Marcus Aurelius then,” thought Nathalie, with another quick glance at the abbé and a satirical curl of the corners of her mouth. —

“ ‘ Suppose that men kill thee, cut thee in pieces, curse thee, what then can these things do to prevent thy mind from remaining pure ’ ” — he hesitated — the abbé gently prompted: “ wise ” — “ ‘ wise,’ ” resumed the marquis, “ ‘ sober, just ?’ ” —

" Marcus Aurelius was a pagan," warned Nathalie dryly.

" 'True, but a man of faultless breeding, — a man *d'élite,*" replied the marquis with a conscious air, as if whoever attacked Marcus Aurelius might unwittingly kill two birds with one stone.

Nathalie's intense gaze followed him as he walked with grandeur from door to door. He was laughable, yes, but infinitely pathetic; a most lonely figure in the universal ruin, — his happy village deserted, his beloved country in danger from foes within and without, his party overthrown and suffering in silence, so that had his emaciated hand the force to draw his sword, he, a gentleman, and the child of a heroic race, would scarce have known in what direction to strike. Old, broken, no wife or child to clasp to his breast for comfort, the enemy in possession of his fair lands and his sacred fireside, his only help was to wrap himself in his mantle of conventionality, and lean upon the far-off shade of Marcus Aurelius.

" And is it not better so ? " asked the deep eyes of the Abbé de Navailles. " Is it not better than to let him suffer ? Am I not prompted by affection and wisdom when I seek to reconcile him with the inevitable ? "

Nathalie with a new tenderness and self-reproach moved swiftly towards the marquis. "I have not loved him enough," she thought, and slipped her hand within his thin, half-paralyzed arm. "Uncle," she said, "I understand. I admire. But I am only a woman, therefore it is hard for me to come to dinner to-day."

"You are a Montauban, therefore you should triumph over your weakness," replied the marquis proudly; not actually displeased at her impulsive demonstration, yet looking down at her hand with some wonder.

"Uncle, let us suppose Marcus Aurelius had had a niece. Not a grand person like him," — her face was enchanting in its unwonted pleading and play-fulness, — "but an ordinary, quite insignificant niece, with nothing heroic about her at all, nothing elevated and noble; and suppose she was so commonplace as to feel that there was a kind of — indelicacy — for want of a better word she was not clever enough to dis-cover — in her, one woman alone, receiving as guests an irksome group of men to whom her least bitter wish was that they might all be honorably shot dead on the field of battle," — her voice grew low as she went on, and all the winning smiles had left her face; "and suppose she should say to her illustrious uncle, 'Pray excuse me, for I have no heart,'—what would he reply?"

"He would reply,"—the withered frame of the Marquis de Montauban vibrated strangely; the fires of long ago leaped in his sunken eyes; he seemed to grow tall as he spoke;—"he would reply, 'Have I, then, nothing to bear? By the years in which I cared for you, by the calmness and confidence of our affection, by the sacred tie of blood, you, youngest of my ancient race, leave me not alone in my misfortune!'" He sank trembling into a fauteuil, his hands concealing his face.

"Marquis,"—the calm voice of the abbé recalled him to his duties,—"General von Aarenhorst and his suite are about to present themselves. I hear their tread on the stairway."

The marquis sprang to his feet. His features assumed their wonted expression of mild arrogance and unruffled composure.

"You have no choice, countess," whispered the abbé. "Courage!" as the Germans entered the room.

The meeting of General von Aarenhorst and the marquis was courtly and significant. A deferential and manly greeting, a few brief words, a shrewd and kindly glance on the one side, on the other an indistinct response, a deprecating wave of a frail hand with a manner of old-time elegance, and the dreaded moment passed. The officers one by one as they were presented straightened their broad shoulders, clicked their heels, inclined themselves before the elegant old gentleman, and saluted. Madame de Vallauris, cold and pale, stood by her uncle and seemed to see no one; but beautiful women in the great world often look cold and pale and see no one, and the lieutenants found her no less entrancing on that account. The marquis began to feel singularly at ease, and warmed visibly under the genial influence of von Linden. "After all, it pays to be a heroic figure," he thought. On the village street the men were lounging and smoking. German gutturals sounded powerful and all-pervading. German soldiers possessed the land. Countess Nathalie listened. A squad of men for forepost duty marched by with a lieutenant. Her heart resented every separate tone, every color of their uniform, as a personal injury; but she wore her air of still and immeasurable distance, and asked herself if it were a bad dream, when she heard her poor uncle's familiar laugh,—

the mechanical laugh of the complaisant host approving his guest's anecdote whether he quite hears it or not.   And when Jean, his spirit writhing in impotent rage, his manner the ideal of butler-perfection, flung open the folding-doors and announced that dinner was served, and General von Aarenhorst gave her his arm to take her in, she wished, as many a quiet-looking woman too well-bred to be tragic often wishes as she assists at some unavoidable ceremony, that the earth would open and swallow them all.

But the earth remained obdurate; and she, like the bride after the solemn marriage ceremony, like lovers in their first pure rapture, children in their hot and honest quarrels, faithful hearts mourning their dead, — like all of us, sinners or saints, bowed before the inexorable necessity of dinner. Dinner is indeed a stern tyrant. Its hideous, gregarious rites impose themselves upon us at supreme moments when the primeval-savage germ in us asserts itself and longs for air and freedom, space and solitude. The dagger suggests amorous tragedies, dim Venetian canals, and gliding gondolas; but the ponderous silver fork, weighed down like many a dull soul with the sense of its own respectability, — with what suffering, the more cruel because prolonged, is it not associated! The immaculate napkin, bristling with conventionality in every rigid fold, — what agonies has it not led on, like the gallant pennon of a forlorn hope! All honor to the unnumbered victims on the terrible field of a slow dinner! How their stout hearts faint and desperately rally before the invincible soup-tureen, the deadly pauses between the courses, the ubiquitous attack of the waiters, the fatal volleys of small talk! How they die a thousand deaths, yet bravely smile! If, when the spirit flies aghast from the dinner hocus-pocus, the outward man might vanish too, what a significant array of vacant chairs, in our most genteel dining-rooms, would commemorate the triumph of nature over civilization!

"How false it all is!" thought Nathalie. "What a tribute to the great god Hypocrisy, that I stay and break bread with the enemy! Savages would have more honesty and self-respect!" She watched her uncle. His face was excited, and the old, half-cynical, urbane smile of the man of the world flitted over it; but the expression of his eyes was uncertain, and his memory faltered now and then, when she observed he depended upon the abbé, whose low voice gave the missing word, whose manner encouraged and sustained.

Again a pang of self-reproach troubled her conscience, and an anxious look stole into her composed face. "How selfish I have been, not to know how old and weak he has grown! How strangely blind I was not to observe, in the quiet days when he was near me, what I see so plainly now that we are separated by these strange men! Or is it this one day that has aged him? No, I cannot escape this; I should hear the horses and the soldiers, the voices and the constant sounds, wherever I should go. I cannot escape, and I would not; for I must stay with him." Her solicitous glance, leaving her uncle, touched here and there upon the group, the trouble still in her eyes, and met with directness the intent gaze of a blond man in a light-blue uniform, who sat at some distance from her. Involuntarily her look paused, arrested by the strength and deep interest of his; then she dropped her eyes, turned away, and for the first time of her own accord addressed von Aarenhorst. Most eyes at the table were turned, as often as propriety allowed, towards the beautiful woman, with her indifferent air, beside the general. There seemed to be a tacit understanding that staring her out of countenance would be an unfair employment of their privileges; and admiration was therefore meted out to her by each according to his own measure, — light, bold, flippant, respectful, tempered by the demands of the situation and the presence of dignitaries. The inflammable lieutenants conducted themselves with gentlemanly discretion; but it must be admitted, had they met Madame de Vallauris on the street in a German capital, their self-command would have been less, their visual organs more, exercised. As she hardened her heart against the strangers, she had looked up and met the gaze of a friend. Nordenfels' face, grave and self-contained, intent yet not bold, inquiring, seeking, demanding, satisfied neither with himself nor yet with her, seemed in the midst of this strangeness something long known and familiar as her own thoughts.

So Madame de Vallauris had turned instantly to the general with a conventional inquiry. The Abbé de Navailles, his long hair brushed back as if the better to expose the ingenuousness of his clear profile and scholarly face, made vivid mental notes of the incident as he unobtrusively murmured the marquis's missing word. Von Nordenfels in his turn, moved by the subtle instinct that whispers an enemy is near, carefully studied the abbé. The eyes of the two men also met in a long, well-balanced look. Thus nature laughs at the solemnity of etiquette and dinner, and our spirits, free still in blessed moments, look out of our eyes, declare war, and offer love, in spite of our worldly harness.

Von Aarenhorst responded generously, forgiving her for the frequent cold repulses his own conversational efforts had met. Being a tall man, he bent slightly towards her, and thinking of his dear daughter, he looked at her indulgently. In his gallantry was a benevolent protection which would have softened anything less obdurate than her prejudices and sense of wrong.

"No, I have never been in this region before," he said. "Often enough in Paris, of course; and I have made many excursions out of the city, but not in this direction."

"It is not interesting here, unless it is one's home," she added. "It is flat and monotonous, and the village is as rustic as if it were far away in the mountains or on the coast, and not close to Paris; but the park —"

Ah! it was not easy to talk. The most commonplace topic but lightly concealed an unhappy significance. The calm rusticity of Aulnay! Where was it now? And Paris! Who could discuss Paris with the enemy about to storm its walls?

In her discouragement her glance again wandered coldly about the table. "I understand; I would help you if I could," flashed from the grave, watchful eyes of the stranger friend, while the bright-faced young officers offered the open homage of their quick, admiring looks.

"The park is a noble one, and the landscape, under happier circumstances, must have an idyllic charm of its own," returned Aarenhorst's kind voice. "I too have a country-house standing among tall trees."

"My uncle is much attached to Aulnay. Aulnay idolized him," she returned stiffly.

The general looked at her closely.

"Madame," he said, "I have a daughter at home, fair like you, about your age. She and her good mother miss me, and I miss them already many weeks."

"I presume so," was the icy reply.

Von Aarenhorst smiled indulgently beneath his twinkling eyes.

"Madame, may I relate to you a little experience? We were obliged to quarter in one château where it was made evident we were exceedingly unwelcome. The owner received my adjutant with such extreme rudeness that he was tempted to draw his sabre. Naturally, when I arrived I was not in an amiable frame of mind. I demanded my host somewhat, madame, as I demanded the marquis to-day, when you fronted me so gallantly until I cried quarter." Nathalie listened, her gaze direct and unsmiling. "War is not good for us, madame; it brings out all that is harsh in us. A campaign puts us in terrible moods. There is something ghastly in living in the midst of rough men, sad sights, danger and death, and for months missing the sight of a woman's face, the sound of a child's voice; one grows grim and unnatural. I have known times when I felt I would give a year of my life to hear a child laugh."

Countess Nathalie's honest nature was touched by his simplicity. She forgot for the moment that he was an enemy, and did not speak, but listened attentively, her eyes on his, her face lovely in its unconsciousness and interest.

"But I was telling you about the other château. The count, they said, was ill in bed. You see, madame, that often happens; therefore pardon my slight incredulity this morning. I insisted upon seeing him. He appeared, white, not I think from illness, but from rage."

Nathalie raised her head haughtily.

"I don't blame him," continued the general's kind voice. "The family had suffered much. His aged mother, eighty years old, had literally died of fright. After some conversation his manner changed. He introduced me to the countess. She was a beautiful, stately woman, white as marble as she entered. Do I weary you, madame ?"

"No, no," replied Nathalie, strangely interested in the other château.

"There was a gradual change in her manner, a gradual appearance of color in her face as we sat talking. The door opened. A splendid boy of eight sprang in, darted back, stared at the uniforms, then, open-mouthed, at his mother.

"'Come in, René,' said the countess. 'Come and give your hand to this German general.'

"The boy advanced on tiptoe, — one foot well back, ready to spring in case I should roar, or show my teeth, or stand threateningly on my hind legs, — and gave me a timid little hand.

"'What does René do?' I asked the countess. 'His instruction, of course, must be interrupted.'

"'I have him commit poetry to memory, that he may not lose the habit of learning. It is all we can do for him now.'

"'I am sure you know "Maître Corbeau"?'

"'Yes, I know that.'

"'Will you say it for me?'

"René looked at his mamma.

"'Repeat it, my child,' she said.

"René repeated it, and several fables. His hand was nestling confidently in mine by this time.

"'Can you say "Le Paysan du Danube"?'

"'Shall I, mamma?'

"'Yes, René.'

"'It is a very long one,' remarked René, hesitating.

"'If you forget, I will prompt,' said I.

"René forgot; I prompted. The child stared. The count and countess exchanged glances, and asked us to dine. It was a simple repast, but gracefully prepared with a flower or two, as here, madame; and a pleasant thing it is to us, — the dainty touch that betrays a woman's hand. Their provision was slight enough. They had no meat except what we brought, and our men cooked in their kitchen, as here, madame; but they gradually learned, if you will permit me to say so, that they had to do with a chivalrous set of officers and well-disciplined troops. Our relations grew friendly. When we parted, believe me, it was with mutual esteem and regret. Madame, I have hopes that our experience here may be similar," said the general cordially. "It is for that reason I have ventured to tell you so long a story."

"But there is no René here to act as mediator," returned Countess Nathalie quickly, with a little laugh; "and although you speak French admirably, and I have no doubt could surprise us with your knowledge of our poets, you must resort to other means."

"I do not despair of finding them; I only regret that I am probably not here for long. Colonel von Linden must represent me."

But Nathalie was already drawing herself up stiffly, repenting of her momentary naturalness. "That is the way of women," mused the general. "They nurse a theory of implacable hatred. They forget it quite, and smile on us, and treat us well, only to remember and freeze again. She's a pretty creature, and honest. I think we shall be famous friends."

He then calmly neglected his fair neighbor and devoted himself to general conversation. Jean stood behind his master's chair, his holier feelings outraged by the cheerful and frequent laughter, and by the sight of meat mysteriously provided, cooked in the Montauban kitchen by unknown foreign men, and served by creatures of unheard-of insolence, who marched in and out as if he were thin air; and much more substantial poor Jean indeed was not.

Madame de Vallauris answered a few civil conversational sallies from the other side with discouraging brevity, and in her turn scrutinized the company which fate had sent into the old château. As yet she had had no time for thoughts of them; only feelings had occupied her, — hot, vehement, unreasoning feelings. Now, no one was speaking to her; no one seemed to be watching. She leaned back quietly and thought about them all. "It will never make any difference to me what they are or are not. They are enemies of France; that is enough for me. But I will read what each face says as best I can. I will see if they are enemies to be feared or scorned. It is surely well to have an intelligent idea of one's enemies; perhaps more essential than to know one's friends categorically," she reasoned with a half smile. "Friends? I have no friends. That is what happens when girls marry at seventeen and travel with — older people from hotel to hotel, from Monaco to

Baden-Baden, from Nice to Rome, always seeking a perfect climate, and the fountain of youth. Then, some of my experiences and consequent moods were not conducive to friendship," she thought bitterly. "Had I met a friend then, how would I have known her? How would she have known me? Did I meet her and pass her by carelessly,—I, who would be thankful in my soul for her this day? Was she in the long row at some table-d'hôte, or one of the fashionable throng, drinking waters and taking baths to kill ennui or rejuvenate age, or was she among my formal visiting acquaintances? Well, well, I never found her. Perhaps I never deserved her. At all events, here I sit, young in years, and with at least no crime on my conscience to shut me out from ordinary human relationships,—and criminals, indeed, have friends,—but not a friend have I in this world except my poor old uncle. Claire and Diane are married,—presumably happy. They were little sentimental convent friends. What do they know of me, or I of them, beyond a couple of empty letters a year, and an appropriate exchange of felicitations and condolences? Would we know each other better for living under the same roof? Does my uncle know me better than I know these strangers? Do I know him? Dare I pretend to know him? Is it only in books that one nature rests fully in another in sympathy and comprehension? Do we each go about in this world speaking, like Jean and these German soldiers, different languages, only understanding one another awkwardly in regard to superficial things, as they now make rude, half-intelligible signs about the platters? Is this life? Is this all, then? It is all I have known, and it is dreary. I would like to think for the sake of others that something else exists, though not for me."

A little weary, too simple and brave to pose for the misunderstood woman, young still, inexperienced, and fresh in spite of her conviction that life had made her old beyond computation and had no new thing to offer her, she indulged in her rapid, wandering thoughts as she prepared to make her discriminating study of her enemies. The abbé had taken their mental measure; but he was a close student of that occult science, physiognomy. While her quick fancy and instinct arrived often, like a witch-hazel wand, at magical results.

The general had intellect, was therefore dangerous, she decided. Colonel von Linden was a brave, strong man, impulsive, and liable to be misled by a hasty opinion to which he would obstinately cling. She made her fine feminine guesses as to the significance of a square chin, a high nose, a subtle line of cruelty, a benevolent smile, a striking profile, a noble head. She underrated the younger men, as a woman often underrates men of her own age: found von Gerhardt, with his white mustache and dandy air, insipid; von Wedell insolent and supercilious; von Bergen commonplace. Forstenau she rather liked for the honest schoolboy look of his smooth face, and his sullen and awkward manner as he glowered in his plate, speechless, and like her alone, though surrounded by voices and laughter. When she came to the tall man in blue, she met with an obstacle. He had been quietly noting the indifference, melancholy, and pride in her face, the deeply thoughtful yet feminine line of the brow, the restrained warmth in her expression, the mockery of the smile. "What has made her so?" he wondered; and had not satisfied his searching eyes, when hers, taking their inventory, reached him. The enemy otherwise gave her every opportunity to reconnoitre its weaknesses. They were discussing some rare wine which, at a sign from the marquis, waxing more and more genial, the reluctant Jean produced from its hiding-place, where it had been stored with silver and other valuables before the coming of the Germans. "The older men are distinguished types," she concluded, with a consciousness that pictorial justice need not lessen her patriotism. "A little square-headed, a little heavy, but resolute and strong. General von Aarenhorst, if he were not a German, I could almost like. He says he has a daughter. A father like that would not be bad."

"I beg your pardon, madame. Did you speak to me?" said the general, turning to her quickly, his true face, stern in repose, almost affectionate as he now waited smilingly for her answer.

"No, I said nothing."

"Then your beautiful eyes spoke, countess," returned the dignified general as he turned away, his expression softening into a pleasant familiarity and protection which she nevertheless had the tact and good feeling not to resent.

"Yes, you were wise to stay," he remarked across the table to the marquis. "If all the château-owners had remained, they would have done better. When our men find a place occupied, they are very decent. Even an old decrepit woman who cannot run away fares well, while a vacant place exasperates them. Our warriors tend babies and help bring wood and water. They are glad of something to do when not on duty. They are the easiest men in the world to tie to a woman's apron-strings," with a smile at Countess Nathalie. "We are not a warlike nation, except from necessity. We are lambs. But you were wise to stay, marquis. I wished to drive over from Clichy to Vert Galant the other day in a pelting rain. The soldiers had appropriated the carriage-top to patch their shoes. My Schützen regiment have deprived the billiard-table of its green cloth to eke out their uniforms. The iron frame of the conservatory has been worked into horse-shoes; and cold evenings, when green wood won't burn, beautiful carved doors and heavy old furniture unfortunately will. Therefore, as I say, marquis, though our troops are upon the whole well meaning and well trained, if all the château-owners had remained to guard their property, it would have been better."

"Such was my opinion," responded the marquis placidly, "and the advice of my esteemed friend here, the Abbé de Navailles."

"Ah!" said the general, looking attentively at the abbé, who inclined his handsome head with deference.

The marquis smiled benignly round the table. A shade of reserve was of course desirable,—a firm yet unmistakable implication that the situation was delicate in the extreme. But the abbé was right, as usual. It was no use to rebel against fate, and this was no campaign which involved Bourbon honor. He had hoped to be spared. Up to the last he had believed the turmoil would rage around, but not in, sacred Aulnay. Now it was upon him, he took heart of grace. He was an old man. He could not struggle. These officers were gentlemen and cavaliers. The good old wine warmed his blood. He raised his glass.

"Gentlemen," he said with his courtly air, prepared to give a two-edged toast which would define his position and theirs with a trenchant and deft stroke. Suddenly his face fell. He put down his glass.

"God bless my soul!" he exclaimed. "We are thirteen at table! I am not in general superstitious," he added, as people are apt apologetically to state in the very act of yielding to abject superstition, "but if there's anything to which I have a deep-rooted objection, it is to thirteen at table." He half rose, looking very uncomfortable.

"Is n't it rather late to discover it, dear uncle?" asked Madame de Vallauris demurely.

"Under the present circumstances you can surely give yourself the benefit of the doubt," von Aarenhorst remarked heartily. "We military men monopolize all chances of the doom."

"May it not still be averted?" Von Nordenfels rose. "I must in any event beg to be excused."

"I hope —" stammered the marquis politely.

"I have duties," explained the adjutant, rapidly leaving the room with the simplicity and elegance which it was Gerhardt's fondest aspiration to attain.

"That young man is Lieutenant von Nordenfels," said the general, looking after him with kindly interest.

"Ah!" returned Nathalie indifferently.

"Do you know what an adjutant is?"

"Not precisely," she answered, without a trace of interest.

"An adjutant is — I'll tell you later what an adjutant is, madame," laughing a little, "when you ask me; when you wish military information."

"Very good. I shall wait without impatience," she rejoined.

"Every one has a pet superstitions which he keep mostly out of sight," von Linden was declaring.

"Yes," said a blunt major low to his neighbor; "sometimes it's dreams, sometimes it's looking-glasses, sometimes it's cats, or candles, or howling dogs, or haunted houses.   One is as unimportant as another."

"You may laugh, gentlemen," resumed the marquis with dignity, "but I never knew thirteen at table to fail."

"Did you ever know fourteen to fail?" asked the colonel, smiling.

"Great men are often superstitious," remarked the abbé blandly.

"True, true," said the marquis.   "Great men are usually superstitious; in fact, almost invariably so," he announced.

"Marcus Aurelius?" inquired Madame de Vallauris in a low voice, smiling at him past the lieutenants.

"Undoubtedly, undoubtedly," he returned with his grand air.

"I am not superstitious," von Aarenhorst said thoughtfully.   "I know the bullet that is not meant for me will not reach me."

"But that also is superstition," retorted the countess quickly.

"You are right," he said, smiling.

Catching her uncle's eye, she rose, coldly acknowledged the salutation of the company, and passed out on von Aarenhorst's arm.

The officers withdrew. The marquis played a rubber of piquet with airy cheerfulness, well pleased with his Aurelian philosophy. "Everything in life can be borne, — everything, if you cultivate true dignity," he declared. "Nathalie, you observed everything?"

"Everything, uncle."

"You were satisfied?"

"With you? Perfectly, dear uncle."

"Nathalie, cultivate true dignity. You are a Montauban. You can attain to it."

"Yes, uncle."

Somewhat fatigued, the old gentleman went early to his room. Nathalie, high in her turret, looked long at the stars and the dark Tower, and listened to the movement below and the voices of the watch. She was left at last alone with herself.

Pierre the fisherman, detained late in the sacristy, at the abbé's suggestion remained quietly there until dawn.

CHAPTER IV.

THE beautiful autumn days passed at the château
in comparative quiet, disturbed now and then by a
little skirmishing, particularly near Bondy. The
relations of the marquis with the detachment of German officers quartered under his roof became most
friendly. His library was their favorite resort, and
afforded them great enjoyment. Whist, chess, and
piquet, he and they depended upon evenings, — lovers
of games being a sect apart, who forget jealousies, strife,
and personal animosity in the pure delight of winning
the rubber. Their zeal and enthusiasm covered all
political questions, which were indeed seldom or never
touched upon. According to the Marquis de Montauban's interpretation of Marcus Aurelius, true dignity
should avoid perilous discussions with persons in authority. The German officers, sure of themselves and
their cause, never troubled themselves to inquire the
meaning of his reticence. They were content to accept
his courtesy and friendliness. The frail and fine old

marquis seemed to them the personification of grace. They were unsought guests in his house, their troops tramped through his courts, their orderlies galloped in mad haste to his door, their shrill bugles sounded in his ears, their commands, their evolutions, disturbed his peace of mind but never his repose of manner; and this they appreciated. The suspicion that the family were spies, which had been at first entertained, soon vanished. Nothing so improbable, unreasonable, incredible, could be imagined. Love of country beat high in every heart. But the marquis in his delicate way — and all his shades of meaning were as exquisite and polished as a rare miniature painting on ivory — did not scruple to make manifest his extreme distaste to the proclamation of the republic. His sentiment, as a matter of course, was understood to be the sentiment of his house. Neither Madame de Vallauris nor the Abbé de Navailles expressed or seemed to entertain any political opinions whatever. They were both, it was evident, tenderly attached to the marquis. Their thoughts centred in him; his comfort, health, and pleasure were their chief care. The abbé avoided all intercourse with the strangers, but that occasioned no remark. What could a bookworm have in common with men of action ? He seemed to be a harmless, thoughtful nature, and wandered alone in the park early and late, apparently lost in religious meditation. Sometimes, with a book in his hand, Colonel von Linden and his officers would discover him unexpectedly in some shady corner or remote walk to which they had withdrawn for consultation; but his gentle, hurried greeting, his mild and somewhat absent expression, betrayed clearly enough his desire to forget the interruption and to return with all speed to the higher realms where his pure spirit soared, far from worldly men and hate and war. The marquis and his niece went regularly through the covered way into the little church, and scrupulously observed all the ceremonies of their religion. They were devout Catholics, and naturally under the influence of their spiritual guide. The marquis's complete dependence upon him was conspicuous in every tone of their intercourse, and Madame de Vallauris was frequently seen with him, engaged in earnest conversation. He scarcely spoke except to them and to the two fishermen from the Ourcq Canal. To those poor men the good abbé was most gracious and kind. " I have never seen so consistent a religious man," von Linden remarked one day. " He fits his vocation like a stone in the wall. That's what I like. Every man where he belongs.

He's a born parson, I'm a born soldier. It couldn't have been otherwise."

"Not in your case, assuredly," von Nordenfels returned; "but the abbé's eyes are not strictly ecclesiastical."

"Eyes, eyes! What's the matter with the man's eyes?" said the colonel, disinclined to accept anything he himself had not perceived.

"Nothing whatever. They are admirable eyes for seeing, and he sees all there is!"

"Why shouldn't he see?"

"I certainly have no objection."

"Well, I don't suppose we any of us can help our eyes," von Linden rejoined somewhat testily. "For that matter, whenever I look at him, his are buried deep in a book."

"Those eyes buried? Then I only happen to observe them in the moments of their glorious resurrection."

"Come, come, Nordenfels, what have you got in your head against the poor abbé? Does he monopolize Madame de Vallauris too much for your taste? Look at your own eyes."

"I can't very well, without a looking-glass. Not being Gerhardt, I haven't one in my pocket."

"I mean to say the abbé might equally well take umbrage at them, and say they are not military. I presume you will admit there ought to be military eyes as well as ecclesiastical eyes. Now, you are a cavalry officer through and through. Reduce you to dressing-gown and slippers, and still every movement suggests the Gardereiter. You can't disguise yourself. 'Army' is written on your brow; 'army' is stamped on your long legs; 'army' sits on your broad shoulders. But your eyes, — they're a disgrace to you. At moments they are the eyes of a schoolboy mooning with sentiment; the eyes of a visionary philosopher. Confound it, Nordenfels, I don't want to hurt your feelings, but they might almost be the eyes of a— poet!"

"Don't insult me," returned Nordenfels, smiling.

"Then let my good friend the Abbé de Navailles possess his eyes in peace, without your animadversions."

"Men's eyes don't deserve so much discussion," the adjutant said lightly. "The only eyes worth talking about are the eyes of a beautiful woman."

"The sentiment is sound, and does you credit."

Upon which the adjutant dropped the subject. But as the young German was given to quietly working

out problems, he occupied himself more or less with
the unknown quantity in the Abbé de Navailles' eyes,
and speculated also upon the nature of the spiritual
advice which necessitated so prolonged and earnest
tête-à-têtes with Madame de Vallauris. He envied the
privileges of the saintly man. Yet not infrequently the
fantastic idea sprang into his mind that the thoughtful, attentive face which the beautiful woman turned
towards the abbé as she listened to his homilies
betrayed more keen watchfulness than simple liking
and trust. Why should she not like and trust the
family friend? Why should she put herself mentally
on guard in his presence? Why should her clear
eyes resolutely question his? Why should she
shrug her shoulders with impatience or weariness?
Why, nevertheless, should they be apparently on
the best of terms, so that without minute scrutiny
no one would have suspected the tiniest flaw in
their companionship?

One evening when Madame de Vallauris and the
abbé were talking low in the bay-window, von Nordenfels concentrated so much thought upon this
grand "why," with its innumerable ramifications,
that the marquis triumphantly checkmated him in
three moves.

Whatever the Abbé de Navailles might be in his innermost soul, Madame de Vallauris, in the opinion of the tall man in blue, was, so far as outward manner was concerned, perfection. The one lady among nearly a thousand men, she glided in and out with incomparable simplicity and reserve. To the younger officers she remained pale, frosty, and beautiful as a moonlight night in midwinter. General von Aarenhorst was now at Clichy. In spite of her strenuous efforts to keep her manner at the freezing-point, she frequently forgot herself during his stay at Aulnay, and charmed him with her naturalness and grace. Colonel von Linden's animation and kindliness had also now and then caused a sensible relaxation in her frigidity. It must be admitted that perfect consistency was not her chief attribute at this time. Her theory of conduct was loftily immovable, but in her practice was a perplexing variableness. If she deigned to smile at the genial colonel's wit, and treat him, as he expressed it, "like a fellow-creature" one day, she was sure to repent before morning, and relegate him at their next meeting to the misery of neglect. To the younger men she was from the beginning relentlessly unapproachable. But in spite of their lamentations, they were of the unanimous opinion that she was filling a difficult position uncommonly well; and her extreme reserve, fairly considered, seemed a duty, a privilege, and another charm.

Regularly in the chapel, often in the more secluded alleys of the park, and gradually among the soldiers, as illness claimed her pity or an occasional wounded man was brought into Aulnay after a skirmish, her fair, grave face and black-robed figure were seen, always followed by the brilliantly illuminated Manette. Colonel von Linden's generous heart had repudiated the bare suggestion of possible treachery on the part of a perfect gentleman of the old school, like the Marquis de Montauban, his most lovely niece, and so unworldly a person as the Abbé de Navailles. The indignity, as it seemed to the good colonel, which they had at first suffered in being restricted to the château and park, he had long since withdrawn, merely requiring their parole as a matter of form. The invalid marquis smiled gently, but remained at home. Countess Nathalie and the abbé made use of their freedom only when they could do some good work among the men. Such characters, bearing the great discomforts of their position with dignity and resignation, winning profound esteem from every side, were indisputably what they seemed to be. Any thought of double-dealing was preposterous. Moreover, had they had the desire to communicate with Paris, where was their opportunity? No; every step they took was visible; every unsuspicious, unsuspected act, before the gaze of hundreds. The colonel's confidence never wavered; his attachment to the three strengthened each day. "Spies, spies," he would say, "of course there are spies, German as well as French. But it's arrant nonsense to push the spy theory too far. If there are spies at Aulnay,—I'm one myself!"

Madame de Vallauris was known among the troops as "The Lady,"—not "The Countess," not "The gracious lady," according to their pretty and civil German form of speech; but, as if the rough soldiers were glad to see something finely feminine passing in their midst, and to acknowledge its unique charm, she was to them always "The Lady." Her beauty won them, as beauty is apt to win, without effort or desire; and if she had been quite as good to them, but possessed of ugly features and a croaking voice, they would undoubtedly have been grateful, but in all probability their gratitude would have been less impregnated with enthusiasm and personal devotion. To be as beautiful as Helen of Troy no one need perhaps desire, although what woman would disdain the fatal gift should the great gods proffer it? But the beauty that made Countess Nathalie's kind deeds seem kinder, lent a nameless grace to her slightest ministration, and softened rude men as she passed, was surely a blessing to her and to them. Then, her gentleness and indulgence were boundless. She never condescended to them with the evident intention of displaying amiability, never awkwardly sought to bridge the distance between them with phrases of studied benevolence. She heard a complaint or a request looking the man honestly in the face with her air of intelligent consideration and respect for his needs. Her simplicity came, saw, and conquered. A vulgar duchess — the type, in truth, is not unknown — would have found her haughty. She was endowed with the power of instantly congealing a displeasing conversational current; and the rash being, whether placed by the accident of birth high or low in the world's congeries, who should presume to be familiar, intrusive, or curious, — who should, like an ill-bred, giggling woman, nudging with a rash elbow to attract her neighbor's attention, dare mentally to nudge Countess

Nathalie's sacred personality, — would have had reason to repent.

But the soldiers in Aulnay offended her neither by presumption nor pretence; and as she learned to know their wants, they occupied her much. Energies which had been lying dormant awakened, and her empty life grew replete with interest and duties. Mornings, in her high turret-room, she listened for the bugle, the tramping feet, the voices and calls, the swift coming and going of the orderlies. Adjutant von Nordenfels brought the command from Vert Galant. Sometimes, early, she would hear his voice in the court-yard at dawn giving his Bursch an order. She knew his horses too. Naturally, she could not be so wholly blind and deaf as she would fain have made herself to all things appertaining to the staff. She apologetically admitted to her own conscience that, being a person of average intelligence, she was scarcely able to escape from the necessity of observing which of the officers seemed cleverest, most zealous, the best soldiers. Von Nordenfels was evidently considered a rising man, and was indefatigable in service. In his unassuming way he now and then sought to approach her. She could talk with him easily and would have forgotten that she must not enjoy his conversation, if she had not peremptorily forced herself to remember. Curiously, the ungainly and coltish Forstenau was surest of a friendly reception. She was somewhat uncertain to him also, but at times seemed to have an unlimited fund of patience for his awkwardness and stammering. In return, she gained from him much information about horses and racing. Next to his horse, von Forstenau loved von Nordenfels; and occasionally, in a moment of unwonted expansion of soul, the superior topic yielded to the secondary, and the adjutant's valiant deeds and kind and manly qualities were warmly if uneloquently descanted upon by the young Centaur, who paraded his friend's points in full gallop, as it were, before the quiet countess.

Manette, after her own fashion, did likewise. Her incisive mind had rapidly arrived at von Nordenfels as the most fitting knight elect for her mistress, and with von Nordenfels it faithfully abode. She was as sure that he was the man for the countess, as she was sure that Johann Wackermann, the big and burly, exactly suited her own fancy. But while she had fully determined to subjugate and in fact finally marry the huge Wackermann, and already had him in a state of dough-like submission to her moulding touch, Madame de Vallauris did not raise a finger towards any cavalier whatever. "Anything so unnatural is wicked, and that I shall declare to the day of my death!" Mamselle Manettechen, as the soldiers called her, vehemently affirmed. "It is a crime, and the day of reckoning will come," she concluded tragically. "Ah, if madame would but take counsel by me! I've got Wackermann, bless him! safe and sure. He's the man for my disposition. He grins when I make eyes at Corporal Heinrich, looks proud of me when he catches me coquetting in the dusk with Scheible, and is calm as a May morning when the lieutenants make hay while the sun shines. And who can blame the beautiful dears for liking their bit of fun with a cheery little thing like me, when they get nothing but cold looks and haughtiness up-stairs?

"But all the same Wackermann is the jewel I've been looking for and never found till now. And now I've found him I'll keep him. For Wackermann will let me have my little fling and won't be jealous. Any man who could possibly be jealous I should make jealous. Wackermann is the sure haven where I'll always come back to rest after my various enlivening little excursions. Wackermann is a dear, sweet-tempered as a lamb and brave as a lion,

big as a giant, and a very handsome man withal.
Yes, he's the man of my choice, and what comfort in
the thought! And oh, if Countess Nathalie would not
harden her heart! Many maids, being themselves
provided for, would never trouble their heads about
their mistresses; no, not they, the selfish things! But
the more I associate with madame, the more attached
I grow to her; ideas descend upon me in torrents. And
when I think what a picture we two make, — she so
elegant and graceful, so all that a countess should be,
and I with my basket tripping jauntily along behind,
and all the men watching, and Wackermann smiling
most affectionately, and all my other lovers making
such eyes, and 'Mamselle Manettechen' here, and
'Mamselle Manettechen' there, — why, my devotion
to Countess Nathalie is beyond all bounds; for if I
had n't been her maid, would I ever have found
myself in such a heavenly situation?

"But she, — she might as well be a dairy-maid at
Grosley Farm, so far as simplicity goes! And she
does n't act it, either. Not in vain have I made my
nice observations at the theatre, as well as been maid
to ladies of high degree, who mostly act as well off
the stage as others do on it. There's many who
would play the rôle Countess Nathalie's doing now

quite natural, but I should find them out. A woman may deceive the mother that bore her, the husband of her choice, the friend of her bosom, her brother, her lover, but she never can deceive the maid who buttons her boots in her moments of energy, and brushes her hair in her moments of languor."

Late one night Madame de Vallauris leaned back thoughtfully in her chair. It was scarcely what could be denominated a moment of languor, but she looked graver, more preoccupied than her wont, and held her half-closed book listlessly. Manette's dexterous fingers had loosened her mistress's hair preparatory to brushing it. As the little maid daintily arranged the toilet implements, turned up the lamp, and moved a footstool, a great resolution seized her.

She was about to speak, when Madame de Vallauris said, " Manette, I am afraid that poor boy is going to die."

" I 'm afraid he is, madame."

" He has a mother, and a sister, and a sweetheart, at home."

" That 's as it should be," Manette returned stoutly, " especially the sweetheart. I don't care what leads up to it," she thought. " By hook or by crook I 'm going to have my say to-night."

"But it's surely harder for him to go if he must leave what he loves."

"And I should say it would be harder to go if he'd never had anything at all. What you've had you've had, and nobody can take that much away from you. But if you've never had anything you ought to have had, and the time comes for you to leave this world, — and a very pleasant world it is, after all, madame, with compensations even in war-times, for such as look for them, — why, then your soul has a right to get up and protest, and say, 'Begging your pardon, I'm not ready, for I've never had my chance!' Not that there are n't such as have their chances and throw them away," she added with marked significance.

"I promised," Countess Nathalie went on gently, not noticing the girl's tirade, "to write a letter to his people if he does not live, and to send them a lock of his hair."

"Well, I'm sorry for him; but he's kissed his sweetheart, and stepped out well to the music with his flag flying, so if he must go, as many another brave boy must, he's had the foam of the moment. Good-by to him. It is n't he that occupies me most."

Countess Nathalie was rarely surprised by Manette's

eccentricities, but now she turned her head slightly and glanced up at her.

"May I speak, madame?" demanded the girl in an excited voice.

"Certainly. Why not?"

"But may I speak not precisely as madame expects? May I speak my mind?"

The countess looked doubtful.

"I hardly think it would do to give you plenary indulgence, Manette," she responded, smiling. "Your 'mind' might be so very extraordinary. It is late, too; you must be tired. You'd better go now," she said very kindly. "You need not brush my hair."

For her only answer Manette seized a hand-mirror, and coming quickly round in front of the countess, brandished it before her with a tragic air.

"Well, is there anything the matter?" inquired Madame de Vallauris with faint surprise.

"There's everything the matter," returned Manette solemnly.

"I seem to look very much as usual," said her mistress in an uninterested way. "Put it down, please."

"But no, madame," cried Manette with pathos, and actually a tear in her hard black eye, "not until I once, even at the risk of madame's displeasure, introduce madame to her own self;" flourishing the mirror wildly before Countess Nathalie's eyes, which, however, were looking over its rim in much astonishment at her agitated maid.

"Madame sees her beautiful face, her long, fair hair. Madame will not attempt to deny that there as she sits, with no aid from the pleasing arts of the toilet, wrapped in a loose white dressing-gown made before my time and of no particular cut, she is as lovely as a dream. What would not be the feelings of those officers to behold madame at this moment! What would not be the feelings of any man of sentiment and soul! But I demand, if a bullet should lodge in madame's breast this night and carry her off, like that poor German boy, to whom would madame send a lock of her hair and her last loving message? And so I say he is better off than madame. He must lose, but madame never had."

Countess Nathalie stared at the girl in amazement, yet struck by her words. "Are you mad, Manette?" she murmured.

"And when I see madame's face, and think what that face would be to a man that loved it, — and what I say is only nature, and true, and no harm at all, for madame is a woman; a countess is a woman as much as a maid is, and so I say, and I have never failed in respect to madame and never will, — when I think what that face would be to a man, I could cry to see madame going on in her unnaturalness. What will madame have for it when she is old ? Ah, when madame's bright hair is gray, when her clear eyes are dim, she will say, ' What repays me now, that I did not drink the foam of the moment ? ' The foam of the moment, — it is something for madame, something else for me. Madame is fine, and good, and deep. I am shallow and light, but I am wiser in my way than madame. I make the foam of my moment mine; madame turns away from hers. One goes, another comes. What has madame for all her youth, and goodness, and beauty ? Nothing. No one. And whom has she to thank ? Herself. For though madame is young, if she can resist this she can resist everything always. Madame has taught herself still ways, sombre thoughts. What did madame do before the war but mope, — mope all day long in the park, mope evenings in the library ? Was that a life ? For, with all respect, are an old gentleman of seventy and a holy saint of an abbé proper associates for a young and beautiful woman ? And now what does madame do ?

"It is not that madame should at once decide upon anything uncompromisingly matrimonial. Ah, no! I do not say that is essential. There is a charm in the artistic blending of pale, undecided hues. A strong and pronounced color wearies one sooner. Uncertainty stimulates, mystery beckons. Why, indeed, should madame hasten towards the irrevocable? She has had her little experience. Delicacy forbids me to allude to what I did not personally observe, but more's the pity; for if I had had the honor to be the attendant of madame during her period of dignified tribulation, such as is common in the best families where gentlemen have so variegated a reputation as the late Count de Vallauris, I am convinced that my character and influence and appearance, which contrast so agreeably with madame's, would have in a great measure sustained and cheered madame, and prevented the unnaturalness of her predilections.

"Is this a life, that madame leads? Madame should have a life of noble lines, of warm yet subdued colors. My eyes never deceive me. I know what is appropriate. Madame's life is like a straight monotonous sacque, — ugly, cold, dull drab, and of an inflexible material, — no pliancy, no grace, no freedom; and if madame goes on, she will render herself unable to adapt herself to anything else. Ah, where is the tender blue, where is the amorous rose, where are the glowing purples and royal reds and pure gold, of madame's life? It is all drab, drab, drab. It is the color of a dirge.

"Madame's little experience has depressed her. Very good. It was natural. It was appropriate. But does any experience last forever? Madame, even if I had my way, would still be reticent, softly alluring, vaguely retreating. Ah, the toilets my fertile brain has created for the time when madame awakens from her long sleep, looks gladly at the world, and drinks the foam from the very top of the moment!

"Men, madame, men! Who knows them better than I? Just heaven! Do I pretend they are perfection? But, after all, madame, they are the best there is, and, managed rightly, by far the most entertaining. And if madame were a little, a very little receptive, a very little lenient, would only keep her hand in, as it were, even if she does not deign to produce definite results at present, she would never repent, never! It is not too late. The opportunity this moment presents itself. When, indeed, was there ever before such an opportunity in the history of France — not that I ever read it, or wish to. There are moments one recognizes without big books to help one. The moment and the men are here! Here are the heroes, — tall and short, blond and black, thin and stout, grave and gay, with uniforms of every color and every grade to choose from, and the gardener's house full, and the porter's lodge, besides the whole château, and new ones coming, and changes all the time, and yet the old friends still, and nothing but devotion and readiness on their parts, — nothing; and madame looks at them as if they were sticks and stones and shadows, instead of *men!*

" And if madame were a little friendly and human, would the sky fall? If madame were half as gentle to that beautiful blue one, for instance, as she is to all the ragamuffins in the ranks, would that be a sin or a shame? Does n't his Emperor make him go to war just as much as the rank and file? Is n't the Emperor the servant of the people? It 's nobody's fault. War is war. It 's an accident, like an earthquake. And is this madame's war, any way? Madame's war would be a Legitimist war, and nothing else. And why punish the handsome lieutenants? Is that Christian? The beautiful blue one watches madame.

Ah, and how! He is serious, and distinguished, and silent; and what manners! and what a soldier! There are others, handsome too, and gay, — captains, lieutenants, counts, barons, what one will, — but the beautiful blue one is appropriate. And when he looks at madame, he looks from deep, deep down in his soul, and he thinks, as he stands there so straight and tall, with his face as earnest as madame's, ' Ah, if the beautiful lady would let me tell her my thoughts, would let me look close into her eyes and say, Dear lady, you are lonely and sad, but only let me — ' "

" *Manette !* "

Countess Nathalie rose, staring singularly at the girl. Her fair hair fell about her face; she slowly put up her hand to her head. The maid's torrent of words she had listened to as if to a revelation from another world. She had not thought to chide or silence her.

" Manette! " warned the lady's voice at last.

" I don't care. She 's heard it for once in her life, and it 's good for her! " the girl's heart honestly exulted. " And she can't send me away for my impudence, for there 's no place to send me," her shrewd head added.

"Madame," she returned meekly.

"You may leave me."

"Madame is not offended ?"

"Offended ? No. But you forgot yourself, Manette," said the countess in her iciest tone.

"If I ever remembered myself, it was just now," thought Mamselle Manettechen. "Mostly, when you've prepared your conversation the very things you care about seem to have slipped completely out of your mind. But I struck the nail on the head this time, and from every side at once."

"Yes, madame," she replied modestly.

She withdrew, her countenance demure, her conscience uttering warm encomiums.

Madame de Vallauris stood motionless some minutes in the middle of the room, hesitated, then pulled the bell-rope.

Manette came tripping in innocently, as if nothing more important than a rosette on a slipper had been under discussion.

"Madame desires something ?"

The countess, though very gentle, never looked prouder or more serious as she stood before the girl in her white draperies and loose hair and said generously: "Manette, your words were unfitting, but

I am sure you meant them kindly. For that I thank you. Good-night."

"Good-night, madame. Madame is too good. I wish madame sweet dreams."

Away went the little maid, never indeed much preyed upon by compunctions or doubts of the wisdom of her course, but at this moment in a state of audacious and supreme self-glorification.

In spite of Countess Nathalie's best efforts, she could not forget Manette's extraordinary harangue. There were phrases of it which seemed to have burned themselves upon her memory in indelible characters. She fell asleep only to dream restless and fantastic dreams. "These are the heroes!" cried a loud voice. Gigantic and changing, yet distinct like cloud-forms in wild night-skies, a great procession swept over mighty mountain-tops,— Hector and Achilles and old Ajax, Arthur and Launcelot and the Knights of the Holy Grail, Charlemagne, Theodoric, Romans, crusaders, modern kings, stately warriors of all lands and times. "Choose!" cried the voice. "A countess is but a woman. Choose! Is yours a life? Choose! For what is your youth, for what your beauty, for what the warmth and longing of your heart?"

With strains of martial music the grand procession marched on, sounding the war-cries of ages, waving countless banners of renown. Then it vanished. There was a great stillness. In a cottage of Aulnay, on the narrow bed, instead of the wounded soldier she had pityingly watched that day, a young and stately cavalier lay dying. The familiar face, pallid against the brave blue uniform, looked with strange longing into hers. "Dear lady, you are lonely," he began; "only let me —" He paused, his voice wavered. "Say farewell to my sweetheart," he murmured faintly. "Tell her not to grieve. We lived. We loved. We drank the foam of the moment."

CHAPTER V.

IN bureau-work for Colonel von Linden, whose sword was mightier far than his pen, and whose epistles were a sure means of disguising his thoughts, Max von Nordenfels was indispensable. Indeed, his clerkly duties were so naturally performed, the colonel might have classified him in the ignoble array of lawyers, doctors, pedagogues, authors, and all such as entertain undue interest in the invention of Gutenberg, had not Nordenfels saved his reputation by his spirit and activity in service. His energy, exactness, rapidity of execution, courage, and a certain persistence or toughness, made him invaluable as a leader of men in critical situations. During the campaign the soldiers had had not infrequent opportunities of proving their attachment to him; and there was not one of his company who would not have followed him unwavering to certain death.

He was by no means a Protean genius, but simply a young man well-born, well-endowed, well-bred, well-educated, with a well-grown body and a well-looking face. Fair, tall, blue-eyed, grave with strangers, he was essentially of a Northern type. His manner, always distinguished, merged quickly under provocation from gentleness to extreme stiffness, — a scholarly soldier, a soldierly scholar, cherishing many a fair theory of humanity and benevolence, many a hope of the world's progress towards liberty and light, in spite of the seemingly retrograde motion from time to time of this confusingly mulish planet; and in the deep recesses of his soul hovered an exalted dream of womanhood and home.

Like most young men, he had fallen in love more or less deeply on unnumbered occasions, happily fallen out again, and time had healed his scars. Yet his manner while under the influence of love's frequent young dreams had been so much less demonstrative, expansive, and exuberant than is common to the average lieutenant, that his comrades held strange theories of his insensibility. Some casino-pleasantry had once called him "Tilly," — the man who never laughed and never loved a woman; and the name, in spite of its absurdity, clung to him.

From his gymnasium days, when a succession of maidens with braids or ringlets sat enthroned in his vulnerable heart, through his cadetship and entrance into the elegant world, he was, to speak plainly, in love without intermission.

In the higher circles of conservative countries there is, as all polite people must concede, no such thing as flirtation. Anything so vulgar would not be tolerated or, indeed, comprehended; and only a vague, an imperfect allusion to the alleged practices of a cruder, coarser race ever sullies the innocence of German aristocracy. It is a benign interposition of Providence that four thousand miles of water separates the girl who would unblushingly walk a block with a man at high noon — with two men, if circumstances require — from her sister who would die before she would put her soul in conventional jeopardy by such light conduct.

No, there is no flirtation, at least, flirtation visible to the naked eye, in Leipzig or Dresden. What corresponds to that bold, bad Americanism, means, in truth, in Germany, either less — or more. But what signified, then, the unutterable things many a dove-eyed, languishing maiden looked at Max von Nordenfels, when, held very close against his breast, they whirled madly round to an intoxicating Strauss waltz, while the august row of chaperones against the wall nodded serenely, and tacitly proclaimed to the world at large that all was well in the realm of strict propriety? What meant certain twilight episodes and conservatory reminiscences? Under what head shall tender little missives, slipped into his willing hand, be classified? Why was his private drawer overflowing with plaintive and suggestive notes:—

DEAR BARON MAX,—You looked unhappy at his Excellency's ball. Or was it my fancy? I, too, am most miserable. If you but knew what—but no—I must not write it. I will tell you at the Krawisckys. Of course you will be there. I have not forgotten: every other waltz and the cotillon. How *triste* life is! Always your   A.

Now this authentic effusion betokens neither a heinous crime nor yet a palpable engagement. It is evident that its gentle warmth might have been fanned into a flame by Baron Max, but it was not. In all honesty, he left the privilege of consoling "Always his A." to somebody else, and "A." in all honesty was shortly consoled. But by what name acceptable to all prejudices denominate this effervescing interchange of sentiment?

Then "Always his B.," his "devoted C.," his "everfaithful D.," his "attached friend E.," and all his alphabet of susceptible and perfectly chaperoned sweethearts also honored him with their innocent confidences, — be it understood, not without all-sufficient entreaty and intense encouragement on his part, — until the flowers and gloves and ribbons which he treasured equalled in quantity an eligible young bachelor's collection of similar tender objects in any crude land where the informal exchange of sentimental keepsakes would not be regarded as an anonymous crime. These unimportant facts in his career merely serve to demonstrate that a handsome young cavalry officer in Germany finds now and then something to mitigate the rigor of his lot, and between the heavy and solemn fugues of society indulges occasionally in a pleasing and capricious little intermezzo.

The letters and the keepsakes Nordenfels had long since burned. The looks and the smiles he had, for the most part, forgotten. His calf-love epoch was a time of the gray past. He had had, indeed, deeper affairs since. Then came a lull in his amorous proclivities. He took to hard reading, decided views, found society a bore, and was the despair of his good father, who desired him to marry one of three eligible young girls in Leipzig society whom, with paternal wisdom and unimpeachable logic, he had selected. Max even alarmed the old baron seriously by expressing radical views. He went so far as to say that when he married he should choose only a large, sweet nature that would not measure life with the petty and irritating measure of Leipzig womankind. One of his friends had married an American, a beautiful and rare woman, and made for himself what seemed to Max an ideal home. He found wonderful freshness in its loving atmosphere, a graciousness in its hospitality, a picturesque charm in what elsewhere was dull routine. But there are Americans and Americans. The next type he met was a young girl whose exquisitely pretty face it was impossible to overlook. She wore huge diamonds in her delicate ears, told her mother at the table-d'hôte with the sweetest smile in the world to "shut up," and before a row of electrified lieutenants remarked with perfect ease and ingenuousness, " Ma says there 's no good in these mixed marriages. Ma disapproves. She says they always come to grief; but I 've made up my mind to try one, all the same." Max Nordenfels withdrew. This was not the kind of originality he sought.

For some years now he had conspicuously sought nothing feminine, and his comrades regarded him as curiously indifferent to woman's charms, and in consequence held him for a man of boundless ambition.

Now at thirty he found himself — amid the stirring scenes of a campaign, anticipating no emotion other than the legitimate excitement of war — most violently and seriously in love with Madame de Vallauris.

Moreover, he, the cool, grave, and unimpressionable "Tilly" of the regiment, had fallen in love like a schoolboy, at first sight. From the moment she had stood before the officers in her cold protest and answered Aarenhorst with unrelenting pride, he had found her admirable and lovable beyond all women he had met. He yielded on the spot the last lingering remembrance of the most winning and gentle of his countrywomen; it became instantly a matter of supreme indifference to him that fascinating Americans existed. His ideas of beauty and womanliness began and ended with her; his hopes for the future included her as it included his own soul.

Except for the pleasure of being in love that only a lover knows, — "the joy that is born of pain," — he was truly uncomfortable at this period. In the first place, everybody else was in love with the countess, as a matter of course. As von Gerhardt remarked, no man who respected himself could fail to be in love with her. She was, he declared, Beauty surrounded by a thousand Beasts, Dornröschen and scores of Princes, Little Red Riding Hood and many wolves.

All the heroines of all romantic tales had, according to him, concentrated their fascinations in her unique personality. Not that Gerhardt's ebullitions in themselves were dangerous. He was the best soul in the world, and, in spite of his affected dandyism, which would easily lead the pedantic judge of character astray, in spite of his youthful exaggerations, an honorable gentleman, a brave cavalier. His multitudinous love-affairs were the standing joke of the regiment, — each heart experience, frankly recounted, having the duration of the dew on the blossom. But still Gerhardt would talk, and his talk was repugnant to a fastidious man like Nordenfels; and von Wedell talked, — less agreeably, be it said; and the colonel and the captains and the surgeons talked. Nordenfels longed often to stop their mouths with clay. Forstenau did not talk. Nordenfels liked him the better for it, and owed him a debt of gratitude.

That she was beautiful, that she was exquisite, elegant, stately, graceful, that her dull, fair hair grew richly, that her hands were fine, her eyes thoughtful, that her mouth was too often mocking and satirical, that her whole face was the coldest, her manner the

stillest ever seen, except when she softened marvellously and changed altogether in response to some
wish or whim of the lame old marquis, — Max Nordenfels knew but too well; and it was torture to him
to hear his comrades discuss her perfections. Yet
what earthly right had he to remonstrate or interfere?
They said nothing derogatory or disrespectful. On
the contrary, they admired her vastly, and offered her
their deferential if evanescent allegiance. Since a
pint measure cannot hold a quart, why require of it
more than its legitimate capacity?

Nordenfels would surely have been most miserable
if every man of the whole staff at the château had
been seized with a grand passion for Madame de Vallauris. At the same time their amiable superficial
homage was displeasing to him. He grew unreasonable and irritable. Often evenings, as she sat with her
book, or came and went in her still way, — for the
marquis was uneasy if she left him long, and would
grow nervous at his game until his glance met hers, —
Nordenfels felt a fierce longing to seize her and take
her in his arms and spur his good horse and bear her
away from them all, through the night, out of the
world. Sitting there primly, — he with a book, she
with a book, the abbé with a book, and all their

books most thoroughly unread, von Linden or another playing bézique with the marquis,— von Nordenfels grimly questioned whether we have upon the whole improved our ways, and whether the simplicity and directness of his old robber-knight ancestor, who carried off the lady of his love and flung his rival into the deepest dungeon of his castle, were not admirable qualities. The Abbé de Navailles was, in one sense surely, not a rival. But Countess Nathalie looked at him, listened to him,— reasons enough for removing him summarily from the scene of action. He was accordingly mentally consigned to the mediæval dungeon as often as Nordenfels came to the library evenings.

But infinitely worse than the annoyance caused by his comrades, a greater obstacle than the ubiquitous abbé with his dark, gleaming eyes, was the invincible reserve of Madame de Vallauris. Night and day he asked himself how this was to be overcome. In his impatience he was forced to remember that stronger than bolts and bars and guards is the repelling force of a woman's own heart. "But I love her," he told himself; "I love her with my whole soul. I understand her, now, in all that she does, and I would not have her a shade kinder."

The morning after Manette's surprising midnight exposition, Madame de Vallauris, accompanied by her maid, went to look after the wounded soldier. The poor boy had died in the night, and his beardless face wore the look of a fair young child. Wackermann stood by him, grave and sorry.

"Were you with him?" inquired the countess.

"Yes, madame, and the lieutenant."

"The lieutenant?"

"Lieutenant von Nordenfels. He," with a glance at the still face, "asked for him."

"Ah!"

Wackermann now became the grateful but uncomprehending recipient of encouraging smiles, exciting nods, and vastly eloquent looks from Mamselle Manettechen. The good fellow went on quite innocently: "The lieutenant was abed. But he turned out as quick as if poor Karl had been a general. He knew Karl at home. We're all from the same place, —Karl and I from the village, the lieutenant from the Schloss. We were boys together. The lieutenant was sorry to see poor Karl."

Never had Manette given him such glances of unqualified delight and affection. It was part of her tactics to provoke, to leave unsatisfied, to bewilder;

but now he was basking in the strong sunshine of her full and unreserved approval. It encouraged him to further speech.

"It is n't every young gentleman that 's ridden all day and been writing a mountain of papers all night, that would get up at dawn just to see a poor fellow that 's got to die whether or no, and stand by him as tender as a woman. But the Herr Lieutenant is n't the sort that cares for his own comfort, — for food and sleep and ease, and all that. Colonel von Linden came in yesterday too. That pleased poor Karl mightily. He was proud of that."

Oh the bitter reproach, the dark dissatisfaction, of Manette's pantomime!

On Wackermann's broad face a slow, vast doubt uprose. What had he said to displease his adored Manettechen? With her bright black eyes she was casting vividly imperious glances at her slave and urging him on, to what he knew not. Much depressed, he began humbly, "Lieutenant von Nordenfels — "

At once his inscrutable sweetheart's face beamed with smiles. Vehement but affectionate little nods cheered his dejected spirit.

Wackermann stopped short to consider. Considering involved in his case such ponderous creaking mechanism, that stopping short in any other occupation was a necessity of his being. Manette's dumb-show went on unceasingly. Then Wackermann grinned. Proud of his perspicuity, he stared at her long and cheerfully.

Madame de Vallauris turned quickly and looked at her maid, not in the least deceived by that adroit young woman's innocent repose of manner.

"Only go on!" implored Manette as soon as her mistress's head was turned.

"Lieutenant von Nordenfels —" began the amiable giant, when his face, except for the attentive eyes, suddenly assumed the curiously expressionless look common to the soldier greeting his superior, and his hand flew up in respectful salute as Max von Nordenfels entered the little room.

"Ah, madame, you here? That is kind," he said quietly.

She looked gravely at him, then down at the still, white face. Her strange dream was haunting her incessantly. It had made Nordenfels' features more familiar to her than any in the world. She wished his actual presence had not followed until she had had time to forget the pleading of the eyes, the sweetness of the smile, the pathos and the power of the dream-face. There was something unpleasant and startling in meeting him here and now. "Dear lady, you are lonely," he had murmured in the dream.

"You were with him, I believe," she returned simply.

"Yes, I happened to be here."

"He is young to go. He looks like a child."

"Karl was a brave fellow," von Nordenfels said warmly; "though young, one of our best men. I knew him personally. He came from my own home. He was on the outpost service three nights ago. It was a stray French shot that struck him. When he lingered, I thought he'd get over it. Poor old boy — there'll be many tears wept for you at home!"

"His is not the worst fate," murmured the countess, moved to speak she scarce knew why.

"Ah, no!" answered the young man with a bright smile. "He would say so if he could. Better, too, than if he were a married man with a wife and children depending upon him. The stray balls do not always choose so wisely, do they, my poor Karl? Oftenest they hit the bread-winners," bending with a pitying smile over the dead soldier struck down in his young manhood. Then, turning to Madame de Vallauris, he said, "He bade me say farewell to his sweetheart — "

"And tell her not to grieve," said the countess in a low, distinct voice, repeating the words slowly, mechanically, and looking absently at Nordenfels, who, with much surprise, asked, "But how could you know that, countess ? "

Up to her hair mounted the warm accusing color, as she realized how singularly she had spoken.

Nordenfels noted it with curious satisfaction. He knew no just cause why she should blush. But as her very eyelashes were important to him, and whether she looked to the right or the left a significant and interesting fact, he could not fail to regard this evidence of feeling as a revelation and a phenomenon; and he stood staring at her speculatively, quite forgetting that direct looks indefinitely prolonged were the privilege of an intimacy he had not the honor of enjoying with Madame de Vallauris.

"I beg your pardon," she said at length. "I interrupted you."

"You anticipated merely. 'Tell her not to grieve,' were his very words."

"But she will grieve."

He nodded gravely.

"Some one died last year in this very house, — an Aulnay man. I was quite indifferent. Yet I am sorry for this stranger," she continued.

"The other had his people round him," he suggested.

She shook her head. "No, it was not that." She did not indeed know what was stirring in her soul, making her sympathies larger and more tender.

She stooped and cut a lock of the boy's bright hair. "I promised to send it to his people," she explained.

"You, madame !"

"Ah, yes, our château manner," piped Manette shrilly, "is not our cottage manner by any means; and what the fine officers lose, the common soldiers have in abundance. Not that one begrudges it to that poor fellow. But, in general, is it justice ?"

"Hush, Manette !" said the countess. "I cannot write German very well," she continued to Nordenfels, "but they will understand, at least. He seemed to wish me to write."

"Then I will send your letter with mine," he returned, moved to think their words would go together to the sorrowing old mother in the village that nestled in the valley below his own home.

"That a woman's tenderness ministered to him at the last, — they will remember that."

"I do not feel that he is a German," she said suddenly.

Nordenfels smiled slightly. "No; dead, we are all pretty much alike. It seems hardly worth while to hate one another in this world."

"You say that? A soldier?"

"What has war to do with hate, madame?" he returned quickly. "Cannot a soldier be a man of intelligence and heart? War is a necessity; but the war of civilized people is not the expression of personal animosity. What had this poor boy against France? What have I, for that matter? I revere France, madame!"

There was much that she could have replied about war and life and death. Questions trembled on her tongue. It seemed to her they two had much to say to each other. But men were looking curiously in the window and crowding into the house. She could do nothing here.

"I must go," she said, thoughtfully fixing her eyes on Nordenfels' face. The vivid dream, his manly, sympathetic voice, the still form of the young soldier, touched her strangely. Life seemed vast and incomprehensible and infinitely sad. Often enough she had been only sorry for herself. In this moment she sorrowed for the whole sorrowing world. All her gentleness revealed itself, and the muscles of her mouth played sensitively. He had never seen her like this. He felt that he adored her. She leaned in her exquisite womanliness over the young face, calm and beautiful in death. Did his spirit see the green fields of his childhood, or was it wandering in undreamed-of realms of bliss, that he wore that mysterious look of peace that passeth understanding? "For his dear home," she murmured, touching her lips to his brow.

Wackermann gave a great honest gulp and coughed. Manette threw up her eyes with a kind of theatrical ecstasy. Nordenfels made one eager step forward, then, with his accustomed self-restraint, "Madame," he said, his voice trembling but a little, "madame, I thank you for his old mother, who must mourn her last-born, bravest son. I thank you for the young heart that has lost its Love. I thank you — for myself."

A moment more, and she had left the cottage and passed out among the soldiers, who made way for The Lady respectfully, and looked after her with gratitude and strong approval. She went rapidly down the middle of the village street and on to the château. Manette fairly scintillated with satisfaction.

Nordenfels tried to remember what he had said. It struck him, too late, that he ought to have made more of the occasion; ought to have been cleverer, more impressive. But it had seemed so perfectly natural for him and the beautiful Countess de Vallauris to be standing in a rude room adjoining an ex-grocer's shop, looking into each other's eyes over the body of poor Karl Radi, that he had not considered the possibilities and significance of the moment.

He gave his last orders for the burial, and spoke considerately with Wackermann, and remembered old days kindly, yet went from the chamber of death with a strong new joy possessing him. "The Lady," he heard a man say as he passed. The Lady, in truth, — the Lady of his love, the Lady of his heart, the one dear Lady of the world to him!

CHAPTER VI.

"I THINK, my dear, that the abbé is right," said the marquis.

"When was the abbé not right?" returned his niece gently.

"True, Nathalie, true! I am glad that you recognize his qualities; sometimes I have fancied you fail to appreciate him; it is merely an idea, but it has distressed me, absurd as it is." He laughed feebly, by way of reassuring himself.

"Then do not be distressed, dear uncle, for I am convinced that I appreciate the abbé."

The marquis looked at her smilingly. "That is well," he began, with a shade of condescension. "Appreciate — appreciate — one uses the word relatively, of course. To appreciate him fully, one should be, indeed, a man of intellect, a man of scholarship, a a man of the world; for the abbé is deep."

"Very deep," echoed Nathalie.

"But you women have tact and instinct," he

remarked, with his smile of faded gallantry. "Often you intuitively arrive at our results, at the results which men reach through cold calculation, — that is to say, by means of our intellect. A woman's heart —" He stopped a full minute; his eyes looked wandering. "Bless my soul, Nathalie! What was I talking about?"

"About man's intellect and woman's heart, dear uncle."

"Yes, yes! A woman's heart has its own method of procedure. It is rapid, contradictory, and essentially lacks —"

"Logic," said Madame de Vallauris patiently.

"It lacks logic," continued the marquis with urbanity; "and logic is our strength. Yet the importance of this distinction, you, my dear child, can but indistinctly perceive, and the — the — I may well say, the absolute monarchy of logic in human reasoning a woman rarely or never recognizes. You follow me, Nathalie?"

Madame de Vallauris laughed. It was seldom enough that her young face lost its extreme gravity. But who, with the best will in the world, can be always solemn? Sometimes, when quite alone with the marquis, he amused her irresistibly, in spite of her patience, her deference, her constant effort to adapt herself to his mood, so that not the smallest annoyance through any fault in her untiring watchfulness and attention should trouble the old gentleman's mind.

The marquis looked surprised.

" Was I saying anything witty, Nathalie ? "

" Assuredly not, dear uncle."

" I made use of a serious term, I may modestly say an exceedingly apt term, — the absolute monarchy of logic.   I was not aware that I had conveyed the slightest suggestion of a pleasantry."

" It was I," Nathalie said repentantly.   " It suddenly occurred to me, a woman refuses to acknowledge absolute monarchy because she 's a republican, or even a rebel."

" A woman — yes," returned the old gentleman, with an expression of extra-refined disgust hovering over his delicate features.   " A woman, but not a Montauban.   You were no doubt alluding to some remote possibility, to some fact observable in the lower strata of society, or to something you may have read or unavoidably seen on your travels."

" To something I have read or seen on my travels," said Nathalie, now quite sobered.

The marquis looked discomposed. "I have always doubted whether a woman should travel much. But that is past. Moreover, it was then your duty to the count. My dear, would it not, however, be advisable for you to submit your reading to the abbé?"

"I think not, uncle. Why?" she replied serenely.

"Because, while I would not for worlds wish to restrict the choice of—"

"Of a woman who is no longer a young girl," she threw in quietly,—"of a woman who was married five years ago."

"To restrict your choice, at the same time I am of the opinion that a woman of delicate associations, a woman of rare susceptibility—"

"In short, a Montauban." She smiled at him affectionately.

"A Montauban, and the exceeding few who are privileged to be classed with her, should accept advice; should lean upon a stronger mind when she enters so perilous a region as a library."

As Madame de Vallauris had long since braved all the perils of her uncle's library, and found there unspeakable solace and strength, and made close friends of the very volumes he would have pronounced her fatal foes, she could do little at this moment but demurely reply, " If you personally have any wish, dear uncle —"

" Say no more, my dear Nathalie," he responded graciously. " Your docility reassures me. Pardon my fond fear; I am happy to observe it is unfounded. I have a horror of indiscriminate reading for a woman. We men must study the wickedness of the world, must know the weapons of our adversaries. Since they seek to destroy our holiest temples, our most sacred rights, our established, God-given —"

" Ah, dearest uncle, why excite yourself? Indeed, you are not well enough. You have been so wise, and avoided these topics for so long, and now your face is quite flushed, and your poor dear hands tremble. You will not grieve me by being ill? Think, uncle, whom would I have to protect me if anything should happen to you? Dear, dear uncle!"

He had seated himself and fallen back in the large fauteuil, a frail, bowed, and broken old man. Nathalie, beautiful in her strength and youth, leaned over him, smoothed his hollow temples with her fresh touch, murmured her encouraging and tender sophistries.

" You are right, Nathalie. Who would indeed take care of you? But have no fear. I am not ill, I am strong," he said with dignity, rising and resuming his measured and somewhat spasmodic walk. "Old memories,"—he waved his withered hand airily,—"old times, recurred to me. It was but a passing emotion. I am fully aware of the duties which at present devolve upon me in my unusually responsible position. I have to protect a young and lovely woman, my niece, and a spiritual and unworldly man, my friend, from annoyance, possibly from danger. I have to preserve the dignity of the Montaubans."

"And that, at least, can never be difficult for you," she exclaimed cordially.

"Nathalie,"—the confused, forgetful look crept into his eyes,—"was there not some remark of yours which I found unsympathetic, uncongenial? Was there not an implication which even risked—"

"Ah, how well he jumped!" She went quickly to the window. "Did you see, uncle? It was Lieutenant von Gerhardt. There are five of them leaping the hedge."

"Those young men ride very well. We had in our time, it may be, more grace, more elegance, a more chevaleresque bearing. But they ride well. They ride well. The tall one in blue, Baron von—"

"Nordenfels," suggested Nathalie.

"Baron von Nordenfels, yes. How well you remember all their names! He rides well. There he goes now."

" He is not there, uncle."

" Ah! indeed! Then it's some one else. But I have noticed him. He is a young man of distinction. One can converse with him. He is not flippant. Have you observed?"

" I may have, uncle."

" But, to resume," he continued with unwonted pertinacity. "Nathalie, I forgot what the remark was, but I have the distinct impression that as you made some allusion it occurred to me your aunt would never have thought of such a thing, would never have used a word — I forget it. I am a little *distrait* this morning."

" I am sure she would never have thought of anything that could in the remotest way be uncongenial to you." Ah, how kind and generous the young voice sounded!

" She was a good woman. I miss her," said the old marquis simply.

" I am sure you do, dear, — always." She remembered how the passivity of her gentle aunt, her sure and serene conventionality, her mind, like her chair, always where it was expected to be, had satisfied his highest ideal of womanhood; and she realized that when a great gulf separates two natures, the suppression of one's opinions, while it makes the distance less conspicuous, by no means bridges it across. She longed to throw her warm, strong arms around his aged form, to beg him tear off his mask, get down from his Montauban stilts, let her help him, love him, reach him. "I do not love you enough," she thought remorsefully, "but I want to love you. Take me nearer, and I shall surely learn. We are all there is left, we two, and my heart is full of pity and affection and understanding for you,— you poor, forlorn, self-deceived old man!"

But the Marquis de Montauban would have found nothing in life so undesirable as to be "reached." Merely being reached after, bored him. If a human emotion betrayed itself at rare moments in him, it was at least at his volition, not that of another. One could allow one's self certain liberties. One knew one's own delicacy and principles of self-restraint; but emotions in general were vulgar, and apt to lead to distressing exhibitions.

Madame de Vallauris therefore assumed the tone that she knew would most please him. "No one could ever be to you what she was," she went on in a composed voice tuned to society pitch.

"She was perfect," responded the marquis with lofty conviction.

"But remember what advantages she enjoyed in her intercourse with you."

"My influence was no doubt educating," he admitted modestly. "But she availed herself of it. She adapted herself."

"Aunt had rare gifts."

"I was satisfied with her, Nathalie." With his phantom-like gallantry he added, "I am sure, upon reflection, that you could make no remark which would jar upon my taste."

"Be quite sure," she returned, "that for no consideration would I intentionally, by word or manner, cause you one moment's annoyance. Your wish is my law," she said calmly and sincerely.

"Now that reminded me of your dear aunt," he remarked, well pleased. "But where were we? One trait of your charming sex is a tendency to digression. That, one always notices when one attempts to converse with you upon any serious topic. You are not consecutive; but it is by no means a fault, in my estimation. On the contrary, the light butterfly motion of the feminine mind gives grace — grace — Where were we, Nathalie ?"

This was a perplexing inquiry to Madame de Vallauris. "We were speaking of the abbé, I believe," she answered after a slight pause, in which her graceful, feminine, butterfly mind did some solid thinking.

"Of the good abbé in general, my dear ?" doubtfully.

"Of the good abbé in particular. You were about to honor me with some of the abbé's views, had indeed begun, when you expressed a doubt of my appreciation of him, and I begged you to be perfectly at rest on that point. Afterwards — I digressed, uncle."

"A proof, a proof !" exclaimed the old gentleman in laughing triumph. "Ah, my dear, what did I tell you of the woman's heart and the man's intellect ?"

"Much that is edifying, and which I shall not forget."

"But," he continued in great good-humor, "when you digressed, Nathalie, I was about to admit that a woman's perception of character is often more delicate than a man's. Therefore it would indeed be preposterous if with your intuition you should in any respect fail in esteeming him according to his merits, — merits which, you understand, I merely repeat to point the argument. I, as a man, analyze and prove; you, as a woman, feel."

"It would be quite incredible, dear uncle. And the abbé said — Tell me what he said, and I will try to make the movements of my mind more sequacious."

"The abbé said — "

"He was alluding to my conduct, you remember."

"Perfectly. The abbé said your conduct was most exquisite. He merely wished my opinion. I have great influence upon the judgment of the abbé in worldly matters. He depends upon me — Did you speak, my dear?"

She had uttered a little indistinct sound, something between a groan and a quick note of scorn, the involuntary cry of her overcharged heart, pushed almost beyond the limits of its forbearance.

"I have dropped my shawl," she answered, stooping.

"Permit me," he returned, arranging it with stiff and feeble hands and circumstantial courtesy.

"He depends upon my judgment, as is natural — quite. And he modestly inquired if I did or did not think that now, after this long trial, in which your dignity of bearing has been incomparable, you could with perfect discretion and grace deign to be a little more affable ? Perhaps to follow, in a certain sense, my example as head of the house ? "

" He suggested that I should follow your example ? " she asked with dangerous quiet.

" Suggested ? Far from it. As I say, he merely intimated his desire to acquaint himself with my views. It was a purely intellectual question, a casual discussion between the abbé and me."

" Ah ! " said the countess, with a deep, long-drawn breath.

" The situation is peculiar. It is unique. There is Paris. You know my views as to the present Paris. I will not agitate you by recapitulating. I simply do not recognize Paris. Paris is for me a travesty, a mummery or less. Let us say less. Paris is for me — *air*. Take pains to follow, Nathalie. I do not say *my* Paris. The Paris of my youth, of my ancestors, the Paris of the Bourbons, the Paris of history, the pride of all civilized nations, the glory of the world, *that.* Paris exists, will always exist for us. But this Paris, with its degradation, its unsavory odors of the mob, its unholy aims, its irreverence and revolutionary taint — "

"Poor, misled, struggling Paris!" murmured the countess.

"Struggling,— did you say struggling, Nathalie? You read that word in a newspaper, of course?"

"Yes, yes, dear uncle, I read it in a newspaper."

"Ah, these newspapers! But let us resume. On the one hand is this unconscionable Paris, which will nevertheless without doubt hold its own —"

"Does he really believe that?" she demanded impetuously.

"He? Who? I am at a loss to understand. Is my endeavor to instruct you inopportune, or —"

"Ah, no, no, dear uncle! Pardon, and pray continue."

"On the one hand, then, this Paris, which cannot claim the sympathy of a Montauban — indeed, I can only treat Paris with silent contempt. On the other hand, Germany, with which I must own I have in general small sympathy. It is a rude nation, I have heard. These gentlemen, it is true, take pains to present themselves at their best. They have done fairly well. They have a tolerable idea of civility. I regard them in a certain sense as my guests."

"Oh, uncle!"

"And therefore I endeavor to mingle dignity and

condescension in my treatment of them.　I should be sorry, Nathalie, if you could not follow me.　My château, I regret to observe, has grown very shabby with the coming and going of orderlies and the free uses to which it has been subjected.　The stair-carpet is painfully threadbare.　Look at the lawns, the court-yard. Where are my horses ?　Where are my servants ? And my wine and silver literally *sub rosa*, — being buried under my rose-bushes.　My larder is empty. Potatoes and rice are, I believe, still there.　Otherwise, for food we depend upon our guests, do we not ? "

" Yes, uncle," Nathalie answered huskily.

" But, as the abbé frequently remarks, it cannot last forever.　The Germans will retreat.　We shall rehabilitate ourselves.　In the mean time, with dignity, with philosophy —　You follow, Nathalie ? "

" Perfectly, dear uncle."

" We impress the strangers ; we command the situation.　*Noblesse oblige.*　Therefore I would beg you to permit the conversation to flow more fully in your presence.　Make your *salon* evenings, my dear.　It will be beneficial to those young Germans, and in no wise compromise you.　Never imagine I have not found your manner up to this time beyond criticism. A certain hauteur sits well on a Montauban — and there were many strange men here, I admit. But, as the abbé justly remarks, I, the head of the house, am always present. We know, too, the characters of our uninvited guests. Evenings, there are but few at once in our drawing-rooms. Why not lend to what is enforced an aspect of social pleasure ? Why not encourage those stiff young Germans to an unreserved expression of their sentiments, their plans, their actions ? Why not use your prerogative as a charming woman to draw them out, and at the same time to learn of them something of their politics, their war-designs, their daily practices ?"

"Uncle!" exclaimed Nathalie, with a startled and suspicious look. But no — the old gentleman was innocent. Pleased with his eloquence, he meandered placidly on, not so much as noticing her interruption, repeating with parrot-like assurance all his inoculated wisdom; and as he spoke in his measured accent, his manner encased in an indestructible veneer, Madame de Vallauris perceived in it all the terrible and gentle omnipresence of the abbé.

"I would not, of course, advise intimacy. Pardon the word, my dear," he said airily. "It escaped me unawares. You do not indeed need any warning in that respect. I would merely suggest that we create, evenings, so to speak, an atmosphere."

"An atmosphere?" repeated Nathalie.

"Yes, my dear. The word is good. Not the atmosphere of a Hôtel de Rambouillet, but the atmosphere of a Montauban, — in distress, dignified, serene, triumphant."

"Good heavens!" ejaculated Nathalie in consternation.

"I do not wonder at your surprise, my dear. I too was somewhat impressed with the novelty of the scheme when the abbé — that is to say, when we, the abbé and I, happened to stray in that direction."

"Would all this make you happier, dear uncle?"

"It would at least seem appropriate."

"Manette's word," thought the countess.

"It would ennoble our powerlessness," admitted the marquis. In his look, in spite of his grandeur, was a veiled entreaty. She met it gallantly.

"Dear uncle, are you not monarch here? Do we care if German lieutenants leap over our hedges? What my heart can do for your comfort you may be sure of. My head, as you have mentioned, is little worth."

"It is enough — enough, my dear, for a woman,"

said the marquis encouragingly, condescending to pat her hand.

"Now, there is von Gerhardt," he announced with the exactness of a well-learned lesson,—"a good rider, a susceptible, expansive, vain, voluble man,—how instructive he might be made!"

"I should never have thought von Gerhardt instructive," she said meekly. "I should have chosen another adjective for him."

"That is immaterial," continued the marquis. "Let us consider the colonel,—bluff, hearty, admirably informed, a talker. What racy ideas could he set afloat in the atmosphere of our salon! Then a man of that positive temperament is sometimes most easily influenced by a woman."

"Indeed!" said the countess, raising her eyebrows.

"Consider, too, that tall and dignified young man with the graceful manner. He wears a blue uniform. You remember him, surely?"

"Von Nordenfels," Nathalie said softly.

"Ah, yes, that's the name,—a man with private despatches to carry about; a man selected on account of personal valor and cleverness for important service; a man of a certain softness beneath his cold exterior.

I observed you talking very amiably with him last night. That was promising; that was well."

"He did not dare"— began the countess passionately.

"He did not dare anything beyond his orders, so far as I know," said the marquis with facetiousness. "I would merely suggest he is a favorite with his superiors, a marked man for his years, and in our international salon might be an attractive problem. It would in fact gratify me, my dear, if, in consideration of all that I have said, you would do me the favor to unbend in moderation towards the stranger-element, temporarily through a caprice of fate under my roof. If I permit a certain relaxation in your manner; if I, the head of the house, am on the spot to protect, to support,— what more can you desire ?"

"What, indeed ?"

"Then all is said. I shall depend upon you,— a discreet warmth; an encouraging atmosphere. Thanks for your attention. I hope the effort has not fatigued you, my dear. I think I will go out and look at those young men. They are not jumping badly, upon my honor."

"Do go, dear uncle. It will interest you," she said

kindly. "It is mild in the sunshine, and you so rarely go out nowadays. It will do you good."

"Thanks, my dear Nathalie; thanks. I will stroll out and encourage those young men."

Airily making his adieus, he with difficulty walked out into the court.

"Oh, how he is failing, body and mind! When I remember what he once was, and then this conversation!" Tears filled her eyes. She felt inexpressibly helpless and lonely. A slight noise at the door made her turn. It was the Abbé de Navailles whose intellectual and benign presence now appeared.

"Ah, madame," he said in gentle greeting, "I am fortunate to find you here. Pierre has sprained his foot, and I have given Antoine my last bandage for him. Perhaps you —"

"M. l'Abbé de Navailles," facing him and speaking very rapidly, "will you have the extreme kindness to remember that I am not your tool?"

"Madame?" in mild interrogation.

"Will you also remember that my manner, my conduct, my words and ways, are my purely personal attributes, which no mortal may presume to determine or direct?"

"Madame?" he repeated, as if questioning whether he heard aright.

"Will you furthermore have the goodness to bear in mind that while I esteem nothing a sacrifice which may minister to my uncle's comfort, should my scheme for his happiness differ diametrically from another's, I am quite capable of finding my own the wiser and better, and of following it persistently, regardless of consequences?"

The gentle incredulity on the abbé's face merged slowly into equally gentle reflection. "That is all?" he said at length.

"That is all," answered the countess, looking at him with unconcealed defiance, then turning to go.

"One moment, madame," his soft voice begged. She waited, watching him mistrustfully. "The burden of the three — I presume I may say warnings with which you with admirable frankness have honored me, is one and the same. To its somewhat unflattering implication I refrain from replying directly."

"As usual," the slight droop of her eyelids and her satirical mouth responded plainly enough.

Unruffled and sweet-tempered as it was possible for a man to be, he continued: "I would merely suggest to your sense of justice — and I have never met a woman who makes more honest and successful effort to be just than you, or one who holds stricter accounts with herself, — I would simply suggest one question, madame. In your excited and sensitive frame of mind — "

Her look confronted him in haughty challenge.

" Most natural under existing circumstances," the placid voice went on, " when there is no repose by day or night, and every spirit lives in perpetual uproar and distressing uncertainty, might it not be possible for your imagination to exaggerate or distort harmless facts, and particularly to misinterpret the amiable conversation of your uncle the marquis? Charming and interesting as he continues to be, we who know him best and love him most must sometimes hold our breath, observing how his age tells upon him in these latter days."

Sincerity, unwavering affection for the marquis, sounded in every tone of his voice. The manly dignity of his character, softened by perceptible tenderness, in spite of her brusque attack displayed no retaliation. No heat obscured his calm mental vision. Intellectually her superior, he stood before her, and she acknowledged, now as always, that she had no proofs against him. What he said was true. Her poor uncle might easily convey a false impression. And she herself, — could she ever be sure that her old prejudice against the abbé did not blind her judgment even when he was innocent? Whom indeed could she trust? On whom could she lean? Her uncle was too frail and old to hear an unguarded word. However well grounded her charges against the abbé seemed, however indignantly she confronted him, she could not gainsay the tranquillity and fairness, not of his open defence, for he never actually defended himself, but of his tacit refutation. She looked at him now bitterly. "The man makes me doubt my own instincts," she thought. " 'The man's head, the woman's heart,' as poor uncle fondly says. But if the woman has only her intuitions, and they desert her, what will she do then? I wish to be just. I wish to be tolerant. I do not intend to be deceived. My instinct warns me. My head acquits him. But why does he wish me to be friendly with the men he hates?"

"Could there not be some error?" he asked quietly, as if reading her thoughts and responding.

"There can always be some error," she answered.

"Take care you make none from overmuch wisdom. And, that we understand each other once for all, whatever plan you design for the edification of our house, if it includes me, should be communicated directly to me."

"Undoubtedly, madame," he said, smiling as if at the perverseness of a child. "And the bandages?" reverting to his first theme with solicitude.

"Pierre seems to sprain his foot curiously often," she said abruptly.

He shrugged his shoulders. "Yes, he may be a little awkward."

She looked at him troubled, doubtful, uncertain of him, of herself. His face bore her scrutiny without effort. His simplicity was admirable. But as she found herself weighing and measuring, now condemning, now acquitting him, yet questioning what those clear eyes meant to conceal and what that fine mouth desired to express, the thought of a face whose every line she knew rose up in contrast, and she remembered with a great sense of security and peace the tone of the stranger's voice.

"Manette shall bring you some bandages," she said, and went away smiling softly, as if with happy thoughts. The abbé smiled too, but differently.

"She is very young, after all," he reflected.   "All the better."

The only result of the marquis's eloquence was that Madame de Vallauris, far from exercising her charms evenings with the deliberate purpose of drawing out the Germans, was seized opportunely with a slight indisposition, which confined her some days to her room.   The marquis, who had never known her to have a moment's illness, was frantic with anxiety.   This caused her conscience severe reproaches, and induced her to reappear sooner than she had designed.   It was singular how empty the rooms seemed without that one quiet figure in black, and how dull all conversation was without the voice that was but rarely heard.   Von Nordenfels stalked in every evening; looked round gravely and stalked out again, the abbé's eyes not being the depths in which he longed to gaze.

When Madame de Vallauris came down again there was unfeigned rejoicing, and the marquis had quite forgotten his salon scheme.

"You were cruel, madame," whispered the abbé, with his indulgent smile.

"Only to be kind," she returned gravely.

Nordenfels, whose bureau-work had monopolized

him every night of her absence, had now apparently
no more arduous duty than to keep silent guard in
the room where she was leaning quietly back in a low
chair, half shaded by the draperies of an alcove window. It was of no use attempting to talk with her.
The Lady discouraged them all, except Forstenau, with
her monosyllabic indifference.

" Horses can surely compromise no one," she
thought, watching the abbé under her half-closed
lids.

Von Nordenfels was at a loss to understand why he
was relegated to the first hostile conditions of their
acquaintance. Surely she had been friendly, not only
in the cottage, but since at the château ; her eyes had
met his frankly, and with the lingering question he
had learned to read in them. Now Gerhardt, Wedell,
and the chandelier, at which, her head thrown
back, she frequently stared, could claim as much
attention as he. He refused to call her capricious ;
but not feeling in a sufficiently careless mood to enact
the rôle of social supernumerary, rose suddenly, made
his adieus with some stiffness, and left the room.
The countess, as before, continued to listen languidly
to Forstenau and to stare at the chandelier.

CHAPTER VII.

THE autumn sun was shining one morning with unusual warmth upon the besieged city and its environs, where a great stillness prevailed, broken now and then by the muffled tone of a distant cannon from the resisting forts. On every highway and along the narrow riding-paths, marked by poles, indicating for the orderlies the most direct line possible from headquarters to headquarters, were single cavaliers and groups of horsemen, officers and orderlies, all riding towards Vert Galant on the Metz road. They were for the most part strong and sun-browned faces, and powerful figures sitting firm in their saddles. Their uniforms would scarcely have enhanced the effect of a drawing-room; for, like their wearers, they bore traces of wind and weather and many a hard night of bivouac. A sash over the shoulder and the black leather bag at the belt distinguished the officers acting as adjutants. The horses were in a tolerable condition, many of them having been "requisitioned" to fill the very considerable gaps made, not only by the enemy's shots, but by the over-fatigue and insufficient fodder on the unusually long marches.

It was evidently some weighty reason which had induced the commander of the corps to order all the adjutants, with the exception of those occupied with the troops on forepost duty, to report at Vert Galant.

The country-house where the prince had established his headquarters displayed a stately façade, and was still in most respects well preserved. A large garden with an iron railing lay between the house and the broad street. Gradually groups of officers gathered here in highly animated discussion. The entrance-door on the left showed the carriages of the staff in admirable condition. The gardener's lodge on the right was transformed into a guard-house. Before it stood the watch, observing with close attention a group of prisoners who had just been brought in from the foreposts. They were from various infantry regiments, a few from the Garde Mobile, and some Tirailleurs de la Seine. A staff-officer was noting the numbers of their regiments, and endeavoring by severe cross-examination to ascertain as much as possible of their combinations, strength, and position. After the men had had some rest and food, they were re-questioned rigorously. Already there were flying rumors that Paris was destitute of provision.

On a bench by the guard-house sat some lightly wounded prisoners whom two surgeons were bandaging, while a young officer extended his pocket-flask with an encouraging word to one and another of the unfortunates.

Through the broadly open windows on the ground-floor of the pleasant house a breakfast-table, if seen at a sufficient distance, suggested by association an indefinite vista of family life and tranquil joys; but approaching, the remains of the extremely substantial but by no means luxurious repast, and the unmistakable mannish appointments, showed plainly enough this had no likeness to the morning rites of a cheery home. A group of civilians attached to the Saxon headquarters sat there still, leisurely sipping a glass of claret, among them some Knights of St. John, serving under the red cross, two distinguished surgeons who had left their professor's chairs of Leipzig University to give their services during the campaign, and the correspondents of the London "Times" and "Daily News."

Upon the mantel-piece, piled in perilous irregularity nearly to the ceiling, were boxes of cigars, — the so-called " love's offerings " sent generally with the friendliest intentions by some benevolent association, but rarely redolent of the choicest Havana. Many rapid writers were working at their best speed in a room on the right, where a printing-press was also preparing the orders, and a young officer at a side table was sketching on a large scale a plan of the last reported French defences along the Saxon line.

The field post, that blessed messenger between the army and the fatherland, was busily at work in an adjacent building. Two mountains of letters rose conspicuously,— on one side those received, on the other those about to be sent. What anxiety, impatience, anger, and sorrow, what sighs of love and longing, were imprisoned in those paper mounds!

The great hall clock, with its slow, impressive voice marking in peace or war the fatal flight of time, now struck three.

The issue of orders had been appointed for two, and Vert Galant had waited already a whole hour for the coming of the adjutant who should bring the order from Grand Tremblay, the headquarters of the Maas Army. A certain restlessness began to be noticeable among the officers. Some of them, in a truly feminine and childlike manner, went frequently to the entrance gate, and eagerly scanned the road upon which the longed-for adjutant was expected to appear. Others smoked, and assumed a stolidity they by no means felt.

The corps commander, too, had left his room in the first story, and coming out into the garden by a side door, was now walking up and down on the west side of the house in the alley which extended towards the Bois de St. Denis. Every inch a prince, he was an elegant, still youthful-looking man, rather above the middle height. On his right, still taller than he, strode the powerful and noble form of General von Aarenhorst, who had come over from the château at Clichy to discuss some important points with his commanding general. On the left of the prince was the chief of the staff, a short, thick figure, in a somewhat neglected uniform. As he walked, he talked volubly, with free gesticulation and rapidly varying expression of his intellectual face. Close on the heels of the prince followed a magnificent hunting-dog of purest breed. He had lost his French master and strayed to Vert Galant, where with an *aut-Cæsar-aut-nihil* instinct he had attached himself at once to the prince in preference to all others. A single French word of praise or petting delighted the beautiful animal excessively, although his progress in the German language was already commendable.

Presently, not by the Metz road as was expected, but by the narrow path along the Ourcq Canal and through the garden gate in the rear, came the corps adjutant in full gallop. His brave bay was covered with foam, for upon him had fallen the responsibility of making good as far as possible the time lost by human blundering and delay in issuing the orders. As the adjutant passed the dining-room window, one of the St. John knights reached out a brimming glass of good red wine, which the thirsty man, without stopping, swallowed at one gulp as he hastened on to the prince. The crowd of waiting adjutants streamed into the bureau. A staff-officer, after announcing the corps time, by which every adjutant set his watch, read rapidly and distinctly the despatches from head-quarters. Sitting, standing, using the shoulders of the man in front as desk, they wrote at the officer's dictation. Suddenly, in their immediate neighborhood they heard the sound of repeated gunshots. They started and listened, with some excitement. " Don't be disturbed, gentlemen," remarked the dictating staff-officer. " It is only the orderlies shooting the last pheasants of the park for our dinner."

The final detail of the instructions ordered a dislocation of the Saxon corps, Aulnay to be evacuated and occupied immediately by the second division of the Prussian Guard. Von Nordenfels' pencil was curiously unsteady as he wrote this order.

The delivery of the details was completed. The adjutants sprang to their horses, for some time impatiently stamping in the court, and galloped in small groups towards the entrance, where, to their dissatisfaction, they were summarily forced to halt. A long provision column, bringing supplies from Claye, was passing the closed gates of Vert Galant. Strong horses, *percherons*, from the northeast of France, on the Belgian boundaries, were harnessed by threes and fours to the heavily laden wagons. French wagoners in their blue blouses and baggy trousers walked at the side. They held their reins and long whips listlessly, not once giving their peculiar cheery call to their horses, or their loud and jovial whip-cracking. Silent and gloomy they stalked on, every two of them guarded by a well-armed man.

As the last wagon went heavily by the gate, out flew the pent-up adjutants towards all points of the compass. Along the highways and field paths, by wood and stream and meadow, the fleet hoofs galloped through the still country, carrying the important news in every direction.

It was late in the day when von Nordenfels rode into Aulnay with his despatches, the necessity of which arose from the following facts.

The French army was now reconstructed, the armies of the Seine and the Loire had united in the south, where, in consequence, the Bavarian general, Von der Tann, with a large body of troops, had been ordered. This weakened in no small degree the besieging girdle, and dislocations were imperative to cover, so far as possible, the threatened points. Active measures and changes of quarters, however admirable as military tactics, were nevertheless far from personally agreeable to the officers stationed at Aulnay. They were loud in their expressions of regret, and the dismay of the marquis was grievous to behold.

"Bless my soul, gentlemen! Can nothing be done?" he asked in stammering accents strikingly at variance with his usual lofty placidity towards the Germans.

"Nothing, I fear," returned the colonel, smiling.

"But how do I know what the officers of the Prussian Guard will be like?" demanded the perturbed old gentleman.

"You can judge for yourself to-morrow morning, marquis."

"They are a bad lot," Gerhardt took occasion to confide to the marquis. "We are bad enough, but they are incalculably worse. We have injured your beautiful château, but they would have demolished it entirely. A Prussian? Why, a Prussian is a kind of impossible being with a double-barrelled thinking apparatus, not an atom of heart, and truly distinguished manners."

"Distinguished manners are all one really requires for most situations in life," remarked the marquis affably, feeling much comforted.

"Here, Nordenfels, you are a half Prussian yourself; come and tell the marquis to what species of monster the Prussian belongs."

The adjutant had hurriedly entered the room, looked around, and was about to return to the bureau.

"If they are all like Herr von Nordenfels, they will let my poor old château, like a faded belle, console itself with the remains of its beauty." And the marquis, pleased with his eloquence, raised his handkerchief to his smiling lips and gently inhaled the invigorating fumes of eau-d'Houbigant.

"We won't praise them too much," von Nordenfels

said, looking in his cordial, respectful way at the marquis. "We prefer you should think us their superiors. But, believe me, they will attach themselves to the château and be sorry to leave when their turn comes, as we are ; and you will find some good heads for cards among them. So much, justice compels me to say for my rivals."

"Well, well," returned the marquis with cheerful condescension, "a man of my age and my experience must consent to take things as they come. That is true wisdom, gentlemen."

"I can take most things," muttered von Gerhardt in a stage aside, "but I can't take a Prussian. He never agrees with me. He sticks in my throat like a five-pronged fish-bone."

"You remarked?" began the marquis civilly.

"A technical observation to my comrade here," Gerhardt hastened to explain with importance. "We are necessarily uncommonly busy this evening. Strategic problems, vast responsibilities—" And the dandy lieutenant bowed himself away.

"Are you too busy for a parting game of chess, Herr von Nordenfels?"

"I fear that I am. At least, I have some pressing duties. Nothing so strategic as the occupations of von Moltke and my friend Gerhardt, but considerable writing still for the colonel; and there is somebody I must see," he said in a business-like tone, knowing one betrays what one wishes to conceal oftener by an elaborate circumlocution than by an unaccentuated statement of the truth. The marquis, intent on chess, expressed the hope of a game later in the evening. The dark abbé, reading in the alcove, did not once raise his eyes. Various officers came in and out of the room or passed the door upon which Nordenfels had fixed his gaze. Nothing of interest entered. In spite of the onerous duties of which he had spoken, he watched and waited with unobtrusive persistency. Suddenly some bright ribbons flaunted themselves aggressively in the corridor. They disappeared. Nordenfels asked himself a pertinent question. They flashed by again. Nordenfels rapidly surveyed the room. The colonel was conversing with the marquis. The abbé quietly read. "Of course, those eyes of his see everything. See? They see when he's at his prayers and when he's asleep." Nevertheless, the adjutant rose and sought the ribbons. As he advanced, they receded, until they had decoyed him to a place where a low-voiced colloquy seemed to their owner not inappropriate.

The exchange of ideas was brief but significant.

"She's in the acacia-walk," was the welcome information imparted to him in a stage whisper.

"A thousand thanks, Manettechen. You shall never regret that."

The ribbons flew in one direction where a flaxen giant was awaiting them; the uniform moved as eagerly, if with more dignity, in another.

Past the great linden and the thuyas he went, with his long, firm step. His heart beat fast. He knew no words to say to the lady whom he was seeking in the twilight; but in his lover's rhapsody, fearing, hoping, trembling, rejoicing, he remembered only the liquid depths of her eyes as he had met their gaze in the cottage, and forgot their haughty indifference as she stared at the chandelier and nothing. He was glad of the garden, glad of the gathering dimness, exultant that he was drawing near to her lovely presence; and even the morrow's parting seemed a shadowy sorrow, so strong and warm was the undefined hope in the young man's honest soul.

She heard the swing of his sabre, the click of his spurs along the paved walk, and well she knew his step. A thousand conflicting impulses moved her. Should she go? Should she stay? Would he notice that her eyes were wet? How could he venture to seek her here? How could he know? Should she remain where she was on the low rustic seat? Should she rise and walk the other way?

She remained. He came. Impassioned as any lover whose romantic ardor illumines the pages of tradition and verse, had she been an old dowager at high noon instead of his lady-love in the soft twilight, he yet could not have inclined his tall figure, and raised his hand in stiff salute, with more ceremonious elegance; and under no circumstances could she have manifested a smoother impenetrability. He had a confused impression that life was short, that it was folly to let golden moments pass without making them one's own in bliss and forgetfulness; but of such wild thoughts this modern knight, being encased in good breeding as in a coat of mail, gave no sign; and of all the eloquence surging mightily through him, not a word escaped. He only said, "Good evening, madame."

"Good evening, Herr von Nordenfels," replied the coolest voice of the countess.

"It is mild this evening," remarked the ardent lover.

"Yes," she returned, with befitting gravity. "That

is, it was mild. It is a little cooler now. I think
I will go in."

"Ah, don't go quite yet!" begged Nordenfels with
startling vehemence; then he stopped short.

She did not answer, but neither did she go.

The château was noisy with the voices and heavy
tread of men. The village was all astir; but surely
the tumult was of some remote world. Near them
was no sound but the drowsy plash of the fountain and the faintest murmur of the soft acacias
in the evening breeze. Above, the dark Tower kept
watch.

He was not shy, yet he feared the cold mask
she had assumed. He was not bold, yet he felt an
imperious desire to take her in his arms and cover
her haughty face with his warm kisses, until it could
never again, whether in love or hate, look at him
without a flush of remembrance.

At length he quietly said, "You know we leave
the château to-morrow, madame?"

"Yes," replied the cold voice. "I believe I heard
some one say so. They were all making such a
disturbance in the house, that I came out for a
little quiet."

To the refined ungraciousness of this speech

Nordenfels replied in his earnest, direct manner : " I regret every sound and tone that jars upon your ear, every sight that offends your eyes. Our rudely enforced presence in your house seems to me nothing less than sacrilege. Not a day, not an hour goes by, but I feel that with you and for you."

Charmed against her will by his protecting tenderness, her spirit drawn resistlessly towards him, struggling against the strange pain she felt at the thought of losing him, and bewildered by the power of her emotions, she broke out inconsequently, a bitter ring in her voice : " You Germans are terrible. Your war is hard and cruel beyond even the necessities of war. You are relentless, pitiless. From Aulnay to Chelles, with your landmarks and batteries and abatis and palisades, you have ruined our pleasant country. Many a fine estate, many an ancient château, you have sacrificed ruthlessly. You hold that might makes right. You have no other law. You are as inflexible as death. You bring death, — worse than death to us — "

Pained, astonished, Nordenfels stood silent before her, and no instinct whispered : " It is because she loves you that she says this. She seeks to defend herself against herself and you. She has no weapons but these wild words, which she flings desperately on every side."

He bowed his head and listened sorrowfully.

The twilight was closing in dense around them. The fountain plashed on in its cool unconcern. This was not what he had sought in the shadowy garden. He remembered the colonel's pleasantry that first day they rode into Aulnay, and he saw her, proud and pale, facing them at the door of the old château. She was indeed the princess of the enchanted castle. How should he reach her through the labyrinth of thorns? He felt that whether there were only moats and drawbridges between them, or earthquakes and pestilence, tempest and floods, undreamed-of perils and Titan foes, he must go on. And there she sat, so near. It seemed to him there were only they two in the world. So, too, it seemed to the fair woman as she heard the fountain and looked up to the silent Tower. Yet she would not yield.

"You are men of iron, men of stone," she resumed. "Are we not brave? Who is braver than a Frenchman? Our soldiers charge with magnificent force; they are impetuous, gallant, elastic, agile; they have endurance, strength; they are loyal; they are heroes;

but they fall before your cruel, serried ranks of frozen-hearted demons!"

Still he did not speak. He folded his arms and patiently waited for the storm to pass.

"And now you are closing in round beautiful Paris. Nearer and nearer, tighter and tighter, you are drawing your cruel lines. But though you await her downfall, that you will not see. No, that at least will be spared us. You have the overweight of brute force. Whether the triumph of mind is for you or for us, that even your arrogance may not presume to determine."

Her low voice ceased its rapid and indignant utterance.

"Why has she never spoken, and why must it be to-night, of all nights, that she builds this barrier between us?" Nordenfels asked himself.

After a long and painful pause, "I do not understand you, madame," he said with simplicity.

It was no wonder. She did not understand herself, did not know what induced her to pour a torrent of hard words upon the head of this man, whose consideration had never failed to impress her with a subtle sense of protection and rest, whose steadfast eyes followed her with their boundless sympathy and deference, and what beside she had never cared to fully interpret. She only knew her heart was heavy; that a deathly loneliness and dread of the morrow, and of all the dreary morrows to come, had taken possession of her.

Above the sombre Tower, cloud-masses were gathering and breaking. On the west wind echoed faintly the far-off Paris chimes. In all her life she had never known so strong a feeling as this with which she was contending. "He is your enemy," was borne upon the breeze straight from the beleaguered city. Strange and confused voices were struggling for mastery in her soul. "His eyes are true, his voice is sweet, his presence stirs your heart in a wonderful way, and when you look upon him in the strength and beauty of his young manhood, you are moved to place your two hands in his and trust him, and give him what he asks. For something, something he is silently asking, even now as he stands there, pained by your words. But remember he is an enemy, wickedly invading your dear land. He will go to-morrow. Let him go. You are a Frenchwoman and a Montauban." And above this warning sounded the clear voice of her dream. "Choose!" it cried solemnly; while in the dusky clouds she saw a

martial train,—not all those solemn heroes marching down the ages, not all the glory and splendor of
the vision, but majestic, changing forms vanishing
behind the old church-tower; and it was to her as
if the most beautiful of them, the most earnest
and serene, were standing near her and beginning
now to speak in a tone softer than the fall of the
water.

"Countess, much that you say is true."
He hesitated. The position was all false, all un-
necessary, he felt. What had the war to do with
them, with his love for this woman, except that it
had led him to her dear feet, where he longed to
kneel with a thousand impassioned words, only she,
she herself restrained him. "Forgive me if I find
it too hard to answer you; this is neither the time
nor place," he continued. "You cannot wonder that
as a German I love my fatherland; as a soldier, my
calling. And yet, if I could tell you all my thoughts
about war in general, — ah, madame, they are perhaps
not wholly unlike your own, except, of course, I must
contend that our mode of making war is second to
none."

His naturalness and great indulgence were the
most sensible means he could have chosen to calm

her excitement. Instinctively he felt that she was listening more quietly now.

"If you would allow me, some day, in a happier time, I will answer you, countess. Some day there is much I would say to you. I would have said it to-night, but the moment passed — unless — " He hesitated.

He spoke with self-command, but there was love in his voice.

She rose quickly. Her hands trembled as she drew her lace scarf closer round her face.

"Herr von Nordenfels, my uncle will be wondering what has become of me."

"It is early still."

"Yes, but it is better that I go in."

He pulled his mustache and walked along by her side, staring straight before him.

"Why did you tear down Livry?" she asked in a conversational tone.

"I?" said Nordenfels absently. "Heaven forbid!"

Inscrutable nature of woman! At his unexpected reply she laughed a little, low as if to herself, and her lover listened enchanted.

"Livry?" he repeated.

"The château where Madame de Staël lived and

wrote. I was not accusing you of personal animosity," she added.

Madame de Staël, it is to be feared, was to him an object of remote and infinitesimally small interest, but he gratefully blessed her memory at this moment.

"Ah, yes, I remember. Pardon me. I was somewhat *distrait.* It was a necessity, of course. Believe me, we do not destroy homes from a wanton spirit of destruction. We are not barbarians, countess." As hate leaps out in civil, guarded speech, so his love flamed through every light word he uttered.

She said nothing. The twilight and the acacias seemed to cling to her as she walked.

Some subtle fragrance lingering in the lace wound about her fair hair mingled with the fresh earthy smells and the dews of evening. They walked slower and slower.

The lover's voice was silent. His spirit spoke to hers unceasingly. "Do not be unjust, dear lady. It is all a mystery. Human vices and virtues are exaggerated into unnatural prominence in war. In war, as in peace, the noble suffers for the act of the thoughtless and the coarse, and a thousand untrained souls undo the act of the humane and wise. In war, as in peace, the brain plans wisely, the hot heart errs. Is it hard to rule one's own spirit? Is it hard for me now not to fold you to my heart in your loveliness? Do not be unjust, dearest lady. War executes rapidly what peace does slowly but no less surely. In peace, too, strength triumphs, the weakest goes to the wall, and good souls fight a brave fight yet die of cruel wounds. What are the worst wounds? Those of the battlefield? Who can tell? War is pitiless. Is society less so? Does not society make its indisputable requisitions, trample on the wounded, cheer the conqueror whatever his course? And does not society resort to methods not permissible in honorable warfare, to a more extended espionage, to a meaner and more heartless treatment of prisoners, to torture and polite thumbscrews long since abandoned by progressive and merciful minds but retained in society's 'best' circles?

"Some far-off day will a new and noble era dawn? Would that you and I could behold its glory and its justice. In the mean time, my lady, never believe the humane spirit may not exist, even in war; for life is war, and war is everywhere in life and nature. Disease and pestilence are more cruel than the sword, and friendly mother earth is often our worst enemy. Surely, if one thinks, one sees this, and 'Evil saith to Good: My brother, I am one with thee,' so inter-woven are life's threads. Surely the anarchists and all the misled restless beings, seeking to undermine this bad old world in order to build a worse one upon its ruins, are guided by too little, not too much thought; and theirs is the most wicked and most futile war. But trouble your fair soul not at all, lady, walking with me in the twilight, about all these involved questions which the wisest cannot solve. Do not hate me because I come in war. Be magnanimous, be pitiful ! Only love me, and all will be well. Only let me take you to my heart, and the problems and mysteries may circle on for-ever in infinite mazes. Make this moment sublime with the light of your love, and all doubt, all dark-ness, will fall from my soul."

So with lover's logic pleaded the lover's spirit. And he might have said all this and more, for a whirl of fantastic thoughts was rushing through his excited brain; but he could not speak. The day had exacted heavy duties of him. Before dawn he had been faithfully at work. Each hour of service, unknown to him, was bringing him nearer this wonderful moment at the close of the long, hard day. Only one thing seemed important to him, only one thing seemed real; and stronger to him than war and life and death was the love in his heart for this fair woman walking by his side as quiet as the dusk and as mysterious. Yet how could he, on the verge of departure, and after her passionate protest against him, his race, and his cause, turn and declare his feeling? It would be as abrupt and painful as a pistol-shot. That is, how could he insist that she should listen to what she plainly wished to avoid? "If I live, I will come back," he said to himself. "If I die, at least I have seen the one woman I could love with all my strength and all my soul. Yet if I die, I long to tell her once, if only once, that I love her!"

He thought the lady must have heard the loud, fast beating of his heart. Who knows what she heard, or what of all its passionate burden reached her, touched her, thrilled her in the silence? In all the science of unexplained forces, what is so sure and swift as lovers' thought-reading?

The countess suddenly stopped. They were by an opening in the acacias which made a high arched frame for the landscape beyond.

She hesitated, turned to go, gave a little sigh, lingered, and said softly, with an upward gesture, "Look!"

The clouds had drifted on with the far-off dream-heroes; over the Tower gleamed one pale star.

He glanced upwards, then eagerly back to her.

She, looking steadily towards the Tower, went on in her low, quiet voice: "I have watched that star by the Tower many, many times, countless hours, — as a child, and since, — always alone."

He made an impetuous, glad movement, and was about to speak.

"Listen!" she said softly. He folded his arms and obeyed the soft, restraining voice.

"When I was a child I used to wonder if my parents were up there, — if they were looking down and loving me; if there were wax dolls up there that would not melt, and bonbons that one could not eat too much of, and daisies that would never hang their heads though I should clasp them close in my hot little hand a whole summer morning long."

It seemed to Nordenfels that she was faintly smiling; but her voice was sad, profoundly sad. He pictured her a child, wandering alone with her daisies in the great park, and loved her unknown childhood.

"And I wondered if there were uncles and aunts up there that would let one play with village children, laughing and screaming and being happy on the green, while I peered longingly at them, my face pressed close against our gates. A thousand such fancies I had. They would weary you to relate them, — the foolish little fancies that haunt the brain of a lonely child. For I was alone, you know. Later, I used to sit and watch the star over the Tower, a young, young girl, with vague hopes hovering like angels about me, and dreams and illusions beckoning me on. I must have been too staid and subdued outwardly, but my heart rejoiced; and though I was alone, I was then never really alone, for I was like a part of the garden, it was so near, so dear to me. It was my friend, my companion. The plash of the fountain spoke to me; and the breath of the breeze and the touch of the cool and tender foliage on my cheek was a caress, as I pushed eagerly through the shrubbery in the springtime, seeking, finding treasures of blossom and leaf, knowing every bird-note, caring for the hum of the insects and the very dews on the grass, — loving the old park, loving life, afraid of nothing, of no fate, of no beyond."

And he, listening, knew and loved her girlhood.

She paused, considered an instant. "Then I went away from Aulnay," she said simply, her voice still lower. "For a long time I saw the star above the

Tower and the chestnut-trees and dear old-fashioned paths only in homesick dreams.   I was alone still."

He perfectly understood her.   He felt he would give all the years of his life if he might hold her now, this instant, to his breast.   "And then, madame ?"

"And then I came back to Aulnay, and the garden, and all; but I had grown old."

"Old! You, countess ?" He laughed, exulting in her youth.

"What I call old, yes.   And yet here again under the Tower, evenings, listening to the water and to the breeze in the acacias, and watching my star come out, my wishes are more extravagant and wild than when I was young.   A thousand thousand impossible wishes I send floating up above the Tower."

Out on the village street the men were marching down to relieve guard; left, right! left, right!— their tramp echoed through the hollow court-yard and penetrated into the shadowy park.   There were loud, metallic sounds against the paving-stones, hammering, and strong bass voices in abrupt question and reply. She turned her head an instant towards the din and disturbance, then back to the quietness and him.

"You send them floating up to the Tower ?" he repeated tenderly.

"I wish I could live on this fair earth at a later age, when there shall be no jealousies between nations, no hatred, no strife; when the monster War shall have been crushed, and no standing army shall weigh down any people; when we shall sail through space from land to land; when science shall have learned to subdue pain and disease, and soften death."

"And all that on this earth?"

"Why, yes." She laughed a little. "One loves one's home, you know. The star up there would seem quite strange, I fear; and if there are beings on it, they must be different from us, — nobler, grander. I like to think of this earth, this world, transfigured gloriously. It is often such a stupid, sad old world, it is pleasant to imagine it with more light. And if your life has been a mistake, you can always hope for it to be made right in heaven. But all the same you have your fancies about this very planet as it might be, — as it will be, perhaps, one day for others."

He broke out passionately: "Madame, let it come, if it will, — your expurgated edition of this world. I, too, have my Utopian dreams. But let the world go. We are here; and I cannot tell you how my very soul laughs within me when your fresh voice and your young lips speak of your wasted life, like an old crone mumbling in the chimney-corner. What do you know of life? Nothing. Have you been alone? But you need never be alone again. Have you had sorrows, injuries? What cannot youth and love forget! Ah, even in this world there are moments when the soul asks, Can paradise be more? And when a man finds his other self, the life of his life, he craves no unknown world to teach him joy."

"Hush, hush, you must not speak so; you forget," she murmured tremblingly. Then, with a strong effort, she continued, "Herr von Nordenfels, it is unfitting, it is painful and useless to say more."

"But —"

"Spare me. Spare yourself."

"Madame —"

"I could pretend not to understand."

"At first, but not now — never again," he protested. "I can never tell you with words. Unless my life may tell you, you will never know."

Every tone of his voice was a caress for which her soul hungered when he ceased to speak. She answered bravely: "I felt I had not been just and kind to you in what I said. I spoke with strange violence. I wished to make reparation; or, that not being possible, I wished at least to be honest with you and with myself. For that reason, and because you are going away to-morrow morning and I shall never see you again, it seemed to me no harm to talk to you simply as one talks to a friend. I never had a friend. I never talked to any one as I have talked with you to-night. Do not make me regret it."

"I am not your friend; and if I live, you will see me again," the man's voice replied boldly.

Again she ignored in self-defence.

"I spoke harshly. Pardon me. But I believe the greater part of what I said; and though I dream of a world where nations do not hate and kill each other, I am a Frenchwoman, and you are the enemy of my country. Therefore, forget your ungracious hostess. But if you ever think of her, remember she thanks you for your patience with her immeasurable contradictions."

"My patience with you! Good heavens! Madame—"

But she was resolutely walking on. He could only follow. As he was breaking out in eager protestation and entreaty, she placed her hand heavily on his arm. This surprised him into silence.

"Those thuyas have singularly striking forms," she

began, with a complete change of tone, and assuming the descriptive lightness of a ball-room chat. "In winter, laden with snow, they remind me of hooded monks; not upright monks, but stealthy, mysterious, dangerous men."

Little cared he for thuyas at that moment; but he looked at them, notwithstanding, as he passed, and inquiringly at her as they approached the first lantern near the château.

"I thought some one was there," she explained. "I may have been mistaken. You feel an unseen human presence sometimes, you know. I certainly neither saw nor heard anything. It was sheer nervousness."

They were on the lightest portico. The great door was open. No one happened to be passing, but the house was full of movement, steps, voices, doors opening and closing. Any instant some one might come.

"Countess, I have been forgetting that I must go to-morrow. Now, I remember. Surely, this is not the last moment you will give me?"

"It is better that I say good-night."

"But I have said nothing," he murmured, in distress. "I had a world to say. You would not listen.

You have not heard. The precious time is gone. One moment in the library, I beg!"

He moved his arm abruptly. A tea-rose dropped from his buttonhole. He stooped and picked it up.

"It is a pretty rose for this desolate region," she said.

"It is from Vert Galant. The garden and hot-houses there are still full of flowers. This rose is like the one you wore the day I saw you first. Will you not keep it?"

She extended her hand; then, as if repenting, explained, "Ours are quite gone. Thanks, and adieu."

"One moment, madame! Ah, do not go!"

Suddenly she shaded her eyes and looked searchingly into the darkness of the park.

"What is it?"

"Nothing. I am fanciful. I thought I saw a thuya moving across the lawn."

"Countess," he pleaded, "will you not once say you are sorry for this parting, — a little sorry?"

"The change is not welcome to me, Herr von Nordenfels," she returned very gently. "No — assuredly — I do not desire it."

"If I live, I will come back. This is not all, cannot, shall not be all."

"Good-night," she said softly, and was gone.

In her turret-room she locked her door against Manette. She kissed the pale rose, not paler than herself, a thousand times, and her hot tears blurred its velvet petals.

CHAPTER VIII.

THE rose that was kissed and wept over lay the next morning between the leaves of Alfred de Musset's poems, which for safe keeping Madame de Vallauris put under the perfumed laces and ribbons in the upper drawer of her chiffonier. Manette, with the scent peculiar to hunting-dogs and lady's-maids, nosed the object in its unwonted place before she had been five minutes in the room to put things to rights. She opened the book, perceived the rose, and threw up her dancing black eyes with thankfulness. She then placed the little volume diagonally with the drawer, and deftly dropped upon it a violet ribbon and a bit of Point Duchesse, all exactly as she had found them.

"She may have arranged them, she may not. At all events, accuracy 's no crime," was her conclusion as she went thoroughly and swiftly on to her more apparent duties; although she herself considered nothing more incumbent upon a perfect lady's-maid than to categorically comprehend her mistress, — her weaknesses, her virtues, her love-affairs, her glove-buttons, her idiosyncrasies, her dilemmas, her secreted rosebuds, and her innermost desires.

When Countess Nathalie returned, Manette, with the unconsciousness of an infant, was shaking a table-cover out of the high casement window.

"Gently, gently, Manette," said the countess, seating herself listlessly in a low chair.

"Nerves — love-nerves," commented the maid silently. "Don't I know these symptoms? The most amiable mistress, — but the doors must not disturb our thoughts, footsteps shall not sound, and if we could, we would stop all the clocks and roosters. It does not do to give way to this mood. If the world could not make a noise it would burst, and that's the long and short of it. Has n't my soldier marched away too? Have n't I put on blue ribbons, by no means becoming, but, alas! how significant? Blue — faithfulness. With them I remind myself of my attachment to my Wackermann, and, just heaven! I 'd better hang on more of them, for that Prussian Feldwebel going towards the stables is an adorable creature. If I shake the cloth harder, better still the white curtains, he may look up; and how appropriate, — a smiling girl at a window, waving a flag of truce! How endless are the opportunities presented to a fertile mind by this sad war! He sees. He smiles. He salutes."

She fairly gasped with excitement.

" Manette!"

" Madame?"

" Why are you making such extraordinary motions, and flaunting the curtains so wildly?"

" Giving them air, madame; lace is so receptive — so sensitive."

" I think you have sufficiently ministered to the sensitiveness of my window-curtains, Manette."

" Very good, madame."

" There are new men in the kitchen, of course. I presume you have not had occasion to speak to them."

" I created an occasion, madame. It was not difficult. Devoted as I am to madame and to the family, how can I do otherwise than be on the best terms with the men in the kitchen, especially when they alone provide the meat?"

" The half-cup of strong bouillon for the marquis. I wish you to beg them to make it regularly and well. The others were very attentive and reliable. I could send Jean, but they laugh at him, and that irritates the poor old man."

"Madame permits me to remark that Jean's demeanor fails in the tact which is indispensable in one's treatment of cooks in general, and particularly men-cooks. Foreign and military men-cooks require special management. It was, so to speak, on the marquis's bouillon that I sailed into the kitchen. The Prussians had not been installed a half-hour, before that matter was perfectly arranged. Madame may rely upon the thoroughness of my mission. The bouillon will be served hot, strong, prompt, and with vast good-will. The kitchen, I may say, is won, to the last man."

"It is a lamentable fact that we must beg for the Marquis of Montauban a cup of beef-tea from Germans in his own kitchen; and if they did not feed us, I presume we should starve. But the important thing, nevertheless, is that he has his bouillon. I do not doubt your method was efficacious."

"Madame knows that in order to execute all the duties which devolve upon me in the present unique situation I have heroically abandoned all national prejudices. I may conscientiously declare that not a fragment remains in my composition."

Madame de Vallauris smiled faintly. That Manette never had any patriotism to lose was obvious.

A shade of wonder at the light nature of the girl crossed her mind, occupied with dreary retrospection. How could any one be merry to-day? The whole world ought to feel that light and warmth and glory had departed, and in the air was a fatal chill. Manette was a canary-bird, twittering and glancing about with hard bright eyes though death was in the house. No — Manette was devoted and good, blithe, thank God! not old before her time. Let her live her own way and be her own gay self, mused the sad countess, who had grown more attached to her one woman companion, shallow as she was, in this world of men and martial rule, as she had also consciously clung with a warmer, closer affection to her unresponsive uncle.

What should she do with this day, and all the other days stretching away into the colorless future? That the Prussians had come seemed absolutely unimportant. Nothing was important now; and she herself was like a dead leaf, tossed hither and thither on the winds of fate. There was but one thing left, — the duty of each day. Even that reduced itself to minute proportions; for what she could be to her uncle was limited by his requirements. Still, with more tact, with more patience, she might learn to be more serviceable, more necessary to him, to comprehend him more tenderly and wisely.

"I will go to him now. Surely it is better to try to do something, if ever so little, for his comfort, his amusement, than to stay here alone and remember. I cannot read. Strange words stare at me from the printed page,—words I heard spoken in a voice I long to follow and obey. And a presence haunts me, holds me, claims me with its loving mastery. Weak heart, that would give and take in love's improvidence; that trembled before a man's pleading tone and a man's loving face; that would fain have yielded to love's sophistry and flung me a traitor yet rapturous upon his breast, to feel his face above me in the dusk like a god's, and his strong arm owning me who am cheerless and alone! A love-sick village girl could scarce be weaker than I. Because he is beautiful in my eyes, must I yield? Because he is noble and earnest, and his grave eyes seek mine with entreaty and faith, shall I plunge headlong from hate to love? Because I feel his unseen presence in a crowded room, and hear his lowest word, and see him only when scores of men ride by my window, because — because — something mightier than I knew existed in the world rises up in me

and claims him, calls imperiously for him, clings
to him and will not let him go, shall I succumb to
the memory of a twilight hour, to his influence and
his will, and gloatingly live the moments over again
in all their bitter-sweet intensity? Cowardly, selfish heart, reaching for its coveted good over blood-
stained fields where patriots have fallen, — heart
basely longing to take refuge in the enemy's camp,
in the enemy's arms, have you no honor left, have
you no shame?

"He is gone. God keep him! I need not blush
for him. He is a true man. In vague dreams I
have pictured such a man as one with whom a
woman's life might grow large, and rich, and full of
noble purpose. The chances of war led him to our
doors. The chances of war have led him elsewhere.
No, I will not yield to chance. I have been weak.
Now, I resist. I will forget. There is one's duty
every day; and then, they cannot last forever, — the
days, the long, long, dreary days!"

She thought with a sudden longing of the rose.
To touch it once, to kiss it, to hold it to her cheek,
was her instinctive need. "School-girl!" she called
herself, and walked in the other direction and stood
a moment pale and still by the window. But she

did not throw the rose away, and never forgot where it lay, its petals crumpled with tears and kisses; and often she dreamed of it, and much else sweet beside, for dreams are rebels.

"Manette, ask Jean if the marquis has had his coffee."

"He has, madame."

"Then tell Jean to ask if the marquis would like me to read to him, or perhaps a game of bézique, or I could sit and chat with him if he prefers. Or, stay, I will go down myself. But no — you may go, Manette."

While the maid went, Madame de Vallauris remained by the window. She could see a part of the acacia-walk, and it left her no peace. But if she turned, the hidden rose appealed to her with tender magnetism. In the whole château she had no protection against the inevitable swing of her own thoughts reverting regularly as a pendulum from duty to love, except the poor resort of a game of cards with the self-absorbed old gentleman. Bézique may be a perpetual solace for elderly ennuied mortals, but bézique and love? Ah, Love forbid!

Even this sedate recreation was denied her, for Manette came with a kind good-morning and many thanks from the marquis, and another time he would be charmed to oblige her, but his morning was already quite occupied.

" M. le Marquis is in a very cheerful frame of mind," volunteered Manette. " He is gracefully gay, airily excited, like — like a bit of dignified thistle-down."

Countess Nathalie's heart sank. Well she knew the demeanor which Manette's impossible phrase indicated. It expressed a mood of her uncle's most fatal to intimacy or any approach to home-feeling, and which rendered him in his breezy self-sufficiency as unresponsive to actual human needs as if he had been a disembodied spirit. Touch him one could not, and help he would neither give nor take.

"Is he alone ?"

" M. l'Abbé is with him. The gentlemen are laughing together. M. le Marquis is still in his dressing-gown, but Jean is laying out his things that he may prepare to receive the visit of the new officers. Very distinguished-looking they are, too, — I having taken the trouble to meet several of them by pure chance, — but when I think with what sternness and coldness and hardness of heart we thought it necessary to receive our beautiful dears, now gone probably forever, though there are among them true hearts that will return, — more than this it being inappropriate to mention, — and when I contrast that and this, I have sentiments, sentiments, madame, which — "

" Which you would do well to keep for your own edification, Manette," warned the countess gently, " since the marquis has simply his pleasure to consult as to whom he will receive and how he will receive them."

" Madame permits me to remark it is not the warmth of to-day that I regret. Far be it from me to begrudge those handsome Prussians anything. Oh, their square shoulders and their long stride and their blond mustaches and their dignified air deserve all they can get. But there are others with square shoulders and slender, straight waists, and a wonderful way in the saddle, and a long easy swing on foot, and heavenly mustaches, not to mention eyes besides, and kind manners to the lowest; and so I say it's not the warmth of to-day, but the coldness of another day that I regret, because it made us lose time, as well as hurt feelings — feelings that — "

" Manette, have you nothing to do ? "

" Much, madame."

" Then do it."

The countess had been for some minutes attentively assorting silks for a strip of embroidery.

"I do not see my palest green," she said, as if life itself hung upon that tint.

"It is here, madame."

Madame de Vallauris's right hand was now moving with the soft regularity which betokens, among womankind, either a calm spirit or a desire to conceal a troubled one.

"If there is one thing more than another that I dote upon, it's this heavenly acacia-pattern. Is it madame's own design?" inquired the wily little maid in her most deferential tone.

"It is very simple," returned the countess negligently. "I designed it months ago for my uncle's trefoil table."

Manette scrutinized her with sharp but kindly eyes.

"No whimper about her — not an eyelash shakes," she thought. Then, with a sudden womanly impulse, the little coquette said prettily, "If madame permits, I will bring my sewing here; unless, indeed, I should disturb madame."

Countess Nathalie looked up with a half-startled little frown. She would have been grateful for complete isolation. Yet to what end, she quickly asked herself. She was for the moment useless to her uncle, useless to herself, to the world. But alone there, how could she resist the sweetness and the pain of her memories?

"Disturb me, Manette? Oh, no," she returned in her soft, cool voice, "not at all. That is," she added, "if you are careful — you understand; if you are desirous of pleasing me. You are a good child, Manette, but sometimes — forgetful."

Manette raised her handkerchief and patted quite dry eyes with a very good semblance of grateful emotion. "Oh, thanks, a thousand thanks! madame is too good. There seems a certain appropriateness," she murmured. "In high or low circles the heart may be heavy while the needle flies swiftly. So many men below, a turret-room above — ah, it is a picture!"

Madame de Vallauris smiled. She was surprised that she could smile again, but Manette was ridiculous. "I should smile on my death-bed at her extravagancies; and even then she would try to make me appropriate."

"I do not care to know what comedy you choose to play just now," she said. "If you like to come, and will be sensible, I have no objection."

So Manette brought her work, and in spite of an overweening consciousness of her picturesque effect, endeavored, as far as lay in her capacity, to be gentle and good, and to restrain her unruly tongue. " If I have n't a very deep heart myself, I do appreciate such an adornment in others," she thought, sewing her seams with a demure air, and admiring her mistress's noble profile bent calmly above the acacia-pattern. " Here we are at it again, always falling into the most delicious contrasts. Last night there was she in the acacia-walk having a little private conversation, and there was I having my little private conversation in the vegetable-garden; and I 'll venture to say nothing in life could be so unlike as what she was saying to her adjutant and what I was saying to my Wackermann. But human nature 's human nature, and two pairs of us, mistress and maid, were all the same a-lovering in the twilight; and very pleasant it was too, and admitted of the most touching attitudes. And here we two are again, — she suffering like a martyr and embroidering as coolly as if there was n't a blue-eyed adjutant in Christendom; and I suffering less, and therefore, to balance the proportions, looking more disconsolate. It 's strengthening, it 's a constant elixir to the artist-spirit, to study her and me; and if we should be thrown off a precipice together, when our shattered remains were discovered I am convinced we should still be instructive and picturesque in our suggestion of mental and physical contrast."

"I am a little cold, Manette.   Bring me a shawl."

Manette sprang to a drawer.

"Yes, that will do," said the countess; "any little thing for the shoulders."

But Manette persisted in searching for another.

"It is perfectly immaterial which one you bring me."

"But not to me, — ah, never to me.   The inferior quality must be worn by madame to-day," returned Manette with decision, returning after some delay with a small cashmere shawl to her mistress.   "This is the one."

Madame de Vallauris looked wearily indifferent.

"It is the moral consciousness," pleaded Manette, with a virtuous air.   "Have laurel-wreaths no meaning ?   Or bells of victory ?   Or crêpe weeds ?   Then so has the texture of cashmere.   Madame permits me to alter the arrangement ?"

"Never mind the arrangement," the countess said gently.

" Madame knows I cannot help minding the arrangement; and madame would not wish me to do otherwise, for then I should be false to my highest principles. Arrangements ? What is there but arrangements, good or bad ? Is this war not a big arrangement full of little arrangements, and all depending how things are selected, grouped, and combined ? And a book, — what is a book ? When I have dusted the library, I have stood and looked at the big Littré, and said to myself : ' Manette, put down the feather-duster and consider. There is the big dictionary. There are the works of Monsieur Molière. Manette, all the words are in that dictionary. The thing is, how one arranges them. If you knew how to arrange words as well as Monsieur Molière, you could write as good books as he did.' And a poem, — madame will permit me to confess I once tried to write a poem. My only difficulty was the syllables. ·They did not arrange themselves easily. Madame is smiling ? But when all things are but a clever or awkward arrangement, why does madame, so indulgent and generous as she is, repulse my best efforts, and give me a pang in the heart with her refusal to award me her sympathies ? Was Monsieur Molière born to arrange words for books ?

I, no less, was born to select, to shade, to group, to balance, — in short, also to arrange; and even in the privacy of madame's own room the inferior quality of cashmere for the Prussians has a meaning, and is an act of loyalty to our dear departed Saxons."

"Manette, you are a good girl, but you talk great nonsense. If you wish to remain here, be reasonable."

Manette, having freed her mind, was content to relapse into brief quiet, until again her vivacious tongue led her into temptation, and again Madame de Vallauris's quiet rebuke checked her. Day after day the two sat together many hours; for the Marquis de Montauban seemed to have no need of her whatever, except that he desired her presence at lunch and dinner, and evenings always in the library or salon. He rose late, breakfasted leisurely, and usually found some one to chat or play a game with him afterwards; and it was clear nothing she could say or do had the enlivening and happy effect which the abbé's companionship produced.

Embroidering the acacia-pattern, and sitting between the window overlooking the garden and the rose hidden in the book, what wonder that she continually saw one face and heard one voice, and felt against her cheek the evening breeze that had stirred the light foliage and wafted towards her the faint distant chiming of Paris bells! And every day her loneliness increased; and, seeing many a horse and gallant rider pass and repass her windows, meeting many a tall military form whenever she descended from her turret, living among circumstances and pictures which vividly suggested Nordenfels, she grew to regard him with an intimate sense of old acquaintance, as if there never was a time when he had not existed for her; and her lost good became the strongest, warmest element of her life. Against her thoughts she finally ceased to struggle. Solitude and embroidery are not the most efficacious means against forbidden thoughts. She gradually began to reason that she could think of him as a dead friend; yet, realizing he was only at Montfermeil, her heart beat fast with its consciousness of the powerful influence this strong, young, ardent, manly lover exerted over her. Alive he was, thank God! not dead, though his life could never crown her own. Sometimes in dreams she would see his face again, instead of the dying soldier's, and would wake in terror and pray,

"Not that, not that, O my God! Take me, but let him live!"

So, loving him she missed him, and missing him she loved him; and waking or sleeping, her thoughts were all of him.

CHAPTER IX.

In the mean time, while Max von Nordenfels, even graver and more silent at Montfermeil than at Aulnay, plunged into his work with untiring zeal, had apparently no thought beyond his duties, and was gaining that brown, weather-beaten look that sits well on a blond man's face; while Madame de Vallauris, like a fair dame of an ancient ballad, remained patiently in her turret-room and wove her secret thoughts and sighs into her acacia-pattern; while the marquis had his games and stories and chats, and floated with the current, and vastly enjoyed the life and movement about him; while the orderlies flew in and out of court-yard and house, and the distinguished and dignified Prussian officers were very jolly and light-hearted among themselves, and one and all professed themselves abject slaves of the beautiful but unapproachable young countess; while the dark-eyed abbé read his profound books and kept the marquis's spirit in an equable condition;

while Pierre and Antoine continued to bring their
fish to the château; while Manette fluttered and
flirted downstairs, and planned new triumphs as
she bent over her demure seam upstairs; while the
soldiers performed their evolutions like so much
machinery, yet each and every soul lived its indi-
vidual life apart and mostly concealed from each and
every other life; while there was laughing and eating
in the village of soldiers, yet every now and then a
wounded man brought in from the foreposts, or still
worse, covered pitifully on the stretcher, what remained of some happy-hearted, honest boy after a
shell had done its hideous work, — while, in short,
the siege with all its lights and shades and contradictory phases of life was going persistently on, no
less a person than General Trochu within the great
city chose to develop a certain strategy which had,
as results, various historical facts known to the
world, and also a most direct and important influence
upon the lives of our two lovers.

General Trochu, that much harassed man, honestly
doing his best in a thankless task which demanded
nothing less than a hero and a genius, blamed alike,
whatever he did, by friend and enemy, was, it is
needless to remark, unaware of the existence of Max

Baron von Nordenfels and the Countess Nathalie de Vallauris, and of their reciprocal tender attachment. Yet, all unconsciously, he did them the kindest turn in the world, and his grim war-plans led to happy and innocent surprises growing like spring blossoms out of the stains of battlefields.

What General Trochu with inadvertent benevolence did for our lovers was approximately as follows. Watchful of the enemy's movements, he was not unaware that the beleaguering army was more or less weakened by the detachments ordered south under General von der Tann, and resolved to satisfy himself by practical means as to the true condition of things, and at the same time to seize every possible advantage of the situation. He began by repeated bold sorties against the Crown Prince of Prussia. The 28th of October, General Bellemare fell upon the village of Le Bourget, but three kilometers from Aulnay, and defended by Prussian infantry, routed the Germans, and possessed himself of the village, which he strongly barricaded.

Château Aulnay was naturally in a state of intense excitement on account of this struggle, the first in its immediate vicinity. Neither the marquis, the abbé, nor the countess was visible. Two days later the

Germans prepared to regain the village. For this purpose the whole second Prussian Guard Infantry Division, under General Budwitzky, was united in three columns. Several battalions of the first Guard Infantry Division stood in reserve in the rear, while General von Aarenhorst held the Grenadier Brigade, Schützen Regiment, and four batteries in readiness at Aulnay.

All day long the sounds of the severe battle which closed only at nightfall dominated at Aulnay. The marquis, the abbé, and the countess sat together in the library listening, seeing it all in imagination, and realizing that the Saxon officers who had lived with them on friendly terms were engaged in it.

"It is curious," remarked the marquis, who, so far as physical courage was concerned, was imperturbable, "that when you think the most unpleasant thing has arrived, something more unpleasant is sure to follow. Now, this is all a very uncongenial episode. The disturbance is terrific, in the first place. Bless my soul! but that musketry-fire is brisk. Then, one's sentiments are necessarily conflicting. By instinct and principle our hearts are with our brave French troops. But when we remember Linden and Nordenfels and gay little Gerhardt, we don't like to think of them shot through the heart, now do we, Nathalie ? "

" No, uncle."

" That 's the veritable mischief, upon my word. Men you 've met in a friendly way, men you 've greeted with a friendly good-morning and shaken hands with at night, men you 've found good company, men who can beat you at chess, — well, now, you don't want the French to lose, but you don't want the Germans to be shot ; and that 's about it, is it not, Nathalie ? "

" Yes, uncle."

He walked up and down, inhaling eau-d'Houbigant audibly.

" That you can read to-day ! " he said to the abbé, who raised his unfathomable eyes from his book, and smiled at his friend, replying, " I read from habit, not indifference, believe me."

" Long ago, when hot young blood coursed through my veins, with my good sword in my hand, I had no time for thoughts," the marquis rejoined with feverish animation. " But, listening here, I think, I object, I protest, I am in a dilemma ; I don't like it. There is the strife ; here, two men, one weighed down by age, the other prevented by his vows from striking a blow. But what can one do ? "

"What, indeed?" returned the abbé's low voice. "What, but have patience?"

The marquis threw up his head, and listened like an old war-horse who after years of toil hears the bugle-call again. He put his hand to his head with a troubled air. The phantom-like old gentleman seemed to feel his humanity once more. Nathalie slipped her cold hand through his arm.

"That is right, my dear. Cling to me. Women need protection at such times. Women's nerves make them suffer enormously. You are terrified, are you not, my dear?"

"Yes, uncle," she returned with low intensity, "I am terrified indeed. I am most miserable."

The marquis rang the bell.

"Jean," he said to the trembling old servant, "wine for the countess; the old port, Jean."

Jean tottered out and in again.

Nathalie tried to take the wine, tried to smile at her uncle. If only the abbé would attribute her emotion to physical fear! But though no muscle of his face betrayed his thought, and his solicitous, respectful air was perfect, she had an agonizing sense that her precious, sorrowful secret lay helplessly before his piercing gaze, and that the world was not large enough to conceal it from him. And still the hideous sounds went on,— now and then a lull in the musketry-fire followed by a furious burst, the roar of artillery continuous. The château windows shook incessantly with that unbearable tremor, when long continued so wearing to the strongest nerves that a distinguished general confessed he had once in his desperation actually prayed to God that the windows might cease to tremble for a little time, lest he should go stark mad. But the windows shook on, all the same.

"I am most sorry for you, my poor Nathalie," said the marquis gallantly. "But there is no escape. Let us only hope that this unpleasantness may not last long. Courage, my dear, courage! It is most natural that you should be distressed. Nothing can be more uncongenial to a woman's highly organized temperament. You are better now, my love? The eau-d'Houbigant is always so efficacious."

So with port wine and toilet-water he hovered about her; and though such remedies could not minister to grief, anxiety, and doubt, she was grateful that the marquis seemed kinder, nearer, than ever before, and ventured to kiss his delicate, withered hand as it approached her face with his odoriferous panacea.

"A woman has great power of endurance, courage,

too, in some situations; but under fire, so to speak, as we are, it would be undignified, unwomanly, to betray no agitation. There are certain things admirable in woman," he remarked approvingly, "but impossible for us. We are immovable."

At this instant a shell burst through the outer wall, directly over the sofa where the countess was sitting, and whizzed through the alcove window, exploding harmlessly in the courtyard.

The immovable marquis had involuntarily made a surprisingly agile spring.

"That was a narrow escape, madame," said the abbé, approaching the countess quickly, with sympathy and solicitation, "and certainly not adapted to increasing your calm, or ours, indeed."

"That," said the Marquis de Montauban, drawing up his aged frame to its greatest possible height, indignation lending strength to the broken voice,— "that is a damnable impertinence!"

Nathalie was about to speak.

"My dear," waving his hand with his grandest air, "you will pardon, under these extraordinary circumstances, my use of so strong a word in your presence. I repeat, whether that is a German or a French shell, it is a damnable impertinence perpetrated by *canaille.*

I will demand satisfaction. There are some of those people out there now. I will inquire what they mean by it."

"Can I not go for you?" The abbé, rising quickly, followed the incensed marquis. "I can surely express your views to them."

"No, my dear friend; I thank you, no. You will remain with the countess, I beg. Upon me alone devolves the duty of protecting my own house."

Nathalie went to the window.

"Dear uncle, you will at least remember the officer out there is not personally responsible for the shell. He is looking at the fragments, and is as much surprised as we are."

"I shall say what I myself deem fitting," he returned haughtily, as he left the room.

"I hope he will not excite and fatigue himself," began the abbé.

"I think not. It is Major von Schönberg out there. He seems to be gentle and considerate. I have noticed his manner with my uncle."

"The marquis is certainly stronger than he was, and happier. Do you not think so?"

"He has much to interest him. It is natural. He watches the men exercise; he hears the cheerful music; he sees the officers jumping the hedge, the young soldiers practising the goose-step, the others skirmishing by companies in the fields and vineyards. They chat with him, they amuse him. Much seems to happen to him. The worst life must be one in which nothing happens. Then, no doubt at his age he forgets."

"Forgets? What?"

"Who they are."

"That seems an easy thing to forget."

"I think not; at least, not for long," she returned quickly. "When one is young, one remembers."

After a pause he murmured, "Countess, you are a brave woman."

"My uncle thinks the contrary, as you perceived just now," she said with unconcern.

"A very brave woman," he repeated softly.

"How those windows rattle! It grows to seem worse than a worse evil."

"Madame, you have the habit of considering me uncommunicative?"

"That, at least, is quite true."

"You will then smile at my simplicity if I reveal my thought at this moment?"

"Pray do not attempt it. Your thought would

crush me with its weight, and the unusual effort might be injurious to you."

He smiled, and continued gently, " I am thinking how far I may trust you."

" Not at all; because your trust would not be reciprocated. Who can trust a distrustful soul ? "

" Sentiments and opinions are not immutable. We see the strongest natures contradict themselves."

" We do," she returned calmly.

" What was most sacred to us grows indifferent or meaningless; and what we believed was most remote from us suddenly becomes the nearest influence," continued the abbé's gentle, objectless tone.

Madame de Vallauris held herself gallantly, and merely answered: " It is often the case, I presume. We are all more or less iconoclasts."

" Then, merely for the sake of argument, dear madame, — it is surely better to chat a little in spite of this rival din of muskets and artillery, — why assume that even you yourself, so consistent and stable as you are, indeed, might not find the sentiments of to-morrow contradicting those of to-day; might not acknowledge a new force, abandon a crystallized mode of reasoning ? "

" Merely for the sake of argument, there is nothing

of all that which I might not be capable of doing, given, of course, sufficient inducement," she said coolly, throwing her head back on the cushion and looking at him calmly. Her hands were folded lightly in her lap; she wore her usual composed air.

From Le Bourget came on the wind the sound of rapid firing, and her heart was in an agony of fear. But not in her extremity should this man here have any outward advantage. All the old antagonism revived. Her hero was fighting against her land, facing death from a French bullet. She might this instant be listening to his death-stroke. Now, at least, she might acknowledge to her own soul without reserve or doubt that he was her hero. Beneath the shadow of death love uprose royally and claimed his own. But this man had no place or part in her love or in her sorrow. Let him approach, let him surmise what he would, she would face him, and guard her Holy of holies.

To her last remark he had bowed his head in ac-quiescence.

"'Sufficient inducement?' Naturally, the inducement in the case of an honorable woman of your strength of character could be only the sense of a duty to accomplish, the reward of an approving conscience."

She remained silent and motionless.

" A woman of your calibre never yields to impulse, to the temptation of irregular wandering emotions or affections. If such should assail her, — I speak merely for the sake of argument, — she would consecrate them by adapting them to a good purpose."

" And how would such a woman accomplish that ?" she said, her eyes fixed searchingly on him.

A sudden eagerness, a nascent hope, betrayed itself in his face. With controlled warmth he answered low : " I could teach her if she would but trust me implicitly. I would lead her through sacrifices which her noble nature would shrink from, yet endure to a heroic end."

" And what would that end be ? "

" The good of France."

Countess Nathalie started; then, after a pause, she answered by a strange yet simple question. " M. l'Abbé," she said slowly, " are you a good man ? "

" A good man ? What is that ? " he returned.

She made no reply.

" Good ? Goodness is relative. Good ? Who is good ? "

She was still silent.

"Yes, I am a good man, as good men go," he resumed with conviction. "That I do not attain my ideal is my sorrow. My sense of imperfection weighs me down. But I do nothing that I cannot reconcile with my conscience."

"I believe you," said the countess. "That has always been my difficulty." As if she had reached a supreme moment whose inner flame of truth burned all subterfuge away, as if she too, like her German lover, were under the fierce fire of the enemy, she answered, opposing him in loyalty: "The elasticity of your conscience has been my life-long curse. As a girl, I suffered from it. To-day, a woman, I repudiate it. Come life, come death, I will not be guided by you. You are a wise man, M. l'Abbé; your dark hints I do not pretend to understand. But when you count upon me in any respect this day, you err in your calculations. So true as we hear the sounds of battle as if it were at our own doors, I renounce you and all your unknown plans. Whatever you may have in view, you will create no Jeanne d'Arc at Aulnay; and I do not need your interpretation of my duty to my beloved land."

"Madame," he said with his usual gentleness, "it

would perhaps be advisable if I should go to find the marquis. As to our conversation, the excitement of to-day is sufficient excuse for any misconception."

"There is no misconception," she replied quickly, with a woman's last word; but he was gone.

The struggle at Le Bourget continued until nightfall, when the report was brought to Aulnay that the Germans had retaken the village, but with a loss of five hundred men. "And there's no harm done to our beautiful dears," added Manette in ecstasy, this time unreproved.

That night Countess Nathalie for the first time since Nordenfels had gone looked at the rose from Vert Galant, and looking, kissed it with tears of thankfulness and pain.

On account of this action on the left wing of the Prussian Guard, further dislocations were ordered. The positions at Blanc Mesnil and Duguy were strengthened by the detachment from Aulnay. Madame de Vallauris heard the Prussians were to go, knew others would necessarily come. It was all like a hideous dream to her, — a kind of infernal machinery rolling on incessantly. What mattered it who came, who went? They were all Germans. There was Paris holding out. Somewhere in this great mystery of life and war was a man with earnest eyes who had won her boundless love; he was gone, and she would never see him again. Had he come otherwise, all her wishes, all her hopes, her very life, had centred in him. Now she had no wishes more, no hopes; and life was a dull, barren thing, and the sooner it was over the better.

Musing thus, one day she gave no heed to the fife and drum and the marching. She refused to appear when the Prussians begged to make their adieus. Alone in her little room she sat working busily, as a happy woman works, and her face was quiet, not sadder than before.

There seemed to be a great commotion in the village. What mattered that? Why should one listen in pandemonium to a sound more or less? Yet in the martial music approaching was a clear note of triumph that moved her strangely. She dropped her acacia-pattern, threw up her head and listened. A familiar joyous strain floated up to her and made her heart beat fast, for she had often heard it when the Saxon grenadiers were quartered at Aulnay. "How cruel it all is!" she thought. "There is no mercy, no forgetfulness."

Manette sprang into the room with one bound.

"No, madame, no! This is impossible! This is unheard of!" she cried.

"Is my uncle ill?" demanded Madame de Vallauris, alarmed.

"The marquis never was better. But this arrangement, madame, this turn of affairs, this appropriateness!"

The countess stared at her, comprehending nothing.

"If madame will go down herself," gasped Manette with a heroism of self-restraint, "I could explain; I am dying to explain, but I forbear. Madame must go herself to meet the *dénoûment*. O just Heaven! Oh! oh!" ·

"Is there really nothing the matter with my uncle?"

"Madame must see for herself. My feelings overpower me. No, the world is not all bad, when such heavenly things can happen; and nobody need ever say anything against war to me!"

Leaning against the wall, the little maid closed her eyes and smiled rapturously.

"Really, Manette!" expostulated the countess; but rose, nevertheless, yielding to the girl's excitement, and outstretched hand pointing and waving in wild enthusiasm towards the open door.

"If madame does not go down-stairs at once, I shall burst," exclaimed Manette. "Oh, what a moment! I myself could not have arranged anything so perfect. Just Heaven! What an artistic combination!" she murmured, as Madame de Vallauris, wondering and somewhat alarmed, passed down the narrow stairway. , Manette peered after her and listened.

As the countess went down, some one was coming up the lower staircase two steps at once. In the corridor they met face to face. She grasped the baluster in sudden terror, and grew pale as death; but the other sprang forward and held her hands in his strong clasp, and in his gladness smiled like the young sun-god. She, looking up, spoke no word, but left her hands in his, and in her eyes he read his welcome; and a radiance that no one had ever seen in her face dawned gloriously for him.

The Prussians had moved on, and the Saxon grenadiers by a curious chance again occupied Aulnay. This happens to be an historical fact; for the most reckless and inconsequent novelist would never dare to send battalions marching east and west simply to bring a pair of lovers together. But life is more fantastic than fiction; and General Trochu did it all. Had he not just at this period commanded sorties

from the defences, there would have been no changes
of quarters in the Prussian line; consequently Max
Nordenfels would not have been standing in the corridor of the château at Aulnay, holding the hands of
the lovely Countess de Vallauris, and gazing at her
speechless with delight.

CHAPTER X.

THE French along the whole line of the Fourth Army now began to display remarkable energy and renewed strength. An ably organized signal-system, with colored lights in the night, communicated with the forts, which were supplied with guns of the heaviest calibre.

From time to time a signal towards evening would be followed the same night by an artillery attack, in which the whole line of foreposts was swept simultaneously with a hail of bullets from all the French forts and advance batteries. Alarms in the night and feigned sorties were constant, and the German troops were granted no rest.

One day early in November, among the morning reports at headquarters at Clichy came the announcement that a sentinel on the Canal field-watch near Bondy had observed during the night light-signals which seemed to come from the direction of Aulnay.

The commander of the regiment at Aulnay was at

once informed of this and instructed to take every precaution. The Tower was accordingly closely watched at night, and a special guard was placed at the park gates.

At the same time Colonel von Linden wrote privately to General von Aarenhorst that it was an utter impossibility for the family of the Marquis de Montauban to have the remotest connection with the treacherous signals, and indeed he himself entertained the conviction that no signals whatever had proceeded from Aulnay. What was so deceptive as a red light showing itself somewhere in space in the night to a weary and excited soldier? The colonel stated in terms of positive enthusiasm that he had watched the family now too long to be in any danger of error, and he did not hesitate to say that he trusted them, one and all, implicitly. He must indeed appeal to the general's own impression of their harmlessness. So far from subjecting them to the slightest surveillance, he, the colonel, no longer confined them to the limits of court and park, but freely allowed them long walks at their own discretion.

All that they did, indeed, could without effort be followed. The marquis, charming and frail old gentleman, mentally as well as physically enfeebled, was the most harmless person in existence. He seldom crossed the threshold of the château. But Madame de Vallauris went freely wherever she would; he having long since granted her permission, at her earnest prayer, to visit the wounded, of which there was always now a goodly number in the village. She ministered to them all, German and French, like an angel of mercy; was, with a couple of Sisters less expert and tender than she, an immense aid to the surgeons. The slightest reflection upon this beautiful and good woman, who had borne the existing inconveniences with noble patience and a gentleness that had won all hearts, from the highest to the lowest soldier, would seem like assailing the honor of a saint. As for the abbé, he often accompanied Madame de Vallauris in her errands of mercy, and he too in manifold instances had proved himself helpful and devoted. He was on friendly terms with one of the surgeons, and took long walks with him, sometimes as far as the field-watch; but the abbé's whole course of life was studious and harmless. Besides his religious duties, his books, and his friend the marquis, he had neither interest nor occupation. In short, the reports of such signals, so far as Aulnay was concerned, must be entirely erroneous.

That this was indeed possible, General von Aarenhorst was forced to admit. The forepost service for three months was now rendered still more exciting and difficult by the renewed activity of the French. With the outpost duties and the field-watch, the men had scarcely a quiet night, and the effect upon the nervous system of the common soldier was very perceptible. Exaggerations, in fact the purest fictions growing out of night and darkness, were formally reported by excitable individuals, so that extreme caution was incumbent upon those in command. Indeed, as General von Aarenhorst wearily thought, to distinguish between the false and true, one needed superhuman wisdom and foresight.

His position was no sinecure at that time, — in three weeks not once able to undress himself and go to sleep like a Christian; lying half clothed on his bed, and scarcely closing his eyes, when an orderly would enter announcing an attack.

Sometimes the general, roused up repeatedly in one night, would go out to ascertain the veritable condition of things, and riding down the dark icy hill, his horse slipping and plunging in every direction, was himself most painfully in doubt. Simulated attacks were incessant, and often the whole line was one blaze of light.   Should he advance ?   If superfluous, they would say in the rear, " What sort of general is that !   Leaves us no rest, routs us out for nothing ! A little fire excites him, it appears."   And should he not, they would say, " Able general that !   What more does he require ?   An orderly was sent three times in one night to warn him.   There was n't the slightest doubt, and yet he did not move."

Well aware, then, of the manifold chances of error as to place, direction, and distance of the signals, General von Aarenhorst was inclined to share von Linden's views.   The general, too, entertained the highest esteem for the family, and the bare suggestion of treachery on their part was as repugnant to him as improbable.

As nothing whatever of a suspicious nature was discovered at Aulnay, after eight or ten days the watch at the park gate was countermanded.   The general could ill afford to waste the energies of the men at this critical time.

The weather had now grown cold and raw.   Dense autumn fogs obscured the landscape.   The foliage had fallen.   The nights brought heavy frosts.   In quarters the troops suffered almost more severely from the cold than at the outposts.   The small village houses had insufficient means of providing against the discomforts of this extremely low temperature. Moreover, the narrow chimneys were speedily clogged with soot, all the more as the men had no dry wood to burn. They finally availed themselves, in their great need, of doors and furniture, and formed chimney-sweep detachments to prevent accident by fire.

The château grew steadily more and more shabby, the curious life within more natural to the inmates. By the great fireplace in the library many an evening was cheerful with chat and laughter, and many a serious talk took place there. It was a home-like, pleasant room, as a choice library must always be to an ardent lover of books. With its genial associations, its subtle fragrance of the past, and the grand old friends of all times looking down from the shelves, one finds solace and refuge under their immortal ægis, and temporary, restless ills vanish in the calm of their great and noble thoughts and in the vastness of their infinite endeavor. So the library became the natural resort of the quieter officers, while others were making merry with cards and wine in their own quarters, and the marquis was almost never without one or more for his inevitable game. He had welcomed the return of the Saxons as if they were old friends, and they had rejoiced greatly at their good fortune. Their Aulnay quarters were the pleasantest they had known; and they often said to Madame de Vallauris, "One feels more human here, less like a brute." Gerhardt told her honestly, that when he came back and caught a glimpse of her fair hair and black dress at a distance, he felt like saying his prayers, and he was by no means sure to whom. What Nordenfels told her with his deep-set eyes, with his chivalrous manner, with his voice, even in the most conventional salutations, and with words, — indeed, whenever she gave him the shadow of an opportunity, was evident enough to the most careless observer. That it was a serious thing with him, every comrade knew; and one by one they fell back in their efforts to gain her favor, and tacitly made way for him. Or perhaps Nordenfels after his return, emboldened by her first involuntary welcome, calmly made way for himself, without the least consideration of his comrades' presence or desires. Certainly he assumed in his modest but persistent way various rights or privileges to which she grew accustomed, as a woman will, and which were dear to her, although she gave no sign. He secured the place next to hers at dinner. "Why not I as well as another?" he had not unreasonably asked himself, and arranged that matter very speedily with old Jean and his own Bursch the day of his return to the château. Through the valuable aid of that eminent tactician Manette, who deserves public mention in the annals of the Franco-German war, he knew with admirable exactness and celerity whenever the countess intended to take a walk, to visit a wounded soldier,— in short, had any plan whatever which, by adroit stretching, would admit of him. He was very active and busy in those days, often absent long, often sorely fatigued after a succession of arduous duties; but he succeeded, nevertheless, in gaining marvellously frequent chances of being near her; and it is hard to say which he pursued with more zeal and determination, love or war.

They talked much together,— of books, of passing things, of life. They found each other sympathetic and delightful, which is no great wonder, as they were in love; but they entertained each other vastly, and were intellectually charming and stimulating the one to the other, which blissful lovers not always are, but which is surely a most desirable condition of things when two people intend to be life-long companions, and since it is a demonstrable fact that the fiftieth kiss is not quite like the first. Countess Nathalie's life-long companion Max Nordenfels assuredly meant to be.

"She loves me, — not as I love her, for I worship her, — but still she loves me, or she would not have been so exquisite to me as she was in the park; she would not have looked so glorious when we met again. And if she loves me, what shall stand in our way? The war will come to an end soon," he decided with youthful confidence. "Then I may speak; then she will listen; then she will be mine, for she loves me, she loves me!" his heart cried in exultation and thankfulness. "What is a country, what is a prejudice, since she loves me? Love can leap from land to land, and tear down every barrier."

Nights as he rode through cold and darkness with his despatches to and from Vert Galant or Clichy, he was gloriously happy and warm, as if spring sunshine lay in his path instead of chill sleet and storm and danger; and no duty seemed hard to him, so full of light and gladness was his spirit. And always he knew on his return, if it were evening, she would be sitting in her low chair in the library, and would look up quietly and say: " Ah, Herr von Nordenfels,

are you back ? It is a bad night, I fear." For the
nights were mostly bad just then; and each time she
would look more beautiful, more precious, more dear
than even his ardent fancy pictured her, and more
worth a man's striving for and winning for his own,
whatever stood in the way. And what did stand in
the way ? Only a trifle of a war that could not last
much longer, — that might end any day. So he was
waiting for the war to end, with a mighty, throbbing
impatience; for he knew it was useless to urge her
now, and he was tender of her scruples, respected
them, indeed, and understood why she persistently
avoided a tête-à-tête with him. He saw her go her
way among all the admiring men with, it seemed to
him, the least coquetry that ever a woman had. He
saw her winning chivalrous devotion from even the
careless and frivolous, and rousing that rare and beautiful sentiment, a simple and pure affection, from more
than one.

Since he had discerned that glad look of love in
her eyes, there was no room in his heart for doubt.
Before, he had been uncertain and therefore uncomfortable now and then, — not quite happy when others
so much as spoke her name. Now it seemed but
natural they should offer her their tribute and their

homage, as they did, to the last man. If he, approaching, quietly absorbed her attention as soon as possible, it was through no fear of them, but from other easily comprehended motives.

Petty jealousy seemed too mean and selfish a feeling to mar so great a love. He looked in her pure soul that day as in crystal depths. With a strange and sacred joy he felt it was his twin soul revealed in one unguarded moment; his own, now, for all time. Perfect truth dwelt in those eyes, and for her purity he would have staked his life. So if he longed with a lover's warmth for the future and for freedom, he could yet restrain himself and generously consider her position, for she herself had given him the right to hope. He did his duties manfully, and loved her manfully; and if there were no tête-à-têtes, little Forstenau, who oftenest sat near them, was no obstacle whatever to an explicit interchange of sentiment upon all imaginable subjects apt to be discussed by two lovers,—except, indeed, love and war. These two themes, surcharging the atmosphere, were all the more felt for the silence.

There was one single and oft-recurring fact which puzzled him, and which he found not perfectly agreeable, he could scarcely have told why. The Abbé de

Navailles unquestionably exerted some influence upon the countess; at the same time he felt, with his lover's instinct, that the abbé was not a person whom she regarded with unqualified favor. But one circumstance was, nevertheless, undeniable: in the abbé's immediate presence Madame de Vallauris, however freely she had been conversing, relapsed into reserve, if not silence altogether.

Nordenfels disliked the abbé roundly. "What in the deuce does he mean by coming into a room where people are discussing some general subject, and being a restraint? Has he begged her not to talk with me?" Wherein Nordenfels did the abbé curious injustice, for he had begged exactly the contrary. "Never mind," thought Nordenfels, "she'll tell me sometime; or I shall have forgotten by that time, and shall not wish to know. We shall have more important things to talk about. We shall have all this lost time to make up." Still, whenever the abbé drew near and the countess grew silent, Nordenfels speculated more or less, and felt rather savage.

Madame de Vallauris, in spite of principles, prejudices, and struggles, was never so happy in her life as at present. Her struggles had indeed ceased, and she was unconsciously drifting. She believed it her duty to avoid a private interview with Nordenfels, and was grateful that he tacitly acquiesced,— at all events, that he respected her desire. That it would all come to an end some day, she was aware; so would the world. Meanwhile her present joy was vast. It was wonderful that he had returned into her life, and this she felt no less as the days went on. She had bade him farewell forever. In her thoughts a thousand times she had pictured him cold and dead. But he came back to her, living, warm, and full of strength, rich in youth and love. Should she, then, not rejoice? He was great and good. Should she not be glad that his presence for a little time glorified her life,— and that, indeed, however he came, whenever he should go? So she reasoned, when she reasoned, but feeling him near she reasoned no more; and meeting the glance of his honest eyes, which had become so familiar and beloved, she was simply happy, though parting stared them in the face, and the terrors of war were raging around them. It was a strange, sad time. Every day her heart was sore for the woes of humanity; and, shrinking with pity and horror, nerving herself to be calm, she saw ugly sights, heard the groan of strong men in pain, and with her quiet courage and reasonableness gave active help on every side.

Yet amid the tumult and the bloodshed, the madness of brother slaying brother, a fair white temple slowly rose for two quiet spirits. In its stillness they knelt apart.

CHAPTER XI.

SSOMETIMES Countess Nathalie wondered if there would ever be any end to this bizarre kind of life she was leading; if ever again Aulnay could tranquillize itself and resume its rusticity; if the roll of drums and the bugle-call, the tramp of men at arms, the rhythm of horses' hoofs in rapid movement, and the clank of steel would not linger about the Tower like ghostly voices in a haunted house. The Tower had seen so much since the old days when it calmly watched the ripening fields, and the village was at peace, and nothing happened! Nearer and nearer now the waves of war were creeping about its base. Gray and impassive, it surveyed the enemy's line; and its clock, that once had marked the quiet hours of village toil and sleep, was counting now how long heroic Paris would resist and endure.

Ever nearer to the Tower crept the fierce red waves. Countess Nathalie felt in the lurid atmosphere the presage of more woe. On the faces, in the voices around her she read it. A livelier energy was manifest, there were frequent earnest conversations among the officers, and an evident anticipation of active duty. Wounded men from the foreposts and patrol were constantly brought into the village, and the boom of the cannon seemed nearer and more frequent.

"What does this mean?" she asked the abbé suddenly one day. "This something indefinable in the air, — this expectation, preparation, these indistinct omens and rumors?"

He hesitated an instant. "It means — war, madame," he said simply, and read on. He scarcely raised his eyes from his book in those days.

Madame de Vallauris said no more. Later, she knew what the messages of the air signified. It was the close of November, and events were occurring of which the world, comfortably reading the newspaper announcements, expressed its easily formed opinions, awarding praise and blame with after-dinner fluency to hard-pushed generals and overworked troops on both sides.

Like stones thrown into a clear lake, those events in ever-widening circles reached distant shores. Suabian, Saxon, and Prussian homes wept for their dearest and best, or rang joy-bells for the safety and honorable promotion of their gallant sons; many a happy French fireside was darkened forever, many a young heart made desolate.

The French had established on Mont Avron, opposite Raincy, numerous batteries, and gradually provided them with seventy-six guns of the heaviest calibre, which were doing much damage along the whole Saxon line from Chelles to Livry. The blunt-headed summit, lower than the ridge crowned by Forts Noisy and Rosny, wreathed itself from time to time in white smoke against the blue horizon, making so lovely a picture that it was difficult to realize the smoke was the signal of a deadly missile hurled through the calm air to whiz straight on to some brave fellow, tear his stalwart body in pieces, and strike down the bread-winner of a family. The Germans hated Mont Avron, and with bitter reason.

The 30th of November, General Ducrot, with the Second French Army of ninety thousand men, led the celebrated attack against the Würtemberg and Saxon position, southeast of Paris. In and around the villages of Champigny, Brie, and Villiers a bloody drama was enacted, a less important attack being made at the same time northeast of Paris. The excitement at Aulnay was boundless, but the abbé's face, as he went his quiet and harmless way, was luminous and beautiful, Countess Nathalie observed. After the terrible battle of Villiers, General Ducrot was driven back within the French fortifications. The fact was freely spoken of at Aulnay, that the French, though they had inflicted upon the enemy as heavy a loss as they themselves had suffered, had yet failed utterly in their end, — to break the iron girdle round Paris. Then for the first time she reflected that the abbé seemed to possess a marvellous prescience. Not that he ever revealed his knowledge or his hopes. His words, indeed, were his trained servants. But when one sits silent hour after hour in the same room with a fellow-being, and times are troublous, and the air is charged with strange portent, one's mere instincts become at last keener, and one reads aright a momentary pallor or lowering of the eyelids, a cough, a smile. Sometimes, it may be, if we were all dumb we should comprehend one another better; and like dogs, with their wistful, alert eyes and sensitive ears, arrive oftener at the truer meaning, the very heart of things.

At all events, Nathalie felt that while often misled by the abbé's well-turned phrases, she was beginning to interpret, by some unconscious magnetic process his luminous paleness, his eloquent eyes, the very intensity of his quiet. Joy, hope, disappointment, unless her intuition was utterly at fault, he revealed thus tacitly and always prematurely. By the time positive news reached the château, all his soul-flashes had vanished, and he had relapsed into his usual perfect calm.

What did he know, whom did he see, what means had he of informing himself of a French sortie, of a French gain or loss? His life was the life he had always led for years, less influenced than any other at the château by the alarm and continuance of war. Pale and studious, dwelling in the atmosphere of prayer and books, he was unchanged. Who besides the Germans approached the château? Only the two fishermen; and Pierre and Antoine were simple, ignorant men, recognized as harmless by the Germans, and allowed to pass freely to and fro in the twilight as at noonday. But why had the abbé advocated a free intercourse with the officers? For what end would he use friendliness on her part and any influence she could gain? What signified his glowing words when he alluded to service and sacrifice? Surely she had heard aright. But no, she was nervous and fanciful, and pursued by her old mistrust. If the abbé took white wine instead of red, or changed his seat to another window, she was apt to suspect him of ulterior ends and aims, she acknowledged. That he was heart and soul with gallant Paris she knew well. So was she, with every atom of her being. As for knowing more than others, and knowing it first, it was impossible. It was a delusion on her part. Ah, no! No carrier-pigeons with news from the beleaguered city had found their way to the château and the abbé. Once, indeed, one had flown by. The countess saw it, and held her breath with a woman's tenderness for the innocent dove and a patriot's prayer for its mission, as a soldier aimed at it and missed.

December was upon them, and still Paris held out. The Marquis de Montauban began to take a certain pride in the tenacity and strength of the city, as he would have enjoyed a display of bravery from even an unruly child. If he did not uncon-ditionally approve of Paris, still Paris was French, and valiant. He now introduced a facetious tone in his conversation, and made light jokes with the officers as to the length of time he should have the pleasure of entertaining them, assuring them they would be welcome as long as they enjoyed it. He seemed thoroughly reconciled to his surroundings, and entertained the pleasing conviction that whatever havoc war might make, he had remained master of his château, and the most influential being within its walls. At seventy years of age this was a comfort, and added zest to the dry ceremonies of his toilet, breakfast, and daily plans.

Manette pursued her original tactics, combined, arranged, advanced, and retreated with flying colors and huge satisfaction, but one day met with a repulse from an unexpected quarter. In the intimate hour of brushing the countess's hair, towards midnight in the turret-room, she would frequently expatiate upon the continued charm of the situation. "But, if madame permits, one delectable flavor is lacking. Two or three jealous women would make this place paradise. Did I rejoice that there were no women here besides madame and my humble self? I was wrong. I am not too proud to confess that even I can make a miscalculation. Now I at last perceive why an inscrutable Providence has created so many jealous women in this world. By jealous, I mean envious, or anything you please. Jealous, envious — it's often the same thing, and it does n't mean love, by any means; it mostly means selfishness. But I disturb madame?"

"No, Manette. It is possible that you will end by instructing me," said the countess in her quiet way.

"There are points where I could instruct madame," the girl returned, nodding seriously,—"points in which madame has had little experience, in which madame is like a very little, young girl, while I have made my researches, it would be useless to deny."

The countess smiled. So long as Manette would expound her own philosophy, why should she not speak and relieve her mind now and then?

The one danger was, she was apt to suddenly veer round from the general to the particular; and personal remarks were not to the countess's taste. Still, Manette had been very good lately, and was a real comfort, with her inexhaustible spirits and her devoted attention. "What should I have done without my blithe little Manette through all these strange, hard weeks?" she thought kindly. "Why should I not put up with her peculiarities? No doubt she puts up often enough with mine, and finds my grave moods more unpleasant than I find her lightness."

All of which was indulgent on the part of the countess, and honest, too, as far as it went; but if she had cared to analyze her own motives, she would have found also a desire to hear certain precarious subjects approached if not discussed, and a simple human need of sympathy and comprehension in her singular position. There was no one to whom she could or would speak. She was a woman, young, warm-hearted, in love for the first time in her life, and it was a joy to her to even hear her lover's name spoken, though her fair, cold face betrayed nothing. Sufficient to Manette was the shadow of a permission, and her eloquence poured forth with the impetuosity of a mountain brook.

"The situation needs, I repeat, a couple of jealous women to make it paradise; and no doubt the reason the Lord bestows jealousy so liberally upon woman-kind is to prevent monotony," the little maid said, with a shrewd look of reflection.

"I think you do not quite know what you are saying, Manette."

"Madame will pardon. I know but too well; and I repeat, if a jealous woman, that is to say, two jeal-ous women — madame knows my devotion, and that I never consider myself alone — could be set down in the middle of this most interesting circle, madame herself would speedily observe the rich results. Noth-ing whatever could so precipitate desirable but somewhat tardy consummations." Manette here coughed discreetly.

"And I should think nothing could be more thoroughly unpleasant," remarked the countess candidly. "When did a jealous woman ever improve anything, Manette?"

"Ah, madame is no doubt thinking of a tragic jealous woman, with rolling eyes and a dagger! No, no, madame, that kind does the least harm. It is the good and pious jealous, I mean; that's the kind that makes the world go round,—the kind that has awful moral cramps inside when it sees anything superior to itself. One can get out of the way of the rolling-eyed woman with a dagger; but the woman that's jealous of her own pomp and power and authority, and dinners and servants, and husband and children and the stranger within her gates,—one can't get out of her way, and she's as often as not a quiet little woman who does n't know what's the matter with her. We're mostly a jealous set, and that's the truth. When anything's the matter anywhere, I do not inquire, like the great statesman, 'Who's the woman?' I ask, 'Who's jealous?'"

"Perhaps that is what he meant, Manette."

"Madame may be right; yet men are jealous too.

I don't mean jealousy in love. Oh, no! That is a feeling which I respect, even if it leads to stuffing pillows in one's mouth and suffocating; which I am happy to say Wackermann, not being of that temperament, will never attempt. And so I ask if a child falls down a well, or if there 's a war, 'Who was jealous?' I should n't be surprised if jealousy were at the bottom of this very war — jealousy — no more, no less, — Monsieur Bismarck or somebody or other."

Madame de Vallauris smiled. "But why, then, do you wish to introduce it here? Surely we have dreadful things enough already, Manette."

"Madame will admit this situation is inexhaustible. The combinations are kaleidoscopic, meteorlike, and yet — and yet, a cold-hearted, narrowminded, envious, jealous, malicious little woman, the kind who controls her manners and takes away a reputation without blinking, — ah, madame, that is what we need; that would be a boon from Heaven; and I wish she could be set plump down in the court-yard this very minute!"

"I positively do not understand you," her mistress said gravely. "Such a person would be most odious, and would bring unhappiness wherever she appeared."

"It is because madame has never lived in the world. I have lived in the world, and there such women are as plenty as blackbirds in the park; and sometimes it's a marquise, sometimes it's a lady's-maid, — for, begging madame's pardon, a woman's a woman."

"That, at least, is quite true, Manette."

" And it's because madame is so innocent. I — I am not innocent. I know the uses of adversity, and that a hateful person wisely managed often does a world of good. When two hearts, madame," — Manette came forward and eyed her mistress furtively under the flourish of the ivory brush, — "reciprocate yet hesitate, are lofty and noble, and up in the clouds, madame, above all us earth-born worms, and love each other like angels, madame, with acres of blue heaven between, and one thinks of duty, and the other of honor and reserve, and things don't go on as is proper they should, and as those who are interested have a right to expect, — why, there's nothing like a little downright hatefulness to help along. And for hatefulness there is nothing like a jealous, envious, spiteful woman; and I'd bless the sight of her, for there'd be no more shilly-shallying then, and people would find out their own minds, which anybody with eyes can see already, and the jealous woman would make trouble, and out of the trouble would come explanations, and out of the explanations, reconciliations, and one would then not hold so loosely what is too precious to lose and one will never find again, — one would hold the beautiful dear fast and close, and one would say to one's self, ' Not every day does a beautiful blue adjutant with heavenly eyes and a way with him — ' ah ! — and a mustache that — "

" Manette ! "

" Madame ! "

The countess resumed her book. Manette, without another word, resumed her brushing, and soon bade her mistress a demure good-night, which was, as usual, gently returned.

The following evening when the countess went to her room she saw an unwonted sight. Manette, the blithe little philosopher, dissolved in tears, sobbing as she arranged things for the night, moving chairs and toilet articles with a melancholy listlessness.

" Why, Manette, what has happened ? " said Madame de Vallauris much concerned.

" Wackermann," was the response, with another burst of tears. " He's happened."

" My poor little Manette !   Would you like to tell me about it ?   Have you had a quarrel ? "

" Madame is an angel.   I never quarrel, as madame knows.   It was Wackermann who quarrelled in a most glaring and Teutonic manner."

" But, Manette, that excellent, kind-hearted man with his full-moon face like a baby ? "

" Madame will permit me to explain," sobbed Manette ruefully, " that the full moon was concealed by a thunder-cloud, and the baby roared like a giant."

The countess suppressed a smile.   " Then you must have done something very, very bad, Manette," she said gravely.

" Madame will pardon me.   It was not bad.   It was only picturesque and exciting.   It was an interesting study.   It was only Corporal Müller and I in the vegetable-garden.   There is a freshness, a vivacity about Corporal Müller which is exhilarating.   Madame really permits me to relate ?   These bagatelles are hardly in madame's sphere."

" Never mind my sphere, Manette.   You may tell me."

The girl had recovered somewhat.   Through her tears the mischief sparkled again in her bright eyes.

" I thought Wackermann was on duty with the

watch; but, alas! he was watching me. There is, as I remarked, a certain charm in Corporal Müller's vivacity, and I had been sewing all day, as madame knows; and there was Wackermann actually behind the snowy hedge, as Corporal Müller and I sought the solitude of the garden. I would not have thought any man of sense would have made such a fuss about such a little thing as a kiss. He put his hand on my shoulder like a gendarme or a bear, and he walked me off, and he talked to me — yes, he did; and how! O just Heaven!

"He said I might play most of my pranks, and he did n't care — he liked them. But there were limits to all things, and either I wanted to be his wife, or I did n't. If I did n't, well and good; he 'd find another girl, fond as he was of me. If I did, I could behave myself. As to dark gardens and kissing corporals, he 'd put his foot down. And he did — and it 's so long," extending her hands wide apart and laughing. "Madame may believe me, it 's like the foot of a mountain. That 's what my Wackermann did." Her tone was, after all, not without pride in his prowess.

"He did perfectly right," the countess said with decision.

" Yes, it was a beautiful scene," Manette returned. " I am beginning to enjoy it, — he big, threatening, and angry; I crying as if my heart would break. For I was startled, as madame may imagine."

" You would not like to lose him, Manette ? " the countess said gently.

" Ah, no, madame."

" You really mean to marry him ? "

" If he and I survive this cruel yet beautiful war, yes," replied Manette, throwing up her eyes.

The countess hesitated.

" Then be a good girl, Manette, and be a good wife," putting her hand on the girl's shoulder and looking at her earnestly.

The maid turned her head in her quick, birdlike way, and kissed her mistress's fingers.

" I like him all the better for it; and he 's a good soul, and will never spoil my fun. That this combination was a little awkward, less artistic than I usually originate, I must confess; but it has had — its uses," she concluded practically.

" I hope so," returned the countess quite gravely.

That night she wondered much about many things, and, wavering long, she finally looked at the rose and kissed it once only, and laid it solemnly back in its place, and was very lonely,—the fair lady in her turret; yet as she reasoned as best she could about the nature of her little maid, not condemning but granting her right to exist according to the conditions of her being, a thought that had strength to comfort arose in her troubled soul. " Not having, but giving, is true love,— giving all one can; and I would give, God knows, if I might. Life is sad, love is sad, and one does not know the end; but if one has found something worth loving, one has won life's best good. To know him, to love him, to do my duty each day, — what more is there for me? If I might plan my life like little Manette, might say, 'Such a day we will marry, such a day we will go to our home!' Then, the heart speaks, but the heart is exacting. Why should mine have its will, when so many suffer? Who am I, to be crowned in perfect bliss? And the years when I had nothing! And now I have him to love. Ah, God, make me grateful, make me brave to lose him; for since he loves me, I am sacred to myself as if a great white archangel had extended the shadow of his wings over my meagre, longing life." And with the saints of her childhood about her she fell asleep.

The lives in the château fulfilled their appointed way, not all, it would appear, under strict military discipline; and the December days moved on until the 24th, when the French again undertook a great sortie against the Prussian-Saxon lines simultaneously with General Faidherbes's operations in the north. The sortie was directed particularly against Stains, Duguy, Le Bourget, Pont-Iblou, and Drancy; and the battle raged fiercely in the immediate neighborhood of Aulnay, and farther towards the Marne at Ville Evrart and Maison-Blanche. This attempt to break through the German line also failed, although the latter was considerably weakened by the necessity of sending troops north to meet that brave and industrious French soldier, General Faidherbes, who was causing the Germans much trouble. The sortie was of extreme importance to Aulnay, inasmuch as it left the French in firm possession of Grosley Farm, — a dairy-farm close by, which Madame de Vallauris, as a child, a young girl, and a woman, had often visited. She was thrown into deep excitement by the news that her countrymen had established themselves there and barricaded it. "They will soon be at Aulnay," she thought, with a glow of exultation. Then her heart sank; after which she reproached herself.

Meanwhile at headquarters at Clichy, General von

Aarenhorst, in the early reports on the 21st, had again received the statement, by this time somewhat exasperating to him, that a sentinel on the Ourcq Canal had perceived, just before midnight, red-light signals which the man declared positively he could only attribute to Aulnay Tower. Von Aarenhorst felt that it was high time these dangerous signals, which in every instance had preceded a vigorous and important sortie of the enemy, should be suppressed. Since whoever managed them had thus far succeeded in evading suspicion, it was quite possible that he had been sufficiently adroit to display the signals many times unobserved. Regardless, then, of the colonel's enthusiastic defence of the château family, and unmindful of his own friendly impressions, the general requested von Linden to renew the watch on the park and Tower, to have the latter thoroughly inspected, and moreover to confine the Marquis de Montauban, Madame de Vallauris, the Abbé de Navailles, and every member of the household strictly to the limits of château, church, and park.

It nearly broke the good colonel's heart to convey the unpleasant information to the abbé, — for he chose him as victim in preference to the aged marquis, or the lovely countess who had borne her privations

with so much sweetness and dignity. The colonel
had, in fact, no patience or belief in regard to the re-
puted signals. A fatigued, half-drunken, or half-frozen
dazed watch, a level expanse of country, guns blazing
away in the darkness, — what wonder that one sees
signs and wonders, ghosts and signals!

To his communication the abbé replied quietly
that he deeply regretted being forced to make such
an announcement to Madame de Vallauris. As for
the marquis, one might indeed spare him the indignity, as he seldom, if ever, left the grounds. To this
consideration the colonel heartily agreed; and as he
looked at the spiritual face of the abbé, anxious now
about his friend, he deplored this stern necessity of
war. During the day the colonel himself passed
through the gallery and ascended the Tower. In the
small, rough room was absolutely no trace of the
presence of man. The church below boasted some
pillars of an early century, a bit of good sculpture,
and a painting, — the gift of the favorite of a king.
The colonel enjoyed it all, thought it a pity they
must always build on and improve and desecrate such
quaint relics; then he went cheerfully over to dine.

That evening Max Nordenfels sat alone by the
fire and waited. The thin voice of the marquis and

the hearty response of some of his comrades re-
sounded from the adjacent drawing-room. Madame
de Vallauris had not appeared at dinner. She was
not ill, the marquis said, she merely begged to be excused. "The fair sex must have its caprice," the old
gentleman remarked, with his gallant and indulgent
air. But Nordenfels entertained no popular, commonplace view of womankind; he believed that Countess
Nathalie was not capricious, and waited anxiously.

He heard her light step on the stairway, and
the fall of soft folds as she came. The pleasant
sound, heralding the approach of something gentle
and feminine among the spurs and sabres and dominant men's ways, would have been welcome to him,
even if he had not loved her. But as he heard her
coming, — the one lady in this Aulnay world of men,
the one woman in the world to him, — he sprang up,
eagerly looking towards the door with a great joy
shining in his face.

"Ah, I knew you must come down to-night!" he
exclaimed. "Dear countess, two whole days!"

She came directly to him and looked him in the
eyes with a childlike reproach. She was pale, as she
always grew under excitement, and in spite of her
still air he saw that she was agitated.

"Why have you let them do this?" she demanded sadly.

"Do what?"

"You know, do you not?"

"Yes, I do know," he admitted frankly. "Of course I know."

"Then why have you permitted them to do it?" she persisted.

It gave him a wild thrill of delight, that she was instinctively appealing to him for protection and redress; and he felt that it was delicious and dear, and at the same time exquisitely humorous, that she was ignoring principalities and powers, law, logic, and discipline, and holding him alone responsible whether the world went right or wrong.

"Countess," he said with his lover's voice and his lover's smile, perceptible, if somewhat in ambush and an honest twinkle of fun in his eye besides, "'if I were King of France, or still better Pope of Rome,'—but I am only Max Nordenfels."

She colored, and said hastily: "Pardon me; I spoke without reflection. Of course you are not accountable. You will at least give me the satisfaction of knowing you consider it an indignity and an undeserved wrong."

Max looked suddenly grave. "Countess, I think it right."

"You?" she murmured.

"I love you so!" he burst out impetuously. "I would give my life and soul to save you pain."

"Hush, hush!" she implored, "or I shall instantly go in to the others. Be generous, baron; I need to speak with you. Must I fear the slightest tête-à-tête? Are you not my friend?"

"That, too," he returned significantly. "Do not doubt it, say what you will to me. Let me assure you quietly that I deplore every annoyance to you as if you were my" — she trembled a little — "my sister," he went on emphatically; "but that I regard these renewed precautions as right and proper, imperative, indeed. General von Aarenhorst is too clever and experienced to need advice; but my views, such as they are, he was good enough to request to-day. We discussed many things informally. Believe me, it is no indignity offered you; but, on the contrary, regard for your honor demands it. The general entertains the most profound respect for you, and a warm interest."

"Then he chooses an extraordinary method of evincing his amiable sentiments," the countess rejoined with considerable feeling. "Shall I tell you what happened to me? You will say, perhaps, it was an expression of latent approval, a kind of exquisite flattery."

"Tell me first," said Max gravely.

She went on rapidly in her low, controlled voice, colored now and then by fine flashes of her warm spirit. It was a voice with which one could tell State secrets in a crowd and but one be the wiser. The marquis's brittle laugh sounded from the next room. He nodded and smiled at her over his cards, and she smiled brightly back. All the wide doors were flung open. In the music-room beyond some one was playing the "Moonlight Sonata."

"He would not laugh if he knew," she said. "There is much to which he can remain oblivious. Being old, perhaps the past veils the present from his sight. But this would touch him sorely, as it does me. I pray he may never know."

Nordenfels bowed his head in grave sympathy.

"I was going, towards evening, with Manette and my basket to my poor sufferers. I promised Sister Agathe to come again to-day. I had made some sherry jelly, and many of them were looking for me. The French boy with the fever, who is always begging for his mother, grows quieter when I come — but you will not care for such details."

"Dearest," Max broke out passionately, "I care for everything !"

"And we were stopped at the great gate, no explanation, nothing, simply stopped by a sentinel and a bayonet. I went to every gate. The same result. I was a prisoner; we are all prisoners here in the château."

"The thing itself is right," he answered with decision. "The fault was in the method; they should have announced it to you properly, and spared you every chance of outward annoyance. I cannot conceive how such an irregularity could have occurred. I am very sorry." He turned away, and walked thoughtfully up and down the room.

"It is not the method, but the fact itself which I regard as the insult. Colonel von Linden communicated his commands to the Abbé de Navailles. Both agreed that my uncle was if possible to be kept in ignorance of the restrictions. The poor, dear old gentleman would be cruelly wounded in his pride; and as he seldom crosses the threshold of the château, and never goes among the soldiers, why trouble him gratuitously ? Should he by chance attempt to pass the gate, he will be stopped with a bayonet as I was; then he will know."

" Madame !" murmured Max in deprecation.

"The abbé was engaged in the chapel, and could not tell me at once," she resumed.

" Or would not," rejoined the adjutant doggedly.

As she spoke, in her mind flashed simultaneously the same thought; but she refused to discuss the life-long friend of the Marquis de Montauban with any stranger.

" What do you mean ?" she demanded with some coldness.

" Pardon me ; I mean nothing."

While she, haunted by the old suspicion, was thinking, " He might have told me sooner. He had his reasons for letting me be repulsed at the gate. He wished to make me angry and indignant with the Germans. But no, I am not sure ; I am never just to him."

" Listen to me," she began with her peculiar manner of great warmth strongly restrained, — " Hecla glowing beneath its snows," as Linden had said that first day. "Listen ! I have learned in this time to recognize some of your rights, to find some justice in your course. I have learned, for instance, if you appall me by not respecting our ambulance-wagons —"

" It is not always possible," Nordenfels interposed vehemently.

" — that, on the other hand, our forts have had the cruelty to fire on your burial-trains burying French as well as Germans honorably. War grows more hideous, more inexcusable to me every day. It is a monstrous relic of barbarism. I abhor it, and shudder at its work; but I admit you are as humane as we. I perceive that you Germans have sometimes a spark of pity, a magnanimous instinct; but I ask you plainly this, — you whom I believe to be a man of honor, a man of thought, — why is our old and honorable house at this late day insulted with suspicion ? I did not blame you at first. We were simply your enemies, as you were ours. That we were imprisoned within our gates did not surprise us then. Nothing would have surprised us much, — not savages or cannibals. But gentlemen came. We learned to trust them. We saw, in spite of our prejudices, that you were like ourselves ; that you cherished kindness and courtesy in daily life, and deplored every rude act; that war to you too was a necessity, not your choice. We have lived now on an almost intimate footing. Surely you gentlemen quartered here have been able to perceive the harmlessness of Château Aulnay.

Moreover, you have our word of honor to remain outwardly neutral whatever may come. Do you demand more than the word of a Montauban? What, then, do you mean after these weeks of confidence and freedom? Why may I not go freely to my poor, wounded, suffering fellow-creatures? Do I ask whether they are French or German? I who am French in every drop of my blood, have I not forgotten everything where I could deaden one physical pain, make one restless spirit calmer? Am I dangerous? Is my poor uncle, with his weak and withered body, a deadly breastwork against you Germans? Or is it possible that you doubt our pledged word? I tell you plainly, — and I admit to you, Baron von Nordenfels, I have learned to trust you personally, — it seems to me a premeditated insult. In this dreary and terrible experience I have found one consolation. I have been able to give of my strength to weakness, to make some humble mortal — an innocent sacrifice to cruel ambition — happier for my presence. Even this is now taken from me, and the poor men must wait for me in vain. What answer have you to make to me?"

"Dear countess, believe me, it is unavoidable," said the young man.

"Why have they done it ?"

"I cannot tell you why."

"Do you know ?"

"Perfectly."

"You doubt us, then ?"

"Heaven forbid!   I believe in you as I believe in God.   You are the purest spirit I have ever known. I kneel to you, I kiss your feet; and yet I tell you it is right, what they have done.   Though it hurts you, it is right."

"But why ?"

He shook his head.   "Madame," he said, smiling a little, "in the stories, always in a case like this the woman tempts the man.   I have never known why. You tempt me now with your loveliness and innocence, it is true.   You tempt me to take you in my arms, and whisper a thousand love-words in your ear, and never let you go ; but you do not tempt me to forget my duty.   And if I could explain, you would be the first to tell me I was right; so do not ask me. Countess, just now you asked me if I was not your friend ?   Now I appeal to you.   Are you not my friend ?   Have you not faith, though you may not understand ?"

"Of what do they suspect us ?" she said slowly.

"I cannot tell you."

"Does it not seem bitter to you that they withdraw without explanation the confidence of months ?"

"It is no insult.   It is the inexorable necessity of war."

"Whom do they hold capable of dishonor ?"

"Not you, dear lady."

"My uncle ?"

"Never."

"Whom, then ?   Speak out."

"Did it never occur to you, that the Abbé de Navailles could play a deep game ?"

"But not treachery," she said, hesitating.

"There is treachery somewhere.   More, I may not say.   I trust you with this.   Trust me."

A deep thoughtfulness settled upon her face.   In the second room beyond some one had been playing a nocturne of Chopin, and now finished with a long, soft chord.

"Good-night," she said, extending both her hands. He kissed them, and went.

CHAPTER XII

"Ah, Christmas is a sad time for the children at home when the father's not there!" von Linden said with a sigh to Madame de Vallauris, a grave look on his jolly face.

"And a sad time for the father without his children," she returned kindly.

"Yes, madame, I miss them," he said simply.

"What does Christmas mean?" she went on thoughtfully. "'Peace on earth, good-will towards men'? What irony! Two hostile nations in a mighty struggle, the great city there holding out against cold, and famine, and fever, and misery, and your legions. War is a ghastly thing."

Von Linden shrugged his shoulders. "Ah, madame, that may be; but we can't get along without it, you know. It does a world of good sometimes, too."

"Filling the world with death and anguish," she murmured.

"Pardon me, countess, but you have changed your views since I first talked with you. You were more heroic once, more warlike and aggressive. You never said much, but one felt it. You intimidated me!"

She smiled sadly. "I was very ignorant, colonel. I have not changed in my sympathies for my own land, in my ardent desire for France to be victorious. But I did not know the sickening horrors of war. Here, in the midst of it, I have seen sights that have curdled my blood, and that I shall never, never forget; and my very soul protests against such massacre of humanity. To what end is it all,—the ruined village, the homeless wanderers, the poverty and misery and starvation, the bloodshed and the cruelty? The beasts are not so cruel as man. I saw a laughing boy leaning against a wall last Tuesday. There was an angry whiz through the air,"—she shuddered and covered her face with her hands,—"and then I saw what an instant before was a human body—"

"Dear madame, you are a woman and an angel, and sometimes war is hideous for us men. But let us discuss it later. One can argue better in time of peace." He took her hand and smiled, and patted it in a fatherly way. "Some day you and I will meet again; then I will answer you."

"The statesmen have to make peace afterwards," she persisted; "why not in the beginning of difficulties? Why do they insist upon all the cruelty and suffering and barbarism of war? Why not arrange their concessions and payments and diplomatic treaties at first, and prevent bloodshed and misery?"

"Ask them, madame," returned the bluff soldier. "It's their business to pull the wires. It's mine to fight."

"Alas, yes," sighed the countess.

"At least, you have softened a little to us poor Germans. You have not found us wholly barbarous."

"I have found you as considerate as the circumstances permit," she answered with dignity. "But I abhor your war, our war, all war. I believe it is a monstrous crime, and I feel vast and boundless pity for all who suffer from it, for the anguish of body and mind, — here, there," — pointing towards Paris, — "in your own land; and I pray night and day God may have mercy and bring it to a speedy end."

"Amen!" said the soldier solemnly. "We Germans all want to get home, madame. As I said, the little ones are waiting; and when a man has a good wife — " He hesitated. The warlike colonel was evidently very homesick. He took several long strides about the room, making much noise with his heavy, spurred boots.

"That is the irreconcilable feature of it all," the countess said very softly. "A tender-hearted man like you, loving your wife and children, and coming to a foreign land to slaughter French women's husbands and French children's fathers."

"Irreconcilable? Ah, madame, if you would teach the world logic! But I must go; for I feel myself becoming wax in your hands," he added with a genial laugh.

Christmas eve von Linden rode out to satisfy himself as to some reported firing near Bondy wood. It was merely a feint, purposeless, resultless, except that it created anger, excitement, and discomfort. The roads were slippery, the night cold and wet. The colonel, with von Nordenfels and an orderly, rode back to Aulnay in no enviable frame of mind. Approaching the château, they were surprised to see it brilliantly illuminated; and as the two officers entered, Gerhardt sprang towards them. "Don't go up to your rooms," he begged. "Come in here first."

Cold and wet as they were, they went into the great dining-room, where the family and the officers were gathered round a large Christmas-tree; and some of the men were coming in for a peep and filing out to make way for others. A convalescent drummer-boy, one of the countess's patients, sat bolstered up in the corner. Each officer had contributed to the general good whatever the field-post had brought him from home. On a table was a curious array,— cigars and Erbswurst, chocolate, books, trifles from mothers and sisters. A barrel of beer was running freely, and tasted of home to the strong jovial fellows, with their collars turned up and sleet in their hair, who came in respectfully to share the Christmas. Now and then a tobacco-pouch, a few knives, and other trifles were distributed. All could not have a gift, but all could see the tree, with a warm thought of home.

The chaplain made a short prayer, which the most careless of them felt. A man must have his earnest moments when death knocks every day at the door.

Gerhardt was liberally distributing the contents of a large jar of preserved damsons, and Forstenau flourished a ham. Compote, German sausage, and sweet almond and honey cakes all reposed amiably on the same plate, and were consumed together without ceremony.

The marquis moved delicately through the crowd, regarding the scene with ineffable condescension. "It is very amusing, very," he remarked, looking at the tree, the officers, and the men with somewhat the air he would have worn at a spectacular ballet. "I have read of your German Christmas-tree. I never saw one before. Interesting custom, really."

"I did what I could," Countess Nathalie began modestly, "and the lieutenants were so interested; but this must be quite different from their trees — quite."

"I suppose so, I suppose so," the old gentleman returned absently, with an encouraging smile at nothing in particular.

But Nordenfels looked at the odds and ends of candle-stumps, collected and tied on as Countess Nathalie could best manage, and burning with the old familiar Christmas-tree smell on a good straight fir from Aulnay Park. Memories of childhood and home mingled with the incongruities around him, and the weather-beaten soldier-faces smiled in from the doorways, the lieutenants made merry, and the older officers, care-worn, with the troubled eyes of men facing

grave responsibilities, could yet laugh cordially as
Christmas warmed their hearts. The queer keepsakes
from the Fatherland in a motley row touched him
strangely. Even Schinken and Wurst, most prosaic
of all edibles, seemed to convey a tender thought
because packed by some loving mother's hand for
her absent boy. Turning to Countess Nathalie, who
watched it all half anxiously, doubtful whether her
undertaking had succeeded or not, he murmured;
" Who but you could have done anything so gracious ?
It is the most beautiful tree, the kindest tree, the
most perfect Christmas-tree that ever was made ! "

At which she could only look at him and laugh
brightly ; for she knew the candle-ends were few and
ragged and old, and her whole arrangement most primi-
tive. Yet she colored and was happy beneath his
gaze.

They were all grateful to her. " God bless you for
the kind thought ! " the colonel said, taking her hands
warmly, and looking — Gerhardt declared in an envious whisper to Nordenfels — as if he was on the
point of kissing her.

" I made it chiefly for you, colonel," she said sweetly,
— " for you and the pale drummer-boy there. You
confided to me your longing for your wife and chil-

dren; he, his for his parents and sister. There is so much misery everywhere! I thought perhaps I could help you get through your most homesick evening. There is no real happiness in the world anywhere, only now and then a fleeting happy moment," concluded the beautiful woman with conviction.

"Dear madame,— dear child, I may almost venture to say to you, — repeat that to me if you can after three — after five years," the colonel replied, laughing kindly. "Believe me, I know the cure for your pessimism. But I see an orderly in the corridor. Pardon me that I must go, and take my adjutant with me. A thousand thanks, madame, for me, and for us all. God bless you for your kindness!"

"They enjoyed it, Nathalie," the marquis observed later, with a largely hospitable air, as if he had just thrown the château open for a grand ball. "It was very entertaining and creditable. We might do something of the kind often, do you know? It impresses them. It commands the circumstances. The soirée was bizarre, but agreeable, original."

"I am glad you enjoyed it, dear uncle," she said gently.

"It is a pity the abbé was occupied. He would have been uncommonly pleased."

"Could he not have come in if he liked ? What could prevent him ?"

"Nothing more important than scientific studies, my dear," rejoined the marquis facetiously, "which I should be sorry to see you puzzling your pretty head about, even to know the names of them. A clever woman is always a fright. Never grow clever, Nathalie. There's nothing feminine in cleverness. The woman's heart, the man's head."

"Have no fear for me," she said, smiling.

"Fortunately, my dear, I need have none," was his serene reply.

"But what does the abbé study, uncle ? Is he not learned enough?" she asked innocently, feeling with great compunction that she had become a very fox for slyness.

"To exercise his intellect," he replied, with a superior smile. "A man's intellect needs constant exercise, as an athlete's body. Before these disturbances the abbé could run into Paris as often as he pleased. He profits, of course, by my society still. But I am more or less occupied with my guests — and — "

"Yes, dear uncle. And the abbé studies more than formerly ?"

"That is, he interests himself, he exercises. For

the man's mind problems, diagrams, charts, are like the trapeze and parallel bars for the gymnast."

" Charts, diagrams," murmured Nathalie.

" Curiosity — curiosity !" He shook his finger playfully at her. " But it is a normal trait. It is feminine."

" And does the abbé show you his drawings, uncle ?"

" No, my dear child. I have no interest in such things nowadays. But being of an observant, a penetrating intellect, I naturally know in what direction my friend the abbé's mind leans, and what he does with his time."

" And what does he do with it, uncle ?" asked the countess quite bluntly, still feeling like a guilty fox.

" Science," said the old gentleman in a grand and vague way. " Science, my dear."

" Oh — science."

" Astronomy, I fancy. He dropped a little chart, with points and lines, on my desk. Yes, yes, astronomical; but such things are dry to me now, and *per aspera ad astra* has a double signification. You comprehend the Latin, Nathalie ?"

" Yes, dear uncle, — that much, I believe. A little chart, you said ?"

"Bless my soul! You don't want to study astronomy, do you?"

She protested the contrary, laughing a little nervously.

"Yes, we must repeat the soirée," said the marquis, well pleased, "and the abbé must be present. He hardly knows there is a military man in the house. He lives in quite another world. But this was hardly military to-night; it was purely social. The abbé would have enjoyed it. We must repeat it, my dear."

"We will do whatever makes you happy," she said indulgently, bidding him good-night.

But she did not repeat her Christmas-tree, nevertheless, nor was there much sociability at the château after that. The weather was bitter cold, the faces were grave and stern. Deep plans were laid. The Germans were impatient for the end. Paris was making its last brave and desperate effort.

The besieging army now contemplated the immediate bombardment of the city. Partly from conquered fortresses, partly from the Fatherland, heavy guns and batteries were procured. The woods which covered the advanced positions of the Germans before Mont Avron and Clichy had been full of life. Working parties toiled in the dark or by moonlight, and thousands of men were employed those bitter cold nights digging trenches in the frozen ground at Raincy opposite the dangerous batteries of Mont Avron. That the French in spite of their nearness failed to perceive the German activity seemed incomprehensible.

About seventy heavy cannon concentrated their fire on Mont Avron early in the morning of the 27th of December. By noon the French batteries were silent; by night the hill was evacuated. The German fire was now steadily directed against the French forts; while from the south side the bombardment of Paris began on the 4th of January.

Again Château Aulnay was thrown into excitement and distress. Towards midnight on the 14th of January the foreposts at Nonneville Farm, only a kilometer and a half from Aulnay, were attacked by the French. After a hard struggle they were driven back; their captain was taken prisoner and brought wounded to Aulnay. Madame de Vallauris begged to see him, or to have him brought to the château, but was refused. Sister Agathe was with him, she was told, and he was doing well. The countess was on the point of asking for Adjutant von Nordenfels, whom she had not seen in some days. He would take her to see the wounded French captain, she felt assured. Then she remembered that he approved of the order to re-imprison them, and, sad at heart, she decided not to ask for him, but went instead into the empty church, and knelt there long, and sobbed quietly for sheer loneliness and for horror of war.

General von Aarenhorst, at Clichy, was filled with consternation and a grim rage to hear now for the third time the report of signals presumably from Aulnay. They had plainly preceded the French attack on Nonneville, had been perceived by the distant watch on the Ourcq Canal, and were utterly invisible to the guard stationed to watch the Tower and park. "What devils' league can this be?" thought the good general. "A light seen from afar and not seen near by and below must come from the extreme interior of an elevated place," he reasoned. The form of the Tower of Aulnay, the deep room high above the plain, and below the clock and the slender spire, might be adapted by a clever brain to such a purpose. He determined to solve this mysterious and dangerous problem, which had been too long neglected. Lights always preceding French sorties should be summarily extinguished in his territory if it were a possible thing. Von Linden would most

assuredly again defend the Montauban family, assert-
ing that there were other village church-towers, and
that it was a hallucination of the sentinels always to
suspect Aulnay. If Aulnay was innocent, so much
the better; but Aulnay must prove it. Accordingly
General von Aarenhorst had a diopter adjusted to bear
precisely upon Aulnay Tower, and in a square stone
pillar supporting the balustrade of the high terrace at
Clichy a groove cut sharply to hold the instrument,
so that by night as well as day the Tower would be
under scrutiny. An under-officer of the staff-watch
was commanded to look at it every fifteen minutes during the night, and in case of the slightest
discovery to announce it instantly. Horses stood
saddled in the orderlies' stables continually, and an
expert rider knowing the short-cuts could traverse
the distance between Clichy and Aulnay in twenty
minutes.

Colonel von Linden received at the same time
orders to leave the family absolutely free to go and
come as they pleased. Von Aarenhorst resolved to
give them every opportunity to compromise themselves, in case they were addicted to double-dealing.
The abbé received the news of their regained freedom with his usual sweet-tempered indifference;

the marquis had not even suspected the restriction; the countess quietly resumed her visits among the wounded soldiers. "It seems as if they were all struck with blindness as to Aulnay Tower," the colonel reflected, — "even Aarenhorst, clever man as he is. I hope this is the last order. Restriction to château and park, freedom, restriction, freedom. Heaven forbid that restriction should now recur in its regular pendulum swing!"

Countess Nathalie was relieved when the inscrutable power which had forbidden, now permitted her voluntary goings-out and comings-in through the park gates. She smiled somewhat sadly as she realized that she now regarded the right to walk down the village street as a boon. "I must have been wickedly proud," she thought, "if it has taken so much misery to make me humble."

She was infinitely sad in these times, but not selfishly sad, as before in her idle days. Her face wore a look of self-control and spiritual life which made her marvellously beautiful. She always had a smile for the soldiers, however, and for her uncle, and no one found her dull company; only the hope that should have gleamed in her young and lovely eyes was not there to make her radiant. "Duty ought to be sufficient," she thought every day, "and I am a coward to wish it would not all last so very long. The Montaubans are a long-lived race; I am like the Montaubans," she considered with a shudder. "Papa died from an accident; uncle is seventy; fifty years more of duty! One does need courage. To-day there is Robert's bandage and Alexis's soup, and the men to talk with. That is enough. When I think of the fifty years, I am a coward."

She began to watch the abbé now deliberately and closely, but there was nothing mysterious in his conduct. The attack on Nonneville, following Nordenfels' expressed suspicion, her uncle's mention of the points and lines of the astronomical chart, served to make her deeply thoughtful as to the abbé's honesty. Why had they been confined to the château and grounds? Why were they now at liberty? Lately she had not seen Nordenfels for any length of time. He was so glad when he met her for a moment, that it seemed to her the whole world must see and feel the warmth in his manner and in the tone of his voice. But he was scarcely at Aulnay except when writing, or when from her window she would see him mount his chestnut mare in the court and stroke her once or twice, and speak a word to his man with a pleasant smile, then off by lonely wood-road and field-path or leading a detachment into danger and bloodshed. He always came back. He always took her hands as if they belonged to him, and smiled his loving, honest, manly smile straight down into her heart. He would say hastily, "It is always service now. But this cannot last long. Forgive my abruptness, and remember I am coming back in a long, still time."

And she had hardly occasion to do more than look at him with her questioning glance, when he was gone, — so full and hurried were the days.

" What did he mean by his allusion to the abbé? What was it the abbé did with his smooth ways and irreproachable life, and deep, glowing, dark eyes ? "

So she watched him, but found him harmless, studious, innocent.

One night she could not sleep. She was young still, and the restless thoughts most women can express to some good soul and find in return something like comprehension and sympathy, she held back in her own heart. They preyed upon one another, and threw her into an unsettled, questioning mood.

She rose impulsively, and half dressed herself, for the night was cold. Throwing open her casement, she listened to the sounds in the darkness. The atmosphere was singularly clear. In the stables she heard the slightest movement of the horses; not a branch was stirring in the park. She looked up towards the dusky Tower, bold, strong, and broad between her and the night skies. No, it was her imagination! Surely no sudden gleam of light had flashed out like an unbidden thought from that darkness, and vanished as if it had not been!

Startled, she stared through the gloom. Down in the park all was black, only by the yellowish lantern in the court the nearer trees raised their gaunt winter shapes and the snowy hedges leaned forward and beckoned with their cedar fingers in a ghostly way. Sight revealing nothing, she listened, every nerve alert. Why she was awake, why she, above the still park and court, watched by her turret casement open to the night, and breathed the chill of the mid January air, she did not ask herself. Against the illimitable darkness that mysterious, evanescent flash had inscribed itself like the fatal letters that foretold the downfall of a king.

Could she have erred? No. She saw it, rapid and warm as a desire, gleaming vaguely from the Tower into the vast outer world. The stars were

faint, the winds were still. Silence reigned supreme.
Yet she knew that something was in the Tower, and
had sent forth, inadvertently it might be, a swift
reflection of an inward hidden flame far into infinite
space.

She listened. Was it the beating of her heart,
was it the muffled, clanking movement of the night-
watch, was it a deep-chested horse breathing hard
or treading impatiently with his good hoofs, whose
speed had served so well the ambition and the wish
of man in this thing called war? She could not tell.
She seemed to hear everything, — more, indeed, than
there was to hear. Even the armoire behind her
seemed like a sentient thing, and innumerable voices
of the night spoke from within the ancient château,
from the wintry park without, in sudden imperious-
ness followed by a long hush and secrecy.

Above them all she distinguished stealthy movement in the Tower. Did she hear, or did she only
feel? Was the Tower alive? Had it a soul? Two
o'clock was striking now; the premonitory asthmatic
wheeze and gasp of the great works were louder than
usual to-night. One — two — strong and solemn —
floated in broad waves of sound out into the night,
over the still plain. Below, the sentries relieved

guard. The uniform cadence of their step approached and retreated. Stillness far and wide for an instant. How vast night was—and nature! The air was painfully cold. She shivered, with a pitiful prayer for the starving, freezing poor in the great besieged city.

Again the Tower — *moved?* she asked herself, startled, straining her eyes towards its gloomy outlines. No, but something — some one was moving within it. Soft, undefined, muffled, but distinct and incontestable were the sounds which reached her casement.

Her slender turret was highest, nearest to the massive church-tower. It stretched up towards it, eager to penetrate its secret, whatever it might be.

She would know that secret, waking and gleaming there through the night-watches. She had the right to know it. Was it not the old Montauban Tower? Were the marquis not a feeble, aged man, she would call him now to look after his own. Down in a room below there was some one working still, it might be, bending a grave, strong face over piles of reports and papers. He was not aged and feeble, but young, and in the full vigor of manhood. He would help her. He would come with strength to serve, with love in his eyes, eager to do her bidding. But, no.

The quiet writer might write on. He was farther away from her, more useless, more impossible to her need than the marquis; and neither the thought of his good brain nor his true love and knightly strength could be of any avail in this extremity.

She sighed, recoiled an instant. The way was long and dark, the château full of men. Then she prepared to go,—put on soft shoes, took an unlighted candle and matches in her hand.

"No one will hurt me," she reasoned. "Every soldier knows and loves me. I am a Montauban, and always have the right to go into the Montauban chapel—by night, too, if I wish. To whom am I called upon to explain my conduct, except to my uncle? May he sleep soft this night! The chance is, I meet no one. There has surely never been any sentinel on the stairways or at the entrance of the gallery. I shall probably go unimpeded to the Tower-room. If there is nothing wrong there, thank God! If there is, I shall know what. I do not know what I await. Whom I suspect, I know too well. God forgive me if I do him injustice. But I must, I will know."

Quietly and calmly she chose the most practical route, noiselessly descending her own winding stairway, avoiding the corridors nearest the officers' quarters, and deliberately taking a longer turn that she might pass old Jean's room instead of Manette's. "The more Jean should hear, in the dead of night, the less he would stir," she thought; "while Manette is more on the alert when she sleeps than most of the world awake." She stopped in the passage and considered. "Perhaps I should take Manette? No. The Countess de Vallauris cannot go to discover a man's perfidy escorted by her maid. There shall be no chatter. This lies between his soul and mine. If I do him wrong, I will ask his pardon on my knees. But he is my uncle's friend. I go alone. There are moments when a woman, too, must be law unto herself. Who shall dare prescribe to me the etiquette of this night?"

Her soft footfall was scarcely audible along the narrow, intricate corridors of the old château. Where the floors were of stone, she passed like a ghost. When she heard a sound, she stood still, holding her breath for fear, not for herself, but for the failure of her undertaking. If they found her, they might follow, and she alone ought to know what the old Tower was doing this night.

She knelt an instant as she reached her place in

the dark church, the prie-dieu where she had knelt as a child, and prayed with wide-open eyes watching the blue-uniformed children from an orphan school file in noisily with the Sisters, whose black robes and snow-white coiffes and gentle faces moved about quickly until the restless little feet in heavy shoes were all in their accustomed places. She used to wonder why, since she was an orphan, they did not put her in a blue uniform and noisy shoes, as she sat in the great Montauban loge and the breeze from summer meadows ruffled her hair.

Now, in the icy-cold, dark church she prayed a fervent prayer for the old man sleeping the broken sleep of age, for the heroic, resistant city, the very heart of France, and for — ah, yes, in prayer at least she might remember him: one prays indeed for the whole world — for the man she loved.

She passed through the church, feeling her way by the pillars, perceiving faintly the direction of the broad windows, through which not light, indeed, but its dim suggestion came. From the choir she entered the sacristy, and began to mount the spiral stairway which led up, up to the Tower-room. At first the steps were easy and broad, but gradually they grew rough, narrow, and insecure. The ascent would not have been tempting to any woman at high noon; but to that fact she gave no heed, except that she mechanically placed her foot squarely and went slower as the difficulties increased. Before the small door of the Tower-room she paused, breathing fast. Only this screen between her — and what? Under the rough door was a glimmer of light. "God be with me," she said, and knocked.

For answer, she heard a succession of rapid and soft movements. Something like the lid of a box closed with care. The glimmer under the door vanished. Then there was dead silence. She made no sound. The door opened stealthily. A hand, groping, seized her arm roughly; she felt a cold muzzle on her left temple.

The groping hand meeting soft raiment and a woman's form relaxed its hold, wonderingly; the revolver, in dogged defiance and self-defence, still desecrated her fair head with its metallic touch.

"Do not fire, M. l'Abbé," said a cold, proud voice. "You might be surprised; and then — it would make a noise."

"You, madame!" exclaimed the abbé in consternation. Then, as if relieved, "I might have known," he murmured.

There was a strange pause in the darkness.

"Since it must be, come in," said the abbé, pushing the door open.

She, feeling her way, entered.

He closed the door after her, and quickly lighted a candle. The first thing she saw was that the loop-hole windows through which wind and sunshine had played freely were hermetically sealed with heavy wooden shutters. Across every embrasure stretched a wall of silence and mystery. The two stood there as in a tomb, and stared at each other by the uncertain candle-light.

"Countess," said the abbé, not much paler than his wont, not much less calm, less master of himself, "I do not ask why you are here. Since you are here, you are welcome to my — laboratory. Pardon my rude reception. I thought you were a man, a foe. Pray be seated, madame," courteously moving toward her a chair standing against the wall.

"M., l'Abbé de Navailles," began the cold, clear voice, "I do ask you, without circumlocution, why are you here? And I tell you, now and for all time, a woman may be a deadly foe."

He had thoroughly regained his composure. Dark, earnest, with a spiritual calm beautifying his finely cut face, he regarded benignly the lovely woman who stood before him, gallantly defying him here in his Tower, where his intellect laughed to scorn the lumbering evolutions and circumstance below.

"In a certain sense we are well matched," thought the man. "If I am cleverer, she has marvellous insight, an indomitable singleness of purpose, and the courage of a fiend or a Montauban. And am I cleverer, after all?"

"Why am I here?" he answered, raising his eyebrows gently. "I am studying; making my observations, madame."

"Might I venture to inquire what kind of observations?"

His hesitation was barely perceptible. "Astronomical, madame."

She threw back her pale, beautiful face in ineffable scorn. "With closed windows!" she said, with a mocking smile. "M. l'Abbé, consider! A woman cannot always remain poised at fifteen between childhood and life, an innocent lamb, a helpless tool. He who adapts her to his uses may forget the future. But the future comes on apace, — the future, and the day of reckoning. It is here now, for us two. I did not seek it; but we are old-time enemies."

"Not enemies, — never enemies," interposed the sweet-voiced abbé.

"Always enemies!" rejoined the woman's low, passionate tone. "Why strive to conceal it now, here in the old Tower of my race, with the free night-air around us and God's stars above us? What shall we fear, you and I?"

"Dear madame, forgive an absorbed student, if, thrown suddenly out of his occupation, he is at first a trifle inconsiderate, forgetful of ordinary feminine needs. Perhaps a little sal-volatile—" He hesitated.

"You are too wise to intrude society remedies upon an incensed human soul," she rejoined coldly. "Sal-volatile or subterfuge has no mission here in Aulnay Tower. I am no selfish, flippant, pretentious woman, demanding redress for fancied wrongs, making nerves her battle-cry. I am not ill; I am not afraid. I demand of you, face to face, as man to man, what are you doing here in the dead of night?"

"Do I need to remind you that I am the friend and guest of the house, madame?" he asked gently. "When have I been required to give account of my movements?"

"You dare to shelter yourself still behind the hospitality of a Montauban?" she flung at him with unspeakable contempt. "I, a woman, stand here unaided by paltry excuse. Throw off your disguise of years. Meet me fairly, if you are a man."

"So be it," he said, folding his arms.

"What is in that chest?" she demanded, pointing towards it imperiously.

"Instruments. My property. Since when has the Countess de Vallauris become a police-detective?" he replied, the softness of his voice hardly veiling his satire.

"It is enough," she said curtly. "I impeach the chest in general, as I impeach you. I have no curiosity as to its contents."

"Examine them if you will, madame."

She waved her hand in refusal. "Again I ask, what are you doing here in the Tower?"

"Again I answer, pursuing my studies; making calculations."

"You are giving signals to our army," she declared low and rapidly, her eyes fixed upon his face.

After a moment's pause, outwardly unmoved, he retorted, with his usual gentleness, "'Our army,' madame? Pardon me if, knowing your idiosyncrasies, I am forced to inquire which army."

For this thrust she was, in her present mood,

unprepared. She rallied instantly. "So honest a speech as that you have never made to me. Let me be just."

"So unlovely a speech I have never until now had occasion to make to you."

"A truce to speeches, good or bad, from you to me," she cried, with a gesture of impatience. "I accuse you of treachery; of dishonoring the name that shelters you, and your own; of breaking your parole as a gentleman. Of the Church I do not speak."

"Madame, what are so light as words? Your proofs?"

"That you are here."

"A woman's proofs."

"I saw a gleam of light."

"Why not? My candle, as I moved a shutter."

"You have long talks with Pierre and Antoine."

"When was I ever neglectful of my poor?"

"You see and hear all, feigning to be self-absorbed. You watch while you pray. Your eyes burn like smouldering fires."

"Dear madame, you are wandering from your theme. A description of my unimportant personality is no proof of what you call treachery."

" There are sorties all around us."

" Would you have the French less active and less successful, madame ? "

" And — I — I feel through your calmness, through your very silence, your clear foreknowledge of our movements."

" Your feelings, madame, with all deference, would have no weight in any court. When you accuse a man of dishonor, you must be careful to collect your evidence."

She started and looked at him wonderingly. " Not yet ? " she said. " As you say, words are light. Those burdened with most solemn accusation fall imperceptibly from you. I am in truth no lawyer to quibble over terms; and this is no court demanding legal proofs. Yet because I, the child of the house which has extended to you the friendship of years, stand here with no witnesses save our own consciences and God, charging you with base perfidy, with breaking your pledged word, with disgrace to yourself and the honorable roof that shelters you, — I demand, whomever you would evade, that you answer me."

He moved a step away, then faced her again, speaking softly : " Madame, in this world honor and dishonor have variable meanings. I have never failed in respect towards you. I ask you now, is your own conscience clear ? "

She waited silently for his attack.

"In your interpretation of the word ' honor,' " his calm, trained voice continued, " do you allow a violent passion for the sworn enemy of one's native land ? In my turn, I accuse you of hanging with all your heart and soul upon the existence of your German lover. I accuse you of a consuming attachment which makes you weak and blind. Your free, pure thought for France has sickened ; your honest prejudices have vanished. Lukewarm to your duty, you disregard the noblest opportunities. You have lost your strength of moral purpose. You have renounced your land. You love Baron Nordenfels."

A full long minute passed before she answered low, " And if it were true ? If I do love him, what then ? " She was not looking at the abbé now, but beyond him with thoughtful eyes, and a strange calm on her white face.

"To yield to such a love is dishonor ; to conquer it, honor ; to use it with high aims, trampling upon the natural instincts, glorious," he urged.

"How would one use such love ? " demanded the pale woman with slow and gentle utterance.

Like the weird flash of light on the night skies, a sudden flame leaped into his dark face. "How? Do you ask? What cannot a woman like you accomplish if she will? Can one estimate the results, had you from the first been docile, been far-seeing, wise, — you, with your marvellous beauty, your subtle charm, that would make you beautiful had you no loveliness of face and form? Passive, self-absorbed, like a commonplace woman whose highest aspiration is a little billing and cooing and then a prosaic ménage, you have lived now months among these men. They would have adored you, worshipped you, been your slaves and chattels, had you so willed. What is men's adoration? A breath, a brief intoxication, I grant; but the world had never known a better use of witchery than you, madame, could have royally commanded here. Not a movement of your finger but might have signalled the advance or retreat of armies. Every glance of your eyes, every low word of your lips, could have been consecrated to the good of France. Ah, madame, to see your intellect, your beauty, dull, sluggish, and purposeless, while France suffers, struggles, bleeds before your eyes; to see you wasting your God-given powers in cowardice and womanish, weak desire, reaching with every tendril of your heart towards a love that degrades you, — this has been agony to me!"   He covered his face and turned away.

She had clasped her hands closer and closer as his low, vehement words poured on. Now she threw back her head and gazed up in solemn appeal to eternal justice and law.

"A spy," she answered, her scorn so vast it had no vent save in simplicity, — "a spy is what you would have made of me, — what you are!"

"Words, madame, I repeat, have a relative signification. Honor, dishonor, spy, treachery, you use freely. Rhetoric has no power to wound me. A petty measure cannot measure my life. I am accountable only to my God." He too looked up solemnly, as if seeing the boundless sweep of dusky heavens bending over him, and his spiritual rapt gaze sought fearlessly his supreme judge.

"M. l'Abbé de Navailles, even in this moment I am thankful for one thing, — that I have not done you a great wrong, an unpardonable injustice. As I mounted to this Tower-room my soul was on its knees before you, begging you to forgive if I had been so base as to suspect you of such badness. But I need to crave no pardon from you; my soul may stand erect before yours. God judge between us. I am alone, I am sorely tried, a woman without hope. My faults and weaknesses are many; but my spirit craves purity and truth; and wherever I fail, wherever I sin, you may not condemn me, for your praise or blame have no meaning, your prayers, your curse, no weight with me. Your God is not my God. If I were on my death-bed, I would forgive you the wrongs you have done me; but never again shall you influence my life. False and baneful is your light; your smile is a lie, your gentleness a poisonous flower."

"Rhetoric again," said the abbé, mildly.

She extended both hands, palms outward, with a slow, repelling gesture.

"I repudiate you and all the cruel past that was your work. There was a child here once, M. l'Abbé, a lonely child, yet happy enough, being young. You killed her youth, her happiness, her hope."

"Dear countess, if you choose to be romantic in your retrospection." He shrugged his shoulders slightly.

"It is not romance. It is the sober truth. When you brought the Count de Vallauris to Aulnay, had you no pity, had you no heart?"

"Dear madame, of all things I have my own opinions. Matrimony to me and to a milliner's apprentice naturally represents a different force in this world's problems. I would have treated a milliner's apprentice one way. I treated Mademoiselle de Montauban in another. I accredited her with a higher nature, higher needs."

"And for that reason you sacrificed an innocent child to a profligate old man?"

"Madame, I have every consciousness of having done my duty towards you. The Count de Vallauris' frailties have been summoned before a higher tribunal. Peace to his soul! There are some things one can scarcely touch upon."

"And I believe it would be a better place, this cowardly, false world, if a few rare souls should spurn restraint and speak out plainly what they think. What crimes are not committed in the name of tact, refinement, discretion, — what sins of meanness and falsehood! What have I gained by silence through the years? My resistance against you was sure and strong. I yielded to my conventional training. I spared you, sought to shield you from my own distrust. This is the end."

"Countess, even your judgment is not infallible, and

your kindest impulse toward me may be the truest
and the best. Consider; I am twice as old as you,
a thoughtful, gloomy man. How can you probe my
conscience? Admit still you may be unjust. Believe
me, I am, and must remain, an enigma to such as
you."

The music of his voice would have calmed a restless, frightened child. His lofty, ascetic head towered
above her with the spiritual beauty of a Saint Casi-
mir. Even in her deadly opposition she recognized
that he was a man, that his acts were guided by a
masterful intellect, that a less wronged mortal might
have yielded to his magnetism, putting weak hands
in his, with a trusting "Do with me as you will."
But for her his subtle mastery and his eloquent
charm were nought. A strong, sun-browned young
knight with deep-set eyes and fair hair like a Norse
hero, couching his lance in honor though beset by a
thousand foes, stood by her now, unseen, and helped
her to overthrow the abbé's precious casuistries.

"The day he came, the yellow old count with
his evil eyes and double chin, I cried because he was
not like my friend Sophie's fiancé, — slender in the
waist, and with a merry, young smile. Fresh from
the convent, still loving my row of dolls in the glass

case in my turret-room, could I know what horror, what endless misery you were preparing for me?"

"I, dear madame? Am I the instigator of human necessities and social complications?"

"Of mine, yes. Your insatiable planning knows no end, no rest. Your passion for influence is beyond all bounds. Was it fortune for the Church, was it the hope of a human life in your clutches, that made you sacrifice that poor child I once was?"

"Madame, madame, believe me, you do me gross injustice," interposed his gentle remonstrance.

"Do you remember the day they told me I was to marry him? He kissed me on my cheek before you all. I ran upstairs, and with the nail-brush and much soap scoured my face relentlessly, my solemn, sympathetic row of dolls looking on. God knows I would wash away from my life every loathsome touch and word of his that chilled my youth forever."

"Madame!" deprecatingly.

"Oh, yes! I know. In our world everything is admissible save the honest expression of human feeling. But do not fear. The story of my wrongs shall never weary you. I tried to be patient, to endure, to have courage. Yet now as I look back upon that lonesome time, I tell you that you are responsible for every odious moment, for every loveless memory. Did you all wonder that I wept so long when he died? I was weeping, not for him, but for what might have been and was not, — for my lost and desecrated youth, vaguely for the love I had not known, and longing passionately to purify my life from every unhallowed association."

"Milkmaid romanticism!" murmured the abbé.

"He died well shrived. That is the best that can be said. Ah, how well I remember it all, every detail from the beginning to the end. My aunt told me in those first days that very vulgar notions were poisoning the Sacré Cœur. In her time there was no thought of lovers. One took what was presented to one. She was affectionately astonished at my feeble and ignorant resistance. It did not last very long. I said he was old and ugly. 'It did not matter,' she replied, 'he is a Vallauris. In these days of mésalliances, of irreligion and emancipation, it is the duty and the privilege of a Montauban to follow the old régime. The blessing of the Church rests upon the union of a Vallauris and a Montauban.' I listened, and yielded from the mere habit of obedience. I regularly washed off the touch of his lips from my cheek, from my hand, and went to the altar in good spirits, much interested in my first long train. God pity me!"

"Is your fate, then, so different from that of other women?" inquired the gentle voice.

"I do not know. I do not ask. I had one chance. You gambled with it. I had my girlhood, my illusions. You destroyed them."

"Why summon these reminiscences to occupy us now?"

"Because, once before I die, I would like to free my mind of the old weight. Now, for the first time, I know what I have lost, and what your sin against me is. You sneer at what you call commonplace, womanish desires. Know, then, these would comprise my horizon of happiness,—the man I love beside me, and my children on my breast, something near, something warm; not these separate cold worlds rolling on in mysterious space like you and the dear old uncle and me. Is that life?"

"And your ambition is so low? Has the German done all this?"

"Ah," she said simply, "a woman has but one life, but one chance of happiness. It is—love."

"And her country?"

"A woman's home is her country."

"Is there no higher voice than her own desires?"

"God created her to love and to be loved."

"To love a foreigner and an enemy?"

"Who shall condemn? We are foreign to life-long neighbors. There are foes in our own households. Friends are born, not made; and longing souls traverse unwittingly geographical lines, political boundaries, and time and space, to meet. No language, no nation, monopolizes love. Love is boundless, universal, eternal, the spirit of the living God."

"That means, then, you will marry him?"

A strange, wondering look overspread her face. "Marry him?" she repeated softly.

"And forget, between your kisses, the Frenchmen your lover has slain?"

She straightened herself haughtily. "M. l'Abbé, I have already intimated to you that you have no share in my fate. Moreover, not to be questioned, but to question, am I here. What I may choose to do, to be, I determine regardless of you. Leave me henceforth out of your calculations; our ways are apart. You are a false friend, a traitor."

"Madame, you accuse me, I accuse you. But

recrimination is not argument. Let us come to some conclusion."

"You have broken your pledged word. You have betrayed the honor of our house. That is my conclusion."

"As I have previously said, madame, of that you have no proofs."

"Proofs! I *know*. I could expose you to the world."

"But you would not, countess, even if all you say were true," he rejoined quietly. "A friend of the Marquis de Montauban, a lover of France, is safe with you, though he were thrice a traitor. Personally, I trust myself with you as if you were my angel. And yet, remember, madame, for justice' sake, you have no proof."

"You can never deceive me again," she said. "It is well that I came. Now I will go. And what use I shall make of my discovery I do not promise."

He smiled in perfect security. "I know you, madame. I trust you to the death."

"Rely upon nothing. I must think. I shall do what seems right. Between us two is not the shadow of a bond."

She opened the door.

"Softly, countess, and slowly. Will you not take my hand?"

"I fear nothing. Remain where you are."

"As you wish," he whispered. "It is true, you are safer alone."

Down the interminable winding stairs, through the little church, the echoing gallery, the silent corridors, she made her way, unseen, back to her turret-room. Looking round on its innocent four walls, it seemed to her she had returned from the unreal, barren, dreary journey of a terrible dream. "Would it were a dream!" she moaned. "Would I could awake from this oppression, doubt, and loneliness! or would I might never wake again!"

CHAPTER XIII.

The last, supreme, desperate effort of the defenders of Paris took place on the 19th of January, when a sortie from Mont Valérien was attempted with one hundred thousand men. This also failed to break through the besieging lines. The situation of Paris was hopeless.

At the Saxon headquarters they were planning revenge for Nonneville. It was decided that Grosley Farm, since the 21st of December strongly occupied by the French, should be attacked in the early morning of the 19th.

Adjutant von Nordenfels brought the command from Vert Galant towards evening of the 18th. Colonel von Linden conferred with two of his most determined company chefs, and walking up and down in a long alley of the park, communicated to them the instructions. Upon von Nordenfels, thoroughly acquainted with the whole region, devolved the responsibility of accompanying the column in order to effect a junction between the Grenadiers attacking Grosley Farm and the Prussian Guards who were to advance simultaneously upon the neighboring village of Drancy. At four o'clock two companies of Grenadiers were to stand at the south side of Aulnay, and from there take the road along the wood towards Grosley Farm. All details were discussed exhaustively.

Madame de Vallauris, anxious and watchful now as a conspirator, saw the officers stroll into the park and later return to the château. Moved by a curious instinct she quickly started down the path from which they had come. In the dusk she met the abbé face to face, pacing slowly by the thuya groups, his arms folded across his breast, his thoughtful head bent down.

"Ah, madame, have you come out for a little air?" he said pleasantly.

"You have been listening, M. l'Abbé."

"To the wind in the tree-tops."

"To the plans of the Germans."

"The park is large. There is room for them and me. I did not disturb the gentlemen."

"Ah, shame!" she murmured in distress.

"You are trembling, madame," he said kindly.

" It is a chilly evening. Pray do not remain standing here. Shall we not walk ? "

" I tremble from indignation, from pain and horror. You will betray them, now, up there, in the Tower. In some secret way you will reveal what you have heard, and work against them. You cannot deny it."

" Would you wish me to work for them ? " he asked quickly.

"Not that," she said, — " not that, but all in honor."

"Do not be agitated, countess. Let us go in now. Why disturb yourself, indeed ? " he pleaded.

" Promise me not to go up. to the Tower this night. Promise it for all our sakes. Let the victory be as God wills.   See, I am speaking now without reproach, or heat, or rancor."

" You are speaking like an angel," he rejoined, touched by her sorrowful voice ; " but the victory will be as God wills, whether I go east or west."

" I beg, I implore you not to go to the Tower."

" Why should your thoughts dwell continually on the Tower ? ' "

" Do not seek to evade. It is too late."

" You are imaginative, madame."

" On the contrary, I know the Germans have some deep plan afoot. I know you will thwart them if you can. I know, too, we have been watched and set free alternately in an inexplicable manner. Undoubtedly we are still under surveillance. Undoubtedly your mysterious night-messages are suspected. Now I understand what seemed a heartless insult to our honorable house. See, I am talking plain sense, facts. I warn you for your own sake. If you go on, you are in personal danger."

"In any event, the weakest plea to use to me," he interposed gently.

"I grant that," she returned in the same low, hurried tone. "I do not doubt your bravery. Then, for my uncle's sake. He loves you. Peril to you would make him wretched. You refuse to consider the honor of his house. But you are his friend; for friendship's sake, for affection's sake, and long companionship, do not hurt him so cruelly. There are things one cannot do, weapons one cannot stoop to use, no, not to save one's soul."

"You do not know how you pain me," he returned with deep sadness.

"You remain obdurate, insensible to every appeal? Honor has no weight with you, nor friendship and old ties, nor that I come in tears and beg,—that I beg of you! It seems to me that that alone might move you, for I have never loved or trusted you, or asked aught at your hands. In kindness, gentleness, I beg you, let me not plead in vain. I will forget the past, I will forget what I know. Renounce your purpose, sacrifice it to my prayer."

"You grieve me much," he said softly.

"Once more I entreat you."

"I promise nothing; and observe, I admit nothing, madame."

"Then hold me responsible for nothing," she exclaimed desperately. "I warn you. I cannot longer share an evil secret. It oppresses me, terrifies me. The air has murder in it. It is a dastardly, dishonorable thing that you mean to do this night."

"The choice of words is yours, madame. Your fancy leads you far," he returned gently.

"I am free to reveal your course to whomever I will."

"'Free'? Ah, madame, you cannot reveal what you do not know. But if the innermost thoughts of my brain, and the deepest desire of my heart, and my life itself lay at your mercy, I would have no fear of you. No, not even in your lover's arms would you betray me. You are a rare soul. I trust you, I reverence you. Whatever comes, remember that.

Remember, too, a man's whole scheme of duty may conflict with yours, and yet "— he paused an instant —" it is his duty, and he follows it. For this moment's pain, forgive me. It is inevitable. Yet, believe me, I grieve to see you suffer. And now go in, madame, I beg. It is cold here, and you have nothing to gain from me by remaining. All as God wills."

Sad, and vaguely alarmed, she returned to the château and went directly in to dinner, her face extremely pale, her eyes luminous from the air and darkness and her great excitement. The abbé came in shortly after, gentle and unmoved. The marquis prattled like an unconscious child to her, to him, to them all, and afterwards sat down cheerfully to a game of bézique.

Later, Nordenfels and the countess stood in the library, where he had begged her to come. It did not surprise her that he gravely asked, or that she simply came with him, or that he closed the doors, then stood there tall and silent, looking at her. She had never seen his face so earnest. Again he wore a tea-rose from Vert Galant. She fastened her eyes upon it, and felt strangely miserable, and knew not what she feared.

" I thank you for granting me an interview," he said.

" I had no wish to refuse you."

"This will be a critical night.	I need not hesitate to tell you that."

"I feel it, without words," she murmured.

"I do not know why my mood is so heavy.	Action has always roused me before this.	You will not think I am a coward, if I tell you I am depressed and sad?" He smiled a little as he spoke.

She could have wept for grief and fear.	She trembled, but made an effort to control herself.	"You are very sombre.	Does a brave man have premonitions like a foolish woman?"

He came nearer and spoke lower, and took her hands, and drew her towards him.	"There are many things a brave man may fear.	It may be some of us will never come back.	It may be I shall never see your face again.	It may be — who knows what the chances are?" he said abruptly.	"Death may be near or far; but I cannot go from you this night without telling you once more how I love you, how truly and tenderly — with my whole soul."

She grew paler under his gaze, and caught her breath with a suppressed sob.	"Let us go back to the others," she said faintly.

"Not to-night.	Do not silence me to-night.	I love you — love you — love you — Nathalie!"

She covered her face with her hands. How sweet his voice was! Where should she find strength to resist?

Suddenly he put his arms round her, and kissed her bent head, her hands, her hair, with innumerable kisses, holding her close against his breast and murmuring, "Forgive me — dear heart — my love — forgive!"

One moment she lay in his arms, unresisting, then she drew back and raised her sad eyes to his.

"If you would say once that you love me," he pleaded.

"I could have loved you well."

He smiled his radiant, glad smile. "That is enough. You love me, then."

"There is a world of sin and pain between us."

"We will bridge it over," he replied, extending eager arms.

"No, no!" She shuddered and drew back. "There are rivers of blood between us, and graves, and anguish, and the battlefields of France. Nothing can bridge those over."

Thoughtfully he looked at her. Most lovingly and simply he spoke: "Have we not discussed that before? Trust me, it will not last. Trust me, beloved! Let me go from you with your promise."

"I will pray for you," she murmured.

"As my promised wife?" persisted his loving voice.

She looked at him with infinite longing. "His promised wife!" All peace, all loveliness, all bliss, was comprised in those three words. Like a fleeting dream of a lost paradise she saw what might have been. She looked at him and longed to whisper, — "Take me and love me; you are my fearless, perfect knight. You restore to me the freshness of my belief in man's goodness and man's honor. I have no life but you." She looked at him and longed to say as to her other self, "What I know, you must know. Your secret plans this night are revealed. You go to meet a warned and dangerous foe. There is perfidy lurking near. Be cautious; be wise; or, better, do not go." But she only said, "As your friend, no more, I will pray for you."

"Nathalie, there is nothing real between us," he exclaimed passionately.

"There is my country, my religion."

"A woman's home is her country."

Had she not used those very words? But now she answered, "Not mine."

"And religion?" he repeated simply. "What

does that matter ? Why should you not keep your religion and I my own ? "

" I cannot," she cried desperately. " Have pity. Do not urge me." Always she was thinking of the Tower and its fatal secret.

He waited an instant. " You are confused," he began gravely. " You are weary. These war-times prevent you from seeing clearly. But war and winter will pass away," — how his voice thrilled her ! — " and another time will come for us two, — springtime and love and happiness. Ah, do not think me too bold, too sure ! But I love you so, and you have given me the right to believe I am dear to you. Why, then, shall I not hope ? I would be no man if if I could give you up. And for a shadow — never ! "

Should she not warn him ? He stood there so beautiful in his tenderness, so strong in his hope, so brave, so true. If he were going forth to die ! If the very signal flashing this instant from the Tower should bring death to him — to him ! Why not ? It would mean death to many. She could not bear it. Life was too cruel. War, hideous war everywhere, and her soul in agonies of doubt. Should she warn him ? But the signals in the Tower, wicked though they were, would gleam for France.

It was all wrong. Life was one great, cruel, con-flicting pain.

"Are you frightened?" Max resumed lovingly. "Did I frighten you? You are so pale, so wan. Dearest, forgive me before I go, for everything. I have been awkward with you and abrupt. But it has not been an easy time for me. It has been hard for us both. I must leave you. There is so much I thought I had to say. I have forgotten all except that I love you. Ah, the little rose! I brought it for you from Vert Galant."

"I have kept the other," she murmured half inaudibly. "I shall always keep it. It is enough. Wear this one as your talisman." She pressed a long kiss in its heart, and with trembling hauds slipped it again through his buttonhole.

"I shall come back," he said, "and then you will say 'Yes.'"

"I shall say 'No' — always — forever."

The Tower, the cruel Tower!

"Farewell. God bless you! I must go. Your promise would have made me glad and strong. But I can wait. When you are one day my own beloved wife, you will forget that we are not of one land, one race. Believe me. Trust me."

"I who love you, love you so, am letting you go forth to your death," was her whole thought. She trembled violently.

"Farewell." Exhausted from her conflict, hopeless, she felt herself clasped in his strong arms and kissed silently, her forehead, eyelids, cheeks, and lips. "Now — now, surely, I shall come back, my own beloved," he murmured exultingly.

The night was very dark. A bleak west wind blew from Grosley Farm. There was no rest for her, and if in her soul patriotism had conquered love, love struggled still and asked in wild reproach, "Why have you wronged me so?"

No sound came from the black, silent mass. The troops began to muster. She saw them go by. Nordenfels rode under the lanterns of the court, with a long searching look towards her window. She saw the rose distinctly. His face looked gray and stern.

They were gone. What would come from this night? Where were they going? What did it mean? It was terrible to be a woman, to suffer and never to act. She waited with nameless dread a long and wretched hour. She opened her window. There were regular steps down in the court. It struck five. She heard in the distance scattering shots, a long, deep hurrah, more scattering fire, then stillness.

At this moment a rider on a foaming horse dashed into the court-yard, where von Linden paced restlessly to and fro, listening, waiting. The orderly passed the colonel a paper on which were three words, "Aulnay Tower signals."

Colonel von Linden gave a brief order to an officer, who sprang towards the guard-house, and returned immediately with an under-officer and three men, entered the château, passed through it, the gallery, and the church, and ascended the Tower. The door of the Tower-room was locked. They beat it open with the butt-ends of their guns. By the gleam of a blind lantern they perceived two figures. Two shots from a revolver greeted the intruders. Instantly the abbé, pierced through the breast by the under-officer's bayonet, sank lifeless upon the floor. The other figure was seized, disarmed, bound, and led into the court, where he was discovered to be one of the fishers on the Ourcq Canal. Concealed upon his person were memoranda in the abbé's handwriting giving minute information as to the position and strength of the German troops, as well as sketches of the recently constructed batteries near Aulnay and

Fontenay Farm. The fisher Antoine was shot the following day, Pierre placed in safe keeping.

From Grosley Farm was now heard the sound of renewed and violent musketry-fire, which continued persistently, then suddenly ceased. An officer soon arrived at Aulnay with the announcement that Grosley Farm was taken, five officers and over a hundred men prisoners. The renewed fire had been caused by French reinforcements who had been driven back by the Prussian Guards coming from Drancy. Grosley Farm was burnt to the ground. The two Grenadier companies returned in triumph to Aulnay.

It was clear daylight as they marched into the village. Behind them the wounded slowly followed, and still later five ambulances bearing the bodies of the brave fellows who had paid with their lives for the victory.

In this sad group, on one of the last stretchers, lay Max von Nordenfels, living still, but unconscious, and dangerously wounded. A musket-ball had pierced his breast exactly where Nathalie had placed her talisman, the rose of Vert Galant.

CHAPTER XIV

MANETTE, with vivid green satin ribbons fluttering from her coquettish cap, her dainty apron, her sleeves, her skirts, danced ecstatically through château and village.

"But, no! This appropriateness!" she would exclaim to Wackermann, as she and her vast good-natured grinning swain met by her appointment in odd corners and the twilight. Though there seemed to be no earthly reason why they should not meet in broad daylight anywhere, and at any time, as honest lovers on the eve of marriage, Manette insisted upon the rendezvous system.

"The magnifying-glass is death to illusions," she reflected. "A perfect toilet should be a profound mystery, and love also needs subtle draperies, convoluted surprises. Why sit and stare at my good Wackermann by stuffy lamplight, when the vegetable-garden invites us to its shades? Expectation makes a blessing dear; and then in the enhancing darkness

he can think I 'm anybody he chooses, and I can find
in him all the charmers I have known.

"Just Heaven!   I shall rendezvous until I 'm gray,
with Wackermann, — of course with Wackermann!
If everybody knew his trade as well as I do mine,
the world would go smoother.   The toilet and the
heart, — that is the twin study to which I devote
my powers; and, modestly speaking, I am a success.
Mystery, mystery is indispensable in both depart-
ments."

Foolish little Manette, the child of this generation,
may have been wiser in her generation than the children of light.   While her display of ribbons and ideas
provoked a smile, her swift light feet, her steady
hand, her practical, shrewd head, were helpful to an
extreme degree to the Countess Nathalie; and as
well as Manette knew how to count her pennies and
buy her ribbons cheap, she spared neither time nor
pains, nor her energies, nor good hours of rest and
sleep, but spent them all with a grand extravagance
for her mistress.

Sententious, flippant, pretentious, and honest, the
most expert actress, the veriest, most transparent
child, the little maid played her elfish, eccentric part
well in this world's drama, and Nathalie loved her

gratefully. "I do not know what others see in her," she said once long after, "but the comfort she was to me in those terrible months I can never express. Her words and ways are absurd. Her actual being is dear and good. One learns many things in war-times."

"Green ribbons are my duty," Manette announced. "From my duty I never shrink. Green is my most unbecoming color, one distinct step worse than blue. What does it matter? Green is one of the vicissitudes of changeful time. I endure with stoicism, with heroic smiles. I knew enough — few women would have been sly enough for that — to choose satin, not gros-grain. When a color does not suit, satin lends a shimmer, a subtlety. Gros-grain is pronounced honesty, clear and uncompromising. None of that for me! Let my pills be threefold sugar-coated! Otherwise life is unscrupulously disagreeable. Green — green, was that easy for me to swallow, with my sallow skin, my yellow influence, my round black eyes, that demanded a mellow glamour of blinding color and tone? But green I wear, though the skies fall. In the stars it is written. Wait," she said to Wackermann, "till the rosy spring bursts forth."

"Spring is n't rosy," answered her smiling giant.

"Never mind, stupid. You do not understand. All the better. Every great mind works alone. In the springtime, in the springtime you will open your sleepy blue eyes to see the rose-colored ribbons, love's banners, flying everywhere.

"Just Heaven! He dangerously wounded; you slightly wounded! He forced to remain; you permitted to remain! She the gracious countess, I her devoted maid, called upon for different yet similar services! The appropriateness! The arrangement! The unique and perfect picture! Don't talk to me about his not recovering. There is always a *dénoûment*. Things don't end in any slipshod way. What began with trumpets and inspiring flags and beautiful dears in uniforms does n't go out like a tallow dip. Nature, too, has its appropriateness. Mark my words. The doctor may look solemn, the countess may look pale, but the patient's going to recover. Max Baron von Nordenfels will be his handsome, strong self again, with an elegant way of walking, and speaking, and mounting his horse, that nobody ever did see. After the green ribbons of hope will follow the glowing rose of dawning love, — the rose of promise and of passion. Just Heaven! How bewitching I shall look! Ten years younger than in green, and a world more innocent. Wackermann will scarcely recognize me. All the better. The unbecoming, discreetly chosen, has also its uses."

The people were coming back to the village now, wan, hungry-looking beings, to their battered, misused houses. One home had lost a mother during the siege; another, the strong and cheery father; and many a young son was missing. Yet the war was over, spring would soon burst forth from the silent earth, and hope began to blossom in the village heart. The plain grew vast and still again, except for small, rustic sounds. The sharp, cruel musketry, the roll of artillery, the smoke, the flash, the clank of arms, the ominous human tramp, the rhythmical, eloquent hoof,— all was gone. Round the wise old Tower played balmy February breezes, the harbingers of spring; and not one of its gray stones betrayed what it had known and seen.

The marquis missed the abbé at first, but not, indeed, as youth mourns for a friend. "It was a sad thing," he would say. "A fine man in the prime of life. That he should go first and I remain! He had a stroke, you know; seized in the old Tower. Astronomy was his favorite pursuit. A scholarly man, my poor friend the abbé, — a sad, sad loss to me! To think he should be taken first into 'the poppied sleep,' as the poet says, — 'the poppied sleep.'" Then he would smile in his far-off way, and speak of the weather, and the village, in which he took much interest.

In the largest, airiest room overlooking the park, a long, still work was begun, — a work of unwearying care and patience, of inexhaustible tenderness, arduous in its simplicity, exclusive, soul-absorbing. Is it a light task to sit in a low chair hour after hour by an invalid's bedside, to watch his sleep, to renew the cool bandage on a burning wound, to moisten his parched lips with a strengthening drink, to administer a quieting medicine, to deftly turn a pillow making it light and cool to the weary head? Yet who may estimate the weight of anxiety, the painful soul-tension, with which one hangs on every quiver of an eyelash, on every trembling of the lip, on every faint, faint breath? Upon one moment's sleep, one moment's forgetfulness, the life of a human soul may depend. In the solemn night little acts of succor are pregnant with magnitude and meaning. Slowly and heavily fall the otherwise fleeting seconds into the illimitable sea of eternity. The rush and pressure, the striving and noise of the tumultuous world without, grows petty and colorless in contrast to the still, white bed on which the loved one lies. Four walls enclose one's whole future, all one's hope; and the sacred present task is to arrest the cold hand of the weird sister, already poised above the precious vital thread. Like a fragile spring blossom raising its timid head among the snow-drifts, still threatened by the wintry blast, the longed-for convalescence creeps softly on. Then the heart of the watcher in its joy is stirred with solemn thought of the infinite, the unknowable. What is human life? A breath. Yet to what strength, to what heights does it not rise? Whence does it come? Whither does it go, with its capacity for bliss, for sorrow, for power, and for infinite aspiration? Gazing in tenderness upon the beloved face, its pallor warmed at last by the angel of life, the whole world sinks into nothingness, and in the soul rings a vast pæan of thankfulness and love.

Through all these still soul-paths, far from the surging multitude, Countess Nathalie wandered, as day and night she watched by Max von Nordenfels' bedside. Trembling, hoping, fearing, trusting, she performed with outward calm the duties of each monotonous hour, and her great eyes would search with anxious scrutiny every feature of his face. It was long before hope dawned with certainty. But the severe wound-fever was over, the ball had been successfully extracted; now only one crisis remained. Then would come the slow strengthening of the shattered nervous system.

Perfect quiet was ordered as an indispensable condition of his recovery. It was a happy circumstance for him that silence was possible, since, thanks to the capitulation, the thunder of the artillery had now ceased, and stillness prevailed everywhere. In the château court-yard were no hurrying spurred feet; in the village no imperious, metallic sounds, no marching squadrons. The great park stretched itself out in restfulness; the Tower watched and waited in monumental repose. Blackbirds that had dared to brave the bitter winter chirped cheerily in the shrubbery by the broad windows. No harsh tone reached the invalid. Cool, fresh, and airy, his room was made for him as refreshing and as kindly as gentle thought could devise. In weakest meditation he studied the ceiling and the old-fashioned cretonne on the wall. Often the outlines of one pink convolvulus were all his indolent brain could grasp before sinking off into somnolence.

No one might speak to him. No question of his might be answered. Only with a glance, a smile, was she permitted to reply, when his languid spirit awoke sufficiently to manifest any consciousness of the outer world.

But her silent language was rich in eloquence, and a warm, pure light shone from her tender eyes upon the pale face of her sleeping lover, to whose every breath she listened, thankful beyond all measure when at length its soft regularity comforted her soul. After the martial uproar, after the danger, after the strife, the fear, and the agony, she thought she was in heaven when Aulnay grew peaceful all around, and the courageous blackbirds chirped cheerily, and the dear face on the pillow began to wear a look of this world and not another.

Faint yet wonderful was the responsive language of his eyes. Their silent power followed her unceasingly. The eager eyes that had studied the vast firmament with its innumerable stars, that had asked of the everlasting hills their secret, watched the eternal ebb and flow of the restless sea, and with the arrogance of strong young manhood demanded the reason and purpose of all nature, now rested in supreme content upon one form.

Between the lines of the world's sweetest poet remains still unsung what Nordenfels' eyes said to Nathalie in those long, still days of convalescence. Eyes that have beheld the open grave and the long rest beyond, that have grown unaccustomed to reflect the thin and changing pictures of this world, assume a deep and limpid light all their own. Purer, more transparent, more divine the sufferer's eyes became, because their meaning rose unclouded from his soul. A whole history, a thousand passionate poems, they related to her,— a world of reminiscence of happy childhood, and for the future, hopeful, glorious dreams.

And her sweet eyes grew dim and veiled with tears in mute response. She knew all he would say, and in those long night-watches her whole life, spiritual and clear, outlined itself before him. What he sought, what she sought, was the same. She questioned, doubted, struggled no longer. Every transient, fine shade of·meaning on the dear white face she interpreted as the reflection of her own soul.

One day, when she gave him a cooling drink, his long, thin fingers, releasing the cup, clasped her hand, wound themselves so closely around it, drew it so warmly to his breast, that the color mounted to her temples. And after that his gaze rested upon her with so wonderful a meaning, so wistful, longing, thankful, and questioning, that she could never draw her hand away. And he, faintly smiling, would clasp it closer, and so charm the sweet and gracious waking dream into his blessed slumber.

Always richer, more comprehensive, grew their silent language. Many times he sought to speak, but her warning finger on her lips checked his feeble utterance.

But the man's good strength grew with the spring-time. Its balmy, fragrant breath warmed his pale cheek, and thrilled his soul with longing. In the old park the young blackbirds' sweet notes gained fulness, the tender thrush came, and the nightingale's passionate, rapturous song. Life claimed its own. Life in the soft grass crept over the meadows, covering ugly stains and harsh footprints. Life in the village brought laughter after tears. Life stirred mightily in the hearts of the ancient trees, and they awakened and renewed their youth and put forth their myriads of happy, fluttering leaves to drink in the sunshine and the dews. And life throbbed in the pulses of the lover, until at last one glad and per-fect day he opened wide his weary arms with a trem-ulous, "My Nathalie, my wife!" And she for the joy of hearing his beloved voice forgot her colorless, lonely past, or remembered only to bless it with happy tears, since it had led to him.

Daisies whitened the meadow, children's laughter echoed through the village, and the sounds of voices and honest toil from field and vineyard. The wise old Tower watching the turn of fortune's wheel had seen and known much and remained silent; but one fair June day, over the tranquil plain flooded with sunshine, peace, and promise, it roused itself and spoke, flinging its message far and wide in peal after peal of jubilant marriage bells.